Nephilim

House of Mephist

By: Mandy Mad

Edited by: Laurie Williams
facebook.com/HelpYouTellTheStory

Cover art by: Marika Kraukle
facebook.com/raveninkart

Find Nephilim online:
Nephilimnovels.com
Facebook.com/nephilimnovels
Twitter.com/ nephilimnovels
Nephilimnovels.tumblr.com

Dedicated to my Family, especially my Mom, who could have discouraged me when I started showing interest in certain things, but didn't.

Chapter One

Everything happens for a reason. At least, that is what the motivational plaque on the wall, tucked between a beer sign and a poster of a bikini model, suggested. Raven stood in the empty bar, waiting, looking over the years of collected décor covering the aged brick walls. This plaque stuck out like a sore thumb amongst the usual items you would expect to find in such an establishment. Beside the beer signs and a poster or two, there was a guitar, a stuffed boar's head, and a set of signed record albums.

The minutes felt like they were ticking by at record slow speeds. The glow of blue and red neon signs reflected off the large, blank monitor she was standing in front of. The remote in her hand was being idly tapped on her leg. The place smelled like alcohol and old wood, with the faintest hint of cigarette smoke. She was hungry, but the prolonged exposure to the combination of odors was ruining her appetite. Pizza sounded good. Soft, doughy bread, zesty tomato sauce, and hot, gooey cheese. Just thinking about it, she could almost taste it, but the taste was tainted by the smells of the bar, which inspired the thought of pizza and cigarette ashes, an un-appealing combination.

The sound of boots on the creaking hardwood floor broke the silence and brought an end to thoughts of food. "Sorry about that! Had to deal with that call now, you know how it is, right? Where are we at here?" A man, maybe in his lower fifties, made his way over, stopping next to her. A beer in hand, he was dressed in worn out jeans and a shirt from a rock concert from days gone by. Shaggy brown hair was pulled behind his ears, and a tattoo as faded at the print on his shirt was etched on his arm.

Raven looked up at the taller man, her emerald green eyes peering past bangs of thick black hair. "It's ok, Mr. Myrick…." She spoke with a smile, holding the remote up. "I got everything hooked up for you."

"Right on! How does it work?" Mr. Myrick chased the simple question with a swig from his beer.

"When you push this button…" she pushed the 'on' button, which turned the screen on, showing an empty stage adjacent to the main room of the bar. "…the feed starts on the main screen. You will need to turn the monitors in the back on by hand, then hit the record button, and it will start to record the feed in the main office. Hit stop to stop it."

Mr. Myrick watched and listened intently, taking another sip of beer. "And if I want to stream it online?"

"That's on the computer in the office. Once you got everything going, you want to click on the broadcast button on the desktop and click start." She explained briefly with the hope he was smart enough, or rather, sober enough, to know that after starting the live stream, to stop it, you push 'stop'.

He stood there a moment thinking before smiling wide. "You're alright, man, tell your boss I'll send a check over tomorrow!"

"Ok, sounds good," she replied, handing over the remote and heading over to the bar.

"What was your name again, hon?"

"Raven." She pulled the strap of a laptop bag over her shoulder and scooped up a box of extra parts and equipment.

"Hey! Wait up a second!" He rushed behind the bar, barely depositing his bottle on the counter. Raven turned as he came rushing back around with two bottles of beer and stuck them into the box of supplies. "Always tip hard work, I say!" He exclaimed.

"Thanks." She eyed the bottles and debated pointing out that she wasn't 21 just yet. Instead, she just smiled and headed toward the back. She let out a small mumble and huff as she reached the back door. It would have been better appreciated if the man had offered to help get the box to the car instead of giving free beers, or to at least open the back door. With a little careful maneuvering she got the door open and headed to the car.

Raven took a deep breath as she walked. The fresh night air was crisp, clean, and held the lightest hints of the coming summer. The back of the property was poorly lit, leaving it a less desirable place to hang out, and yet there were signs scattered about that told tales of late night partying. A couple of empty bottles, cigarette butts, and food wrappers were carelessly discarded on the ground. A single tree near a make-shift band stand had unlit Christmas lights strung through it. They then stretched from the tree to the back porch.

The thought crossed her mind as she got closer to the car that, despite the place being a bit on the shabby side, good times were clearly had here. It was easy to imagine how cool it must be, all lit up with a band playing and people lingering about just chilling, maybe a couple of people dancing.

Arriving at the car, she set the box on the edge of the bumper, using a knee to hold it in place, and pulled out her keys to unlock the hatch and lift it up. She leaned forward, stretching her arm out, and her fingers grasped at a faded yellow broom handle. Pulling it out, she used the stick to prop the hatch up. As she lifted the box into the trunk, her cell phone started to ring. She hesitated, but pulled it from the laptop bag, answering it.

"Hello?"

"Raven? Where are you?"

"I'm headed back to town. Took longer out here than I thought, and I still got two more stops," she answered as she lifted the hatch enough to pull the broom stick from its propped position and laid it down in the trunk before closing the hatch of the car.

"Are you going to miss dinner again tonight?"

"Yeah..." she sighed. "Sorry, Mom."

"It's ok, you can warm it up when you get home, but I do think you are taking on too many extra jobs."

Raven opened the car door, putting the laptop bag in the passenger seat. "Maybe, but I'm close to having enough money to finish fixing up the car. Then I can slow down.....ok?" She explained, looking the vehicle over with a happy smile. It was an '87 Mustang, slowly rebuilt here and there over the last few years, and all that was left to do was add a coat of shiny new paint to cover up the black and grey patchwork of the original fading paint and fresh primer. The hydraulic hatch lifts were still being debated and, while it made sense to replace them, she kind of wanted to leave them as they were as a reminder of where the car was at before she rebuilt it.

There was silence on the other end for a moment, prompting Raven to head out into the alley, past the trees a little, assuming the signal was being lost. "Mom? Can you hear me?" She questioned as she stood in the middle of the alley just outside the reach of the street light's glow.

"Yeah, I can. Be careful heading home, ok? We can talk about how much you're doing later….right before your Father speaks to you about these college acceptance letters."

Raven let her head fall back, looking at the night sky, shoulders sagging at the mention of the letters. A cool, crisp breeze caressed her fair skin and gently pushed at the flaps of her black leather jacket. "Gaah..really? I don't want to have that talk. How many different ways do I have to tell him that I don't know, I can't decide?"

"Hey don't you grraah or whatever to me, he just wants what's best for you, and if you don't decide—"

"Then I'll re-apply for next semester." She spoke up quickly. "I got to get going, I guess I'll deal with this when I get home."

"Alright, love you, see you when you get home."

"Bye, love you, Mom."

Raven took a deep breath, looking down at the phone as the call ended. "Crap," she mumbled as she noticed the time and the two new text messages from her boss. She turned to head back to the car, and was instantly met with a thud. It was quick and disorienting, some unknown person slamming into her and then awkwardly grabbing her to stop her from being completely plowed over. The two slid as one, kicking up dust and scattering gravel.

"Whoa, whoa, whoa!" The female voice called out, huffing from running down the alley. "You ok?!?! I didn't see you!"

"Just …wha…what?" Raven looked up at the woman who was not much older than herself. Her jacket was torn, and her golden curled hair showed signs of a struggle, or maybe a good romp in the back of a truck, for all she really knew.

"Are. You. Ok?" The woman asked more slowly, looking Raven over before bending down and getting the cell phone that had been dropped in the collision.

"Yeah, sorry…I'm ok. Are you? Why are you running down the alley like that?"

The woman handed Raven her phone, brows rising as she got a better look at her. "In a hurry," she said shortly, bright blue eyes settling on Raven with a concerned expression. "You live around here?"

"No." Raven answered without much thought, brushing the gravel dust off the phone that had surprisingly survived the fall without a scratch.

"Good." She spoke while glancing down the alley. "Get home…and be more careful. I mean that!" The woman ran off in the direction she had been heading, leaving Raven standing in the middle of the alley, a little spooked and confused.

"She literally runs into me as she's racing down a dark alley, and tells me to be careful?" Raven spoke out loud to herself. "Some people…."

Then it hit her, this had been time wasted, and she had to get going. She headed to the car, only to stop and cringe as she heard what sounded like someone running down the alley again. Nothing happened. A quick turn brought her face to face with an empty, dark alley.

With a shrug, she got into the car and took off. She was lucky enough to catch both green lights on the way out of the small town, and was all too eager to hit the gas at the first 55mph sign. With a good song on the radio and a somewhat clear night, it was going to be an easy ride back into Kankakee.

As she drove, she went over in her mind what needed to be done at the two stops remaining. One was fairly simple, and she was guessing all that would be required was to reset the computer system. An easy in an out job, if it wasn't for the fact the customer was a chatter box and could eat up too much time gossiping about random people. Maybe the woman pretended she didn't know how to fix the issue to entrap another into listening to what she had to say?

"Heh…" She mumbled to herself at the new thought. Maybe? She shook her head, deciding not to dwell on it for the whole ride home. It would be best to see what time it was when she got back to town and then decide if calls would need to be made to re-schedule them first thing in the morning.

She turned up the radio, turning the thinking session into a carefree ride down the highway. There was something about the rumble of a Mustang's engine and a good song competing with each other to be heard that she couldn't explain. It felt like in moments like these, there was nothing but the ride and music. Everything would work itself out and life was good. Simple, but good.

As the song finished up, the clouds in the sky started to shift, rolling back at a bit of a crawl to reveal a blood red moon. The silence between songs playing was interrupted by a crackling over the radio airwaves. Raven took a glance at the moon, wanting to see it, but didn't want to take her eyes off the road.

"Yeah, that's creepy, alright."

She reached for the radio buttons, figuring the station was having some issues, which happens, but she wanted music. Her finger didn't make it to the button, however, before a darker cover of Credence Clearwater's 'Bad Moon Rising' started to play. Not only was it not one of her favorites, but the timing was a little creepy. She reached over and hit one of the buttons to try another station.

The song continued, making mention of trouble. She blinked, reaching over and hitting the button again. The song was playing on the next station also. She looked at the station number to make sure it actually changed. It did. Another was tried, the song continued. A knot started to form in her stomach, looking at the station number again. She started to slow the car down as she passed a sign warning the road curved into an s curve ahead, and she tried to change the station one more time. Maybe the stereo was shorting out? It was the first time she had put a new stereo face onto an older car, maybe something had been done wrong and it was malfunctioning?

The radio continued on, the song hitting a part about something taking one's life just as Raven came around the bend of the curve in the road.

"Ok, what the fuck?"

Raven's confusion over what was going on with the radio was swiftly replaced with panic as she found herself face to face with the dual bright beams of a semi truck's headlights, coming right at her. It happened so fast, yet at the same time, it felt like time stood still. The truck was barreling down the wrong lane, or was she? Realizing in that split second that either way, she was about to collide with it, she jerked the steering wheel to try and get out of the way.

Everything became a blur. The song on the radio was drowned out by a blaring horn and tires squealing. She barely saw anything as the semi truck clipped the rear end of the car, causing it to spin as it headed onto the side of the road. The sound of the semi slamming against the steel of the old Mustang overpowered all other sound in that moment. Metal slamming into metal, caving it in as the frame twisted from the impact. It was followed up by the heart stilling boom of the front end as it slammed into a tree.

The force of the impact threw Raven forward, slamming her body against the steering wheel. Just before she blacked out, the sound of tires squealing on pavement led to another loud crash as a vehicle ran into her in their attempt to avoid the semi truck.

The radio stopped playing.

The sound of a car horn continuously blowing was enough to jar her back to consciousness. Two more crashes could barely be heard in the distance over the horn. Her mind jumped to the thought, was she getting hit again? No, the car was still, and after the second crash, all she could hear was the horn blaring.

It took a second for it to sink in that she was resting on the steering wheel, and that it was her own car's horn wailing out into the night. As this detail started to register, so did the pain in her ribs and chest.

"Help…" She gasped out, trembling and reaching a hand up to steady herself as she sat up to look around. All she could see was the tree, the pickup truck that slammed into her and its dead driver slumped over. The truck's windshield was cracked and splattered with blood.

Tears came to her eyes as her mind started to process what exactly had just happened. She had never been in a car accident. She could have died, she still could. It was hard to take a breath, leading her emotions to run wild with fear and panic. More tears rolled down her cheeks as an overwhelming thought gave her courage to move and clarity to function. She wanted her Mom.

Another gasped breath as she looked at the passenger seat where her cell phone had been. Now it was on the floor, and out of reach. More sensations started to rip through her, each pain and wound realized reinforcing fear and panic's grip over her senses. Pain gripped her neck and spread through her back. A severe stinging pain in her side throbbed with any movement. Something wet and warm was dripping down the side of her face. She felt like she was going to throw up as the thought entered her mind that she was going to die out there, alone, never to see her family or friends again.

"That one's moving! That one right there, she's alive!" Someone called out frantically.

Raven moved a little more, looking down at her side. Her mind just couldn't seem to process it, it didn't seem real. There was a piece of metal or something sticking out of her body. The only thing her brain managed to transmit was not to touch it. Then it came to mind that she shouldn't even be moving.

"Miss!" That same voice was now right next to her. "Miss, don't move! Just stay still, we called 911 and help is on the way!"

Raven did as instructed, peering to the side at the man who had crawled through the ditch into the mess of things. Her eyes rolled away and fluttered as a flashlight was lifted to the window.

"Hey, you need to stay with us, look over here!" A new voice drew her attention back to the window. "Do you smell gas?" The new man asked, disappearing from view as he stooped down to look under the car. Popping back up, he grabbed at the door handle. "We have to get her out of here," he said firmly, motioning to the other guy. Raven's vision started to blur. She could hear the two talking, but couldn't understand what they were saying.

Suddenly, everything went black.

Raven came around, laying flat on a cold marble floor. She took a steady, deep breath, able to do so without pain. A hand was lifted and she ran it over the area where, from what seemed just a moment ago, something metal had been sticking out of her. Her vision was blurry, but it slowly cleared to reveal she was looking at a ceiling of peculiar coloring. It was split down the middle, white on the right, and black on the left.

She sat up slowly, looking to either side of what looked like a large gathering hall. The marble it was carved from matched the theme of the ceiling.

Aside from the contrast in color, each side was identical, and contained pillared arches along the wall. Each pillar was smooth, with its connection to the floor and ceiling being seamless. The bases were basic bulky squares, at the top they curved and twisted into ornate carvings of strange symbols, like nothing Raven had ever seen. The space between the pillars and the wall appeared to have just the right amount of room for benches, but it was empty. In between each pillar was an orb of light; just bright enough to illuminate the hall.

At the back of the room there were two doors, each with a marble table in front of it that, like the pillars, seemed to be molded right into the floor. The doors were rather mundane, plain slabs of marble with a simple filigree pattern carved into the corners. Oddly, they had no handles and, if not for the frames, could easily go unnoticed.

In between the two tables was a marble statue of a naked woman. Her coloring was split down the middle to match each side of the room she occupied. She stood tall, her feet flat on the floor. Her right hand was held up, open palm out, with fingertips pointing up. Her left hand was held down, palm forward, her pinky and ring finger folded closed. Whoever created the piece must have spent countless hours carving the intricate details. From the curliness of the hair to the creases in each finger, the statue was extremely life-like.

She was in awe over what she was seeing. But where was she? Was there anyone else around? After a moment of taking in her surroundings, Raven turned to look behind her, only to see exactly the same thing. Her brows furrowed in confusion. It was disorienting to find the room the same, as if you hadn't turned around at all, leaving her to wonder, sort of like when you think about telling somebody something, you mull over how you want to say it so many times that you think you already said it.

"There is no forward or backward, only a choice of left or right." A woman's voice calmly filled the room.

Raven turned back around to face the way she had started. Now, there was a man next to each table. Standing, she slowly walked toward them, staying in the middle of the hall. Getting closer, the details of the men watching her became more clear.

On the right, within the white marbled side of the hall, an elderly gentleman with well-trimmed short white hair stood tall. His tanned frame was draped in white and blue robes that were finely trimmed in gold. The color of his eyes was strikingly blue, matching the brilliant ocean tones of the robes he was wearing. His arms were folded in front of himself, with his hands clasped inside the widened sleeves of his garments. He stood with a humble demeanor, looking forward her without moving, as if he expected nothing at all. The last detail that stood out was his pointy ears.

The man on the left looked more in his forties. Black hair was roughly cut at the shoulders and looked unkempt and greasy. He was pale, dressed in black tattered robes. Serpentine eyes held a yellow tone, and his fingers were tipped with jagged talons. He had an air of confidence all around him, maybe a touch of smugness as he stood also without movement. His hands were clasped in front of him as well, but fully exposed.

"Raven Alexandria Ashlynn," the voice spoke out again, drawing Raven's attention away from the two standing at their respective tables, and to the statue before her.

"The statue is talking?" Raven questioned, but the question was left unanswered.

"You stand in this sacred hall today, faced with a choice." The voice replied, coming from the direction of the statue. Its lips didn't move.

"Choice?" Raven replied. "I don't understand, what choice? What's going on here?"

"You are dead," the voice replied, holding an emotionless tone as it communicated.

"What?" Raven suddenly felt a pain swell through her chest. It was the same pain that had been present when she woke up in the car, hunched over the steering wheel. She looked down and saw that a stain of blood had formed right around where the pain was. It bled through the fabric of the light grey shirt she was wearing. Gasping with the realized pain, she could hear a steady, repeating beep for a brief moment.

"I can't be dead!" She blurted out, almost angry at such a statement. A feeling of dread overcame every fiber of her being at the idea of being dead, but then every sound and graphic detail of the car accident was suddenly remembered like a forgotten nightmare recalled. "What about my family? Do you know how many comic book movies they just announced? Or the—"

"Focus," the voice interrupted.

Raven pushed her fingers against the still forming blood stain on her clothing as her eyes focused on the statue. "What do I have to choose?"

"You have to choose the right hand path of the light, or the left hand path of the dark."

Raven just stood there a moment. It kind of dawned on her that she was talking to a statue, of all things, and that as the conversation took place, two guys were standing there as if she didn't exist as they stared forward. "Why do I have to choose? If I'm dead, aren't I headed somewhere based on the choices I made in life?"

"You are Nephilim."

"I'm half angel?" Raven replied with a pained half chuckle over what was being said. She knew what a Nephilim was. Genesis 6:4; 'when the sons of

God came in unto the daughters of men, and they bore children', the passage came to mind. Was her Father an Angel?

"No," the voice replied.

This brought a grin to the man on the left, revealing jagged, rotting teeth. Raven noticed, and took a step back, eyeing him warily. "How can I be Nephilim, but not half angel?"

"Nephilim can be either half angel, or half demon. You are half demon. You are dark Nephilim."

The pain in Raven's chest started to ease up, her eyes moving to the man on the right. His expression had remained blank so far. "What happens when I choose?" She was almost afraid to ask, given the one man's apparent glee over what the statue was saying and the other man not even looking at her, which started to make sense. His position in the white side of the room, his clothing, he must represent Heaven, and why would he have any interest in someone half demon, unless it was to run them through with a sword, Michael versus Lucifer style?

"If you choose left and walk the path of your birthright, you will join Hell's forces in the war against Heaven and humanity. If you choose right, you will aid Heaven in the war, and help protect the humans."

As the voice explained that going left was her birthright, the man, or demon as it were, lifted his hand out in anticipation. It was clear that this creature expected her to go with him. She looked the thing over, taking a step forward, which widened his grin, a grin that fell a little as she asked a question he wasn't expecting.

"What are the consequences of a…dark Nephilim as you put it, going right and aiding heaven?"

"Don't be ridiculous!" The demon blurted out in a dark and rough voice.

"If you choose the right hand path, your kind will hunt you, not all in the light will welcome you, and your service will not redeem you." The voice spoke out once more, and even in explaining the gravity of that choice, it still presented no emotion.

"Which meeeaaans…." the demon spoke with a dramatic drawl and hesitation, "when you die, you come to us anyway, and we *will* torture you for all eternity for your betrayal." The demon taunted, pushing his hand out further.

Is it really a choice if the attitude of those involved is that you are expected to do something based on what they claim you are? She stared at his hand a moment, thinking about what he said. It wasn't a threat, it was a fact. The situation felt pretty black and white. The irony of such didn't escape her as she stood within the black and white room.

Go with the demon, and then what? What was it like to be a demon? What kind of demon was she? Her nose wrinkled gently at the idea that she could be half succubus, so cliché and stereotypical, but a possibility that was just as unnerving as the rest of what was going on.

Raven looked away from the demon to the other man. Her eyes squinted a bit, looking to the white side of the room was a bit jarring. While it was the same lighting on either side, on the right side of the room it just seemed brighter, especially since she had been looking at a dimly lit wall of black for so long. He was no longer looking straight forward, but was now looking at Raven.

"You have nothing to say?" She questioned curiously, a bit of hope to her voice, maybe this man would offer some form of light at the end of the tunnel of weird unfolding around her.

"What does one say to another, who is faced with such a decision?" The elderly man questioned calmly. His warm voice was aged to a degree that inspired the impression of wisdom. "I will not taunt or make promises." He paused. "I will simply await your decision and hope you will follow your heart."

The vast difference in his approach was hard not to notice. She looked back and forth between the two of them, considering what both had to say. In the elderly man's case, it was not much to go on, however, and what the demon said couldn't be confirmed or denied. Neither choice felt like the end result would be easy, or without challenge.

She looked down in thought, focusing on the split in colors on the floor. It didn't cross her mind that this could all be a drug inducted coma dream. Instead, she thought about the options and events that could follow. Going left…..could be a lot of fun. Her mind wandered a bit over the possibilities. But it wasn't who she was. She couldn't begin to imagine running amuck through the dead of night, terrorizing and killing humans.

Glancing up just a little, her eyes darted back and forth between the two men. It was awkward, the way they were both standing there like someone pushed the pause button and they were frozen in waiting--the demon beckoning her to him with his hand still held up, stretched and unwavering, and the elderly man with the creasing of his gently wrinkled face as he smiled just slightly.

Without another word or further questioning, Raven stepped all the way to the right side of the hall.

"The path has been set" The voice spoke for the last time.

"She belongs to us!"

The demon growled as he came from behind the table, advancing in Raven's direction. Clawed feet burned at the marble beneath them as he moved. Frayed wings burst from his back. The demon crashed into an invisible barrier just before crossing into the white side of the hall. A nerve shattering shriek vibrated from his throat as he clawed at the unseen force.

Raven turned to face the demon, backing away and right into the elderly man's gentle grasp. He had also moved from behind his spot, but in a far calmer and more quiet manner. Gently he pulled on Raven, turning her to face away from the demon and its conniption fit. Not a word was spoken as she was escorted to the door behind his table. The door unlatched and swung open on its own with their approach. The man offered a small smile, motioning for her to go ahead and step through. She looked back at him only a moment before doing so, not wanting to linger too long anywhere near the demon who's screams had twisted to yelling in tongues.

She was going home, or that's what she thought. Stepping through the door, she expected a blinding white light would be seen before waking up. However, when stepping through the door, she fell into what looked like a vast ocean. "Oh shit!" she blurted out just before her body plunged down into the ice cold depths, shivering. A cramping clutched her chest. Severe nausea set in almost instantaneously as her body slowed and she sank under the surface of the water. She swam upward, desperately trying to get to the top. The instinct to take a deep breath was overpowering, bringing a mix of cold water and air rushing into oxygen deprived lungs as the water's surface was broken through.

It felt like she still couldn't breathe. Coughing up water and gasping, Raven barely managed to swim to the edge of the pond and crawl into the grass. Her eyes roamed over the pond, staring at it as she caught her breath. Fall into an ocean, crawl out of a pond, she didn't want to even attempt to try and work through how that happened. She wanted to focus on getting home. Carefully, she looked up to see where she was. A delicate maze of tree branches lush with green leaves and dotted with precious pink blooms provided shade from the golden sun high in the sky.

Standing roughly, a small whisper peeped out. "Wow…" The surrounding garden was breathtakingly pristine. An impressive array of trees, bushes and flowers that were intensely vibrant in their various colors grew everywhere she looked. It was a sight so captivating that the nearby towering structure almost went unnoticed.

An terrace with trefoil archways lined the side of the main building that faced the garden. This made up a series of buildings, made of some kind of cream colored stone that stretched a good distance and towered above the surrounding tree line. Looking to either side of her, it looked like the garden ran the entire distance of the building.

"Don't move!" Someone called out from behind, anger in their voice. "Hands up, turn around slowly."

Raven turned around, lifting both hands up next to her shoulders. Several men glowered, holding swords pointed at her. Their skin was tanned like the elderly man she was just with. These men, however, were younger and clad in armor of gold plate and brown leather. The intricate details of filigree and runes suggested they were some form of royal guard.

Turning around revealed more of the garden. It seemed never ending, a well-planned layout of flowers, fruit trees and plants stretching as far as the eye could see. The span of the garden not lined by the large stone building was lined with trees. The reddish tint of the bark and their height suggested redwood trees, however they were shaped more like oak trees, creating an intertwined living wall of sorts.

"How did you get here?" one of the guards asked, gripping his sword more tightly.

"Identify yourself!" another demanded in a panic.

"Calm down, all of you." A familiar voice spoke from behind the men. "Lower your weapons and let me through," the elderly man requested in a calm, yet commanding fashion. As weapons were lowered and they stepped aside, he stepped forward. "I'm called Andresi. I am the watcher of Eden." Andresi looked Raven over carefully, rubbing his chin in thought.

"I thought I was going back home, to you know, not be dead?" Raven questioned, lowering her hands, relieved to no longer have swords pointed at her.

"Don't worry about that, you are alive and well." Andresi motioned Raven to follow him. "Time moves differently in the outer realms. Your body on Earth has been stabilized by healers and is in the medical ward now."

"Outer realms?" Raven questioned, following behind the man, shooting a glance at the guards that were also following behind her to keep a close eye on her. "Medical ward, you mean hospital, right?"

"The outer realms." He repeated himself thoughtfully. "It's what we call any realm that is not Earth. It can get a tad confusing, multiple realms to keep track of, all moving at different speeds." He explained, speaking from experience. "And yes, Medical ward would be a hospital." He chuckled. "It's a bit of a dated term, my apologies for the confusion."

"It's ok, it's just not a term you hear often, or ever anymore. So…what am I doing here?"

Andresi nodded, agreeing with her observation on his choice of words as he led her out of the garden and into the building. "We must declare your loyalties and assign a guardian to you before we can send you back. Overall, your time here will be brief."

"Where is here? What's….a guardian?" Raven responded with the distracted questions as they walked down a hall. The floors were made of the same stone as the outside of the castle-like building, and lined with a dark red carpet. Tapestries hung on the walls, finely woven silk thread masterpieces depicting certain events. She slowed down a little, taking a closer look at the ones that either stood out to her, or were unfamiliar.

The apple tree in the Garden of Eden. The solitary tree bearing the forbidden fruit was depicted amongst a mix of daisies, roses and a few flowers she had never seen before. Adam stood to the right side of the tree, looking to Eve in temptation as she held a red apple out to him; a snake was wrapped around her leg and up her backside with its tongue sticking out at her ear, suggesting sinister whisperings in progress. The two were a vision, the first humans, according to the Bible. Perfect in every way, the tawny tones of their exposed bodies were offset by black hair and stunning hazel eyes. The detail was amazing, life-like even, it would have taken centuries for someone with exquisite skill to weave such a piece.

Noah's Ark. The massive wooden boat, arranged much like she had seen in images in the Bible. Men and women standing alongside a selection of animals on the deck of the ship, looking down to the land being devoured by vibrant blue waters. Sticking out of the water there were people, reaching out for help. A couple of them had demonic looking features, horns, scales or a tail. Others had Angelic looking markings on their arms or a faded halo over their head.

"You're in Eden, the first demon to step foot here since Lucifer." He stopped walking, noticing she was no longer by his side. Turning back, he cleared his throat to get her attention.

Raven jerked as he startled her out of her reverie, looking away from the tapestry and down the hall to the elderly man. "Sorry, please continue, Guardians?" Raven spoke apologetically as she walked quickly to catch up with Andresi.

"A guardian…." He started back up, turning once more and making his way down the hall. "…is like a guide that will train you and help the council determine which tasks you can handle. He will teach you all you need to know." He came to a stop just outside a large entry way to a throne room, turning and looking at her. "I'd like to ask you something, if I may?"

"Sure…if I can ask something in return?" She replied, curiously.

"Why did you step to the right?" Andresi asked, taking another good look over her features.

Raven blinked, staring at Andresi as the question was presented. "I…don't know?" She replied, questioning her own actions in the process. "I just did what I thought was right." Her eyes then looked over to one of the guards, noticing his pointy ears. All of them seemed to have pointed ears that were just the slightest bit longer than a human's ear.

Andresi nodded. "And that, Raven, is a good reason to do anything."

"Now my turn… are you elves?" She asked eagerly.

Of all the more important things to ask, like, 'how am I getting back to my body?' or 'Where is God in all this?' and she just wanted to know if she was amongst elves. He smiled once more, amused as he turned away. "Are we?" He teased. "You're running out of time, come along!" The elderly man urged, leaving the question un-answered.

Raven followed Andresi into the hall, and the guards were right behind them. Inside, there were other people scattered about, chatting, reading, and doing other various activities. The group came to a halt and settled in front of two large wooden thrones carved with intricate detail from the trees that bordered the land outside, and accented with brown velvet. Seated within were the lord and lady of the land.

"Lord and Lady Lucent," Andresi addressed the two as he came to a halt, nodding his head in respect. Lord Lucent's gaze swiftly fell to Raven, who was looking around, taking everything in.

He held himself with confidence and authority. Lightly sun kissed skin was covered in a mix of fine antique white silks and soft tan leathers.

Golden blond hair gently framed stern features. His eyes were a stunning turquoise blue. Lady Lucent looked a delicate flower, wearing a soft pink silk gown that clung to her slender form at the top, and flowed out into a gentle flare at the bottom. Soft, brown hair was pulled to the side in a braid. Eyes of baby blue held a kindness that her husband's seemed to lack.

Everyone looked like they were ready to film a high budget Hollywood fantasy film, dressed in clothes reminiscent of medieval attire. A common theme was pastel to warm colors, nothing was a shade of darker tones, except for what Raven was wearing. Black sneakers, boot cut jeans, leather jacket, and a light grey top really made her stand out.

"May I present Raven of house Ashlynn, dark Nephilim, pledging to the light, and seeking a guardian," Andresi announced. He stepped aside, giving Lord Lucent a clear view of the new arrival. Raven pried her attention away from a set of children gawking at her, looking up toward the thrones.

Lord Lucent rose, stepping down from the throne, and striding forward, his overcoat flowing behind him. The gap between himself and Raven closed more quickly than she was comfortable with, and the tension in the room was suddenly thick enough that you could cut through it. He stared, looking her over in a manner of inspection. The deafening silence was broken as he finally spoke.

"She is shadow.", he stated abruptly. His voice was warm, with a hint of a holier-than-thou attitude. The announcement brought mumbled whispers and glances amongst those gathered.

"Nice to meet you, too," Raven nervously quipped, as her personal space was still being invaded.

Lord Lucent stepped back, turning from Raven to look at Andresi. "I would like to say the same, however, your very existence disturbs me, your choice this day concerns me, and frankly, I can't in good faith assign a guardian to you." The man took on a blatantly condescending tone that was wrapped in frustration as he spoke.

"Your clothes disturb me," Raven snapped back, narrowing her eyes at Lucent, her actions bringing him to look at her with ire.

"Lord Lucent, please— "Andresi silenced himself as Lucent raised a hand for him to stop.

"I will not...." he started to explain as he lowered his hand. "...*assign* a guardian. I cannot, I will not, ask anyone to put themselves in the position of being around one that will be hunted, as you will."

Raven glanced at Andresi, remaining silent.

"I will, however, allow one to volunteer." He turned from Raven again, looking at those that were gathered. He said nothing else, but the expression he held was loud and clear. This was a challenge, maybe a test? Who was brave enough, or maybe even dumb enough, to step up and take on this task?

"I'll do it." A voice came from behind one of the pillars, low, and filled with amusement.

This brought a crack in Lucent's stern demeanor as his hands were thrown up in the air. "Ooof course, you will." He laughed the telling laugh of a Father who was pretty much on their last nerve when it came to their child. "Go on, then! Run off with the hell spawn and get killed!" Frustration and anger seeped into his tone as he turned and headed back to sit down.

"Edwin!" Lady Lucent finally spoke, her neutral expression now twisting into disappointment as she looked at her husband.

"What did you call me....Eddie?" Raven spoke up, watching Lord Lucent walk away, an action that was halted as he whipped around to throw that ire soaked glare at her once more.

"Whoa, ok, hold on!" The volunteer spoke out as he slinked from behind the pillar. The handsome young man pulled the hood down from his coat, blazing blue eyes dashing back and forth between his enraged father and mouthy new charge. "Don't say anything else!" He commanded, pointing at Raven.

At this point, the crowd had broken up, most who had been observing had already slinked away around the moment Raven had insulted Lucent's attire. Andresi shook his head, and with his task completed, he too silently slipped away.

"I'm qualified. I can do this, Father, please." The young man spoke, trying to convince Lucent to rescind his objections.

"You just got released from suspension." Lucent whipped around, looking at his son. "Do you really want your next charge to be...that?" He questioned harshly, pointing at Raven.

"Something tells me you wouldn't approve, even if she were light Nephilim." The young man shook his head.

"That's enough, please!" Lady Lucent pleaded, looking back and forth between her husband and son.

Raven held her tongue, eyes falling shut a moment as the still unknown man argued with his Father. It started to become garbled, and no matter how hard she tried to focus on what was being said, nothing made sense. She slowly opened her eyes, her vision blurring and darkening.
"Something's wrong." She managed to say, a hand grasping at her chest.

The one who volunteered turned around quickly, running to Raven and seizing hold of her. Lord Lucent even started to react, taking a step forward, but stopped himself and stayed back to observe.

"Raven," the young man spoke firmly. "Raven, look at me." Raven's eyes focused on her new guardian as he squeezed her hand to get her attention. "Remember me," he said desperately. "You need to remember me when you wake up, remember all this and— "she couldn't hear him anymore, the sound of the steady beep emitting from a heart monitor as she flat lined overpowered everything.

The volunteer turned to look behind him and the distorted sight of Lady Lucent rushing from her throne to her son's aid was consumed with a black nothingness as all went silent.

Chapter Two

The sound of metal grinding in the distance echoed through the nothingness of space she occupied. This sound stretched on and on, would it never end? It would, but a new sound took its place, the sound of fluid hitting an unknown surface, the sound of flesh ripping, they both crept through the darkness that engulfed the full span of her vision.

She was unable to speak, but able to feel sensations and taste rancid soaked cotton filling her mouth. She could feel barbed metal strands wrapped around her eyes, cutting into her flesh and blinding her. Finally, the sense of nothingness as she realized her heart wasn't beating.

And through it all, a clicking and clacking, slowly getting closer.
Click..clack..tap…clack..silence.

How long had it been quiet? A minute? Maybe an hour? The thought was lost to the sound of something ripping once more, fluid splattering and the rush of a burning sensation on her arms and legs. Something was ripping at her, pulling her apart with what felt like razors. It struck at her face, then her sides, before it slowly consumed every fiber of her being. She tried to scream, but nothing came out.

The darkness was then torn away, accompanied by a final bout of pain ripping across her eyes as the black void was replaced with a blazing white light. With a turn of her head, things started to come into focus. Something metal; the tray of a hospital work stand obscuring a light grey box with a black screen speckled with green lights.

She closed her eyes a moment and, as she opened them again, everything came into better focus. It was a heart monitor, with all signs indicating no heart beat was being detected. Any questioning of the machine's accuracy was dismissed as her heart jumped at the thought and fear that she was dead, yet somehow able to see what was going on.

Raven lifted her hands up to her chest to find her shirt and bra had been torn open at some point to make it easier for the medical team to work. The heart monitor stickers were still there, but they no longer had the wires attached. Raven sat up, looking down at her body. Her ribs were severely bruised. It looked like something sharp had been slammed into her left side and torn out, leaving a bloody gash that was now stitched up.

Her breath shook as she gently ran her fingertips over the stitches. There was a haze over her mind, leaving her to question everything as she looked around the area. The iv equipment and the syringes on the work tray, especially the alarmingly large one, got her attention for a moment. There were still remnants of clear fluid within the syringes, and bright crimson stained gauze and cloth rested alongside them.

Where was everyone? Shouldn't there be doctors and nurses working to save her life? Did she really die on the operating table? She thought on the situation carefully, trying to peer out into the hall in the hope of seeing someone, but it was empty.

She worked her jaw, pushing her tongue against the roof of her mouth, which tasted like a mix of spoiled milk and moldy air. "Uh...yuck..." she mumbled, cringing and gagging at the taste. She grabbed roughly at the blanket underneath her with the intention of pulling it up to cover herself.

"Ma'am, you need to wait, we need to–" A woman could be heard approaching the room, a bit of urgency to her voice. As her words cut off, she let out a startled scream, causing Raven to jump and drop the blanket. Looking up, she came face to face with an audience of three. A nurse looking absolutely mortified. Her Mom, who stared in disbelief, eyes red from crying. Her Dad, who was in the process of grabbing his wife, in a manner that made it unclear whether it was to steady himself, or her.

"What is this?" Raven's Mom questioned, voice cracking with emotion.

"Dear Lord…." Her Dad whispered.

"Oh my God, oh my God, oh my God!" The nurse repeated frantically as she moved forward, then stopped, then stepped back again, unsure what to do, before finally moving forward to pull the blanket from under Raven and cover her up.

"You said she was dead!!" Raven's Mom cried out, pulling free from her husband's hold to go to Raven's side and hold her close. There was a burst of activity as a doctor and another nurse came rushing in.

Raven let out a short gasp as her Mom clung to her, holding tightly. "Mom...th—that hurts." She groaned out.

"She *was* dead!" The nurse blurted out in surprise and confusion.

"What is this? A sick joke?" Raven's Dad asked.

"Please, you need to leave the room so we can look her over." The doctor frantically pleaded. "Ms. Jones, please."

Raven looked down, trembling a little, still being squeezed. "Come on, Ellie," her Dad urged, gently prying his wife away and out of the room. As soon as Ellie had been pulled away, the doctor and nurses surrounded the bed. She watched as her parents moved out into the hall, her Dad wrapping his arms around her Mom tight as they watched from the doorway. While a nurse checked her pulse, the doctor pulled a small light from his pocket.

"Raven, I'm Doctor Anand, do you remember what happened?" The middle aged man with a light accent questioned her calmly as he held the light up, flashing it back and forth over her eyes to check her pupil response.

"I was in a car accident," Raven answered the doctor, squinting at the light. One of the nurses popped the heart monitor cords back in place, re-attaching them to the stickers on Raven's chest.

"Do you know what day it is?" He asked, putting the light away.

".... the worst day ever?" She replied, looking over to one of the nurses, who couldn't help but smirk at the response as she started poking at Raven's arm to draw blood. "Is that necessary?"

"Yes, I'm sorry. Can you tell me how you feel? Does it hurt anywhere?"

Raven looked back to the doctor, then down at herself. "Here…" She replied, motioning to her ribs. "….and here." She pointed at her side where she was stitched up. "I kind of hurt all over, and…" She trailed off, looking at her hands as she pulled them from under the blanket. "My hands feel funny."

"Do they hurt?" The doctor asked, gently reaching to take them in his own hands and look them over.

"No…it feels like….." She looked up at him, trying to find the words to use to describe what she felt.

"Tingly?" He suggested.

"Kind of, but…" Raven sighed in frustration. "It feels like something is under my skin."

The doctor looked perplexed by what she was describing. "Alright." He nodded, glancing at one of the nurses. "Were you holding the steering wheel in the crash?"

Raven's eyes averted as she recalled the flash of the headlights, jerking on the wheel and slamming into the tree. Her form visibly tensed as she replied. "Yes."

"Alright, we'll figure it out. I'm going to order a couple tests and see about getting you into a room, ok?"

"Yes, thank you, Doctor." Raven looked at him as he made his way out of the room.

It wasn't long before she was moved from the surgical table in the emergency room into a private room with a bed. The unusual speediness of doing so was attributed to the circumstances at hand. It's not every day you pronounce someone dead and, moments later, they are sitting up.

Raven laid there, staring at the ceiling, listening to everything going in the hall outside the room. People coughing, chatting, the beeping of machines and phones calls on hold at the nurses station all mingled in with the Doctor explaining that yes, she was clinically dead, but sometimes these things happen. The word "miracle' was even used at one point as the medical professional tried to reason with the set of emotional parents.

Laceration to the side, bruised ribs, laceration to the head, and something about wanting to do a scan to make sure there isn't a brain bleed was also overheard. Numbness was all she felt to the situation, thanks to a decent amount of pain killers. But one thing did manage to break through the medication induced haze, the deep seated feeling that something had been forgotten.

Raven sat in the bed, watching out the window. Being up on the sixth floor gave a decent view of one of the busiest streets in Kankakee. At nearly 2 in the morning, however, the street was nearly dead. A car or two here and there and a guy crossing the street, all faded into the background as she tried to remember what was missing. She went over and over in her head things she knew needed to be done. College letters, work stuff, household chores, plans with the family over the next week. That moment where you remember and go 'oh yeah that's what I'm forgetting' just wasn't happening. Maybe she hadn't forgotten anything, and the feeling she had was just a side effect of the accident?

"Raven?" Ellie's voice called out as she was finally let into the room. She dropped her purse and coat carelessly into a chair as she ran toward the bed and leaned in, hugging Raven. "I thought I lost you," she explained, bursting into tears.

Turning just as her Mom got to the bed, Raven started to cry and met Ellie's hug. "I'm ok, Mom." She clung to her Mom as tightly as she could and closed her eyes.

"Got room over there for me?" The familiar voice of the man Raven knew as Dad filled the room. Before anyone could answer, he joined in, wrapping his arms around them both. "Thank you, God, for watching over my baby girl tonight," he whispered just before letting them go.

"Yes, thank you, God," Ellie whispered just before letting Raven go.

"I want to go home." Raven sniffled, pushing tears away from her eyes.

"I know, but this is the best place for you right now," her Dad pointed out.

"I think I'll stay the night." Ellie looked over at her husband.

"No, Mom you don't have to do that." Raven spoke up quickly. "Go home, be there in the morning for Myra and Jaden. I'll be fine."

"You sure?" Ellie questioned, turning back toward Raven with concern.

"Might be for the best, that nurse out there seems a stickler for the rules and visiting hours," Raven's Dad pointed out as he looked out the door to see where the aforementioned nurse was, as if she could come in at any moment and shoo them away.

"Yes, go. I'm just going to sleep until they drag me off for tests in a few hours," Raven assured her a bit sleepily.

"Well, alright. But, we will be back first thing in the morning." Ellie leaned over the bed once more, giving Raven another hug.

"Alright, Night Mom, Dad, I love you both," Raven replied as she hugged her Mom.

"Love you, sweetie," her Dad replied.

Ellie smiled at Raven and hesitantly headed out, picking her things up on the way to the door. As her parents left, Raven settled into the bed, looking out the window and up at the night sky. She tried not to think of anything as she closed her eyes to go to sleep. But every time she did, she could hear the squealing of tires. After a few tries, sleep finally came.

Morning soon came, as did a nurse to get her cleaned up and off to have some testing done. They managed to wheel her back into her room just in time for a lovely cold breakfast. However, the morning was saved by a smuggled coffee, thanks to her Dad, who stopped in briefly between morning errands. Raven sipped happily while flipping through the limited offerings of hospital television. The idle pressing of the channel button stopped on the news, as a current report got her attention.

"I'm standing here at the Des Plaines State Fish and Wildlife Area, where around six this morning, fishermen found the body of a woman floating just on the edge of the Kankakee river," the news reporter explained. Other news crews could be seen in the background, along with state police and rescue crews.

"We have limited information available at this time, but here is what we do know. As I said a moment ago, around six this morning, two fishermen were just down past the trees behind me...." he motioned behind himself while speaking ".... setting up at what they call their 'lucky spot', when they noticed what looked like clothing floating just at the top of the water. Upon closer inspection, they immediately called 911. First responders say they were able to find the victims drivers license in her jacket pocket."

The screen switched to blue with an image of an Arkansas driver's license, certain information blurred out. "Megan Green is from Little Rock, Arkansas. Authorities are investigating and ask if anyone knows Megan or has any information that can help, to call the number displayed at the bottom of your screen."

Raven's hold on her coffee cup slipped a little as her stomach turned. The driver's license on the screen belonged to the woman from the alley the night before. 'Get home...and be more careful. I mean that!' Megan's perky, bright voice could be heard in Raven's thoughts.

"Hello, Raven." Someone spoke, having snuck in while the report had her full attention. Raven pulled the coffee cup out of sight as she looked over at the man leaning against the wall, watching her.

"Hello?" She replied, a bit confused.

"You don't remember me from last night….huh?"

Raven tensed a little. "Were you in the accident?"

"No." He replied softly, walking to the side of the bed. "We spoke after the accident."

"After? No, I'm really sorry, I don't remember too much from last night. I think it's all the drugs they gave me." She explained with a chuckle.

The man gave a nod in understanding. "It's ok, I can help you remember."

"Sure, hold on, let me just turn this off." Raven set her coffee down and turned the television off. He lifted a hand, a light encompassing it that was as warm and golden as the setting sun glowing through a cloudy sky. Dazzling brighter specks sparked out as he grabbed Raven's arm gently.

She looked at him with a jump. Pain shot up her arm, radiating from where he was holding her. Those brilliant green eyes fluttered a little. It was as if someone touched her eyes with the tip of an ink quill as ebon tones consumed each eyeball entirely, the same way ink would bleed through cloth. "Let. Go." She hissed out darkly. The tone of her own voice startled her.

"Calm down," he urged, letting go, the vibrant energy around his hand fading away. "I'm going to assume you remember now?"

Raven grasped at where he was holding, keeping a closer eye on what he was doing now. "Y...yes." The black in her eyes receded. "Those were pointed." She stated matter-of-factly, pointing at his ears and following right up with...." Shit, that really happened?" There was a bit of disbelief on her face as she remembered everything. The haze of a dream slowly became more vivid as forgotten moments were recalled.

"A real out of body experience, or something along those lines, at least." He chuckled, pulling himself up to sit on the edge of the bed, facing her. "I'm Aiden, by the way. I don't think I was able to tell you that."

Raven's eyes were glued to him as he moved to sit. "No, don't think so," she replied, narrowing her eyes a little. "Magic?" She pointed at his ears again, stuck on that tiny, pointy detail. He was dressed modernly in a pair of navy blue jeans, heather brown shirt and a black blazer. Otherwise, his ears were the only thing different about him, compared to the night before.

"It's an illusion, a minor one, at that. Can't have people thinking I'm an---"

"Elf?" Raven interrupted.

49

A single brow rose over blue eyes. "I was going to say, logic driven alien. Elf is a human term for what we are. More accurately, we are descendants of the Grigori." With a small chuckle he reached over and snatched up her coffee cup, helping himself to a sip. "We need to go over some basics, so pay attention."

"….excuse you, that's my coffee." Her reply came with an attempt to take it back, a failed one at that, as he leaned back just enough to cause her to miss.

"Mmmm, double mocha and cream?" He took on a playful, mocking tone before becoming more serious. "Judging by the look on your face when I came in, you knew that girl on the television?"

Raven folded her arms with a wince, in the moment forgetting that her ribs were still bruised. "I ran into her last night or, to be more exact, she ran into me."

Aiden took notice of Raven's wince and movement. "No, she didn't," he sternly informed her. "You never saw Megan, you never spoke to her. If anyone asks, for whatever reason, you say no. You speak to no one but me about your encounter with her, understand?"

"That's kind of intense."

"Trust me on this, you can't have any connection to her." He softened his voice as he explained.

50

"Who was she?"

"She was a light Nephilim, and she fell last night. The fact that you had contact with her could cause problems."

"Alright, I never ran into anyone last night. I left the bar and—"

Aiden interrupted, finishing for her. "And had a near death experience. That's the next thing I need to tell you, just to cover all the bases, but something tells me you're smarter than to run around telling *anyone* these things."

Raven unfolded her arms, snapping her fingers. "Shucks! There goes my first social media update, when I get my hands on a computer."

"Oh, darn." Aiden smirked. "Post about how horrible hospital food is, like everyone else."

Raven made a face, laughing a little. Her expression then turned a bit more somber. "What happens now?"

"You could tell me what you were doing at a bar? You're what, seventeen?" Aiden questioned curiously, eyeing her like a big brother would eye a younger sibling caught doing something they shouldn't.

"Little older than that." Raven half chuckled. "I was installing…stuff, I work with electronic equipment and computers."

"Hmm, that could be handy." Aiden, watched her a moment, sitting in silence as he tried to think of the best way to put things. "I'm going to train you the best I can. That is what happens next." He started out, looking at the IV unit she was attached to. "There is a lot you need to learn about yourself. It may be harsh to hear, but part of you is demonic in nature, and demons generally aren't the good guys. I need to get you ready to able to defend yourself against both sides…quickly."

"Your Dad called me Shadow? What does that mean?"

Aiden took another drink of the coffee and offered it back. With the pass off of the cup, he took a deep breath. "Dark Nephilim aren't like light Nephilim. On the light side, you simply have angels. Different kinds of angels, but when an angel reproduces with a human, the result is generally the same, regardless of the type of angel involved."

"So light Nephilim are predictable, power wise?" Raven slipped a quick question in.

"To a degree, there have been some cases of light Nephilim developing light physic ability, or telekinesis derived from the holy light. Then you have demons. There are many kinds of demons, which results in different types of dark Nephilim. One of your parents is a shadow demon."

"Which one?" She questioned, setting the coffee cup down.
"Well, it's not your Mother, I saw her earlier. Where is your Father? I know it's not the black man I saw

raising a fuss at the nurse's station this morning."
Aiden took the opportunity to get up off the bed and
make his way over to the medical charts to look them
over.

"My real father died before I was born."

"Is that what you were told?" Aiden glanced
up from the medical chart, overly curious about the
situation.

"Mom said he was in the army and got called
back overseas. She always said that she found out she
was pregnant a few weeks after he left. He requested
to come back home, but was killed in combat before
the paperwork was processed."

"It's safe to say your Father was a shadow
demon and your Mother didn't know." Setting the
chart back where he found it, he pulled the
conversation in a new direction. "You, my new
charge, will be out of here in a few days."

Raven looked at Aiden like he was crazy.
"They told me weeks."

"The second your body was impacted last
night, the damage…" He rolled his hand as if it might
help him get the words out right. "…pulled your true
nature out of dormancy. You're going to be out in a
few days."

"Is that how it works for everyone? Almost
dying?"

"Not all, no. Some will start their 'awakening'
with puberty or stress. Some go their whole lives not

knowing." Aiden meandered back to the side of the bed.

"That's kind of unsettling."

Aiden shrugged. "In some ways, I guess it is." He gave a small pause. "I'll give you a few more days to rest and then your training starts." He pulled a small slip of paper from his pocket, offering it to her. "I'm staying here and I expect to see you in seven days. Got it?"

"Sure." Raven replied simply, taking the paper from Aiden.

"Raven? Shouldn't you be sleeping?" Ellie, Raven's Mom questioned as she came into the room. Her husband was right behind her with a bag in his hand.

"I'm not tired." Raven answered while slipping the paper out of sight.

"Forgive my wife." Franklin spoke to Aiden, setting the bag down before he turned and offered his hand to the stranger. "Reverend Jones, Raven's Father."

"Dad...." Raven interjected. "No need to be so formal, you're my Dad." She trailed off, eyeing the bag being set down.

Aiden shook the man's hand. "It's nice to meet you, sir, I'm Aiden. No need to apologize, Moms will be Moms."

"Aiden was just leaving." Raven spoke up, looking back at everyone.

"You sure?" Ellie asked.

"Yes, Ma'am." Aiden looked at Ellie. "I have to head to work, but when I heard what happened I wanted to stop in and see if I could help."

"Isn't that sweet, thank you." Ellie responded.

"Heard? We haven't really told anyone yet." Franklin questioned.

"The paper posted an early report online, they got some pictures, one of them is Raven's car pinned to the...." Aiden cut himself off, realizing the topic was better left alone. "I'll catch up with you later, Raven."

"Alright, see ya..." Raven eyed Aiden as he left.

"He seems nice." Ellie smiled at Raven, pulling some things from the bag.

"Yeah, he is." Raven peered over at the bag. "Please tell me my laptop is in there."

Franklin shook his head. "It's still in the car, in pieces."

"And the car?"

He hesitated. "The frame is bent, the engine is trashed."

"Fuck...." Raven blurted out, letting herself fall back into the bed, flinching as she did.

"Raven!" Ellie gasped, looking up at her daughter, surprised.

"The important thing is, you're still here, Raven." Franklin pointed out. "Still here for me to remind you to watch what you say."

"Yeah.... sorry. It was almost done being restored, I'm just..."

"I know, kiddo." Franklin moved to help his wife unpack the bag of things they'd brought from home.

Aiden wasn't far. He had stepped right outside the door and was pretending to text someone. He listened to the exchange, taking note of how close they were as a family. He tried not to let it bother him, but it did. He glanced into the room as he pushed off the wall and headed out.

As promised, in a few days' time, to everyone's surprise, Raven was being discharged from the hospital.

She thought a lot about the events surrounding the accident. The weight of it all was crushing and kept her up at night. She accepted it had been real, as it would be hard to deny witnessing something like a man bringing what she assumed to be holy energy to his fingertips, let alone the speedy recovery. There was an inkling at the back of her mind that it was all imagined. That inkling was brushed aside every time by the simple fact that Aiden was very much real and had spoken to her parents.

On the seventh day, she pulled out the slip of paper Aiden had given her. One line of an address was written with an elegant penmanship. The location was right there in Kankakee, just on the other side of town. Was it a coincidence? Did he already live here, or was the house rented recently?

A quick internet search could provide some answers but. Instead. the paper was crumpled and tossed into the trash. Whatever the case was, it didn't matter. Raven had come to the conclusion that the best course of action was to pretend it didn't happen and move on with life. Warnings of being hunted were disregarded, as in her mind no one would have any reason to do such a thing if she's minding her own business and not getting involved.

Proceed with life as usual. This meant the weekly trip to the comic book store where several new releases would be purchased and taken to a small coffee shop to be read while indulging in her favorite caffeinated concoction. The little shop was quiet most afternoons, making for a good setting for losing yourself in the next stage of a heroes' printed adventure. One of her favorite places, there was artwork on the walls from local artists and a corner with couches next to a fire place and a shelf of books. The front of the shop had large picture windows with window seating and pillows.

The flow of page turning and idle sipping was interrupted as she reached for her coffee, only to grab air. Looking up past the comic book in hand, there was Aiden, finishing the coffee casually, as if his presence was part of the routine.

"How did you know where I was?" She closed the comic book hesitantly as she questioned. Aiden grinned, setting the empty cup down with a bit of force on purpose, allowing it to clunk to the table as only an empty cardboard cup would.

"I got your name off the chart at the hospital. I think you are smart enough to figure out what happened next."

Raven glanced at the barista at the front of the shop, who was oblivious to what was going on, gossiping away with someone at the counter with her. The other tables within the brick walled establishment were empty. "Ok, why are you here?"

"I said for you to be at my place in seven days. It's been eight." Aiden glanced toward the service counter as well. "Did you lose my address?"

"No, I threw it away." She collected her comic books into a neat stack and slipped them into her new laptop bag. "I'm not getting involved in this, whatever it is."

"It's a little late for that." He leaned forward, folding his arms against the table. "Do I need to remind you of the demon that was present when you made your choice? He has your name, knows what you look like. It's only a matter of time before they come for you."

She shook her head, looking away, almost able to hear the mentioned demon's pitched screaming. "Stop."

Aiden sighed. "What would they do?" He motioned a hand toward the laptop bag the comics were stashed in.

"They?"

"The characters in your comic books. How did they react to finding out they are different from everyone else, finding out they are part of something bigger?" There was amusement in his voice as he tried a different approach.

"Well, some of them do exactly like I am. Pretend nothing has changed and they move on with their lives."

"But that never lasts, does it?" He gave her a look. "How many of those stories ended with the character being a hero, despite themselves."

"Some of them became a villain."

He couldn't help it, a smile broke his serious demeanor. "You aren't a villain. You proved that when you were presented a reality few would be able to handle. You were told you could be a villain, that you were born to be one, and you forsook that path."

"I'm also not a hero. I'm just a girl who needs to decide which college to go to."

Aiden gave a thoughtful nod. "Ok." He leaned back, pulling his arms from their fold on the table. "How about, you come with me, let me show you something. If you still feel like the best thing to do is avoid the truth, I'll leave you alone."

"Fine." She agreed reluctantly.

Aiden jumped up, motioning to the coffee shop's exit. With a small sigh, Raven stood, leaving with him. As they made their way around to the parking lot, she eyed the alley way and side street. She knew the streets and could lose him easily. But, what would stop him from approaching her at home?

He led her to his car, a modest model in blue that blended in and didn't draw attention to itself. As she got in, she reached into her pocket and started texting away, which drew Aiden's attention swiftly to her. "What are you doing?"

"Oh…" She started to explain, glancing at him. "Just texting my Dad and letting him know I got into a car with a stranger, to be taken to an unspecified location where I'll be tortured and killed." Her tone was playful as she spoke, with just a hint of seriousness.

He stared at her, his actions frozen at the act of putting the key in the ignition. "That's not funny."

Raven glanced at him again. "Maybe a little bit."

He shook his head, starting the car. "It's not far." Pulling out of the lot, he started driving, side glancing at her as she kept texting. "That's a habit you're going to need to break."

"Huh?" She looked up at Aiden.

"You need to pay attention to your surroundings, not texting." He explained as they turned into a residential area.

Raven remained silent as she tucked her phone away and looked out the window. They pulled up to a two story house lined with wooden shingles. The bushes in the front yard were dying, and the property looked a bit neglected. A feeling of dread came over her as she looked at the front door. The screen was torn and the glass was cracked in two placed.

"I suspected you might have second thoughts, so when I got word of something going on this morning, I asked Father Stevens if he would mind us stopping by." He explained as they got out of the car.

Raven stood in the front yard. She felt drawn to look up, and did so, gawking up at the roof of the house, her form tensing up. "What the heck is going on?" A whisper of a question passed her pale lips. There was something in the window of the attic. Obscure features of a large set of white wings could be seen through crackled glass.

"You can see that?" Aiden asked as if he already knew the answer.

"Yeah." She replied, following behind him into the house.

The home had a strange aroma to it. It smelled almost like buttered popcorn, but also like cinnamon and hints of fresh greens. The decoration of the house suggested humble occupants. Solid muted colored made up the color scheme of the furniture and walls. Decorations were sparse, consisting of a few photos, teddy bear knick knacks and a decorative vase. The couch in the front room was covered in blood. The rusted tones of dried vital fluids were smeared through the carpet and drizzled up the stairs, the sight of which only strengthened that feeling of dread and made her stomach turn.

"What happened here?" Raven questioned, hesitantly looking over the stains.

"An exorcism gone wrong." A calm voice crept down from the top of the stairs. "Come on up."

Careful not to step on the blood, she headed up the stairs, paying no mind to Aiden as she looked the priest over. His simple black slacks, button up shirt, and white clerical collar was right and proper. But he looked tired. "What do you mean?"

"I'm Father Stevens, you must be Raven? Aiden told me about you." The elderly priest managed a small smile.

"Yes, I'm Raven."

"The owner of this home is a parishioner at my church." He turned away, looking through the doorway next to him. Raven moved to stand at his side, following his gaze. The afternoon sun bathed the room in a heavenly glow and danced across the blood stained quilt draped over the bed as a breeze slipped through the trees outside. Two other priests stood over a woman resting in the bed, whispering prayers feverishly. Each had a rosary draped over folded hands and their heads were bowed. "She's dying. Our attempts to free her from whatever has hold of her have failed. Aiden was sent to help." The priest glanced at Aiden a moment. "He was able to detect the infliction upon her soul, but could do nothing more."

"I don't understand." Raven glanced at the priest only a moment. Her full attention was on the woman in the bed. "Why am I here? How will this change my mind?"

"She was possessed." Aiden explained calmly as he joined the two at the doorway, peering over the woman's frail features. There was a darkness around her eyes, auburn hair slick with sweat was pulled roughly into a pony tail and her lips were dry. "As the demon was cast out, it must have lashed out and cursed her in a way no light bearer or prayer can touch. You can remove it, however."

"This seems awfully convenient, the exact day you want to convince me of something, a woman needs help and, oh, look, only I can do the job." Raven looked at Aiden suspiciously.

"This was going to happen, regardless of what else is going on in the world. It happens every day, even right here in Kankakee. Someone goes missing, chances are it was a demon or other supernatural being of some sort. A Mother suddenly starts acting strange, is it drugs, psychotic break, or possession?" Aiden motioned into the room. "A wife, gentle and kind, goes to confession because, from her perspective, she was at the local second hand store and the next second, she is standing over the love of her life, who is dead at her feet." Aiden took a deep breath.

"She killed him?" Raven questioned.

"No, child, the thing that took control of her body did." Father Steven's spoke up.

"Here." Aiden slipped past the two, moving to the side of the bed. "Come here, Raven. Tell me, what do you see?"

Raven glanced at Father Stevens and made her way to the side of the bed. "I see a dying woman."

"And?"

"And…." Raven's brows furrowed. Hesitantly her slender fingers reached out. She pulled the edge of the quilt, bringing the cover away from the woman. "What's that?"

"What's what?" Aiden asked, watching intently.

"There's something in her chest." A silence fell over the room as the two hovering priests stopped their prayers and looked up at Raven with hope. It looked like a black stain just under the skin's surface of her chest. It made no sense, how could she know such a thing? The thought seemed trivial as the dying woman wheezed a groan in discomfort. "What do I do?"

Aiden smiled, reaching for her hand. Met with no resistance, he guided it to hover over the woman's chest. "Here?"

"Yes." Raven whispered.

He lowered her hand, pressing it down over the spot before letting go. "Pull it out."

"How?" She looked at him.

"Follow your instinct, focus on the spot and will it to your hand." Aiden looked at Raven's hand as he offered advice.

Her eyes were locked on that spot as she listened, and focused on wanting whatever it was to exit the woman and ail her no more. A gentle vibration caressed Raven's palm. It felt like pins were pricking at the surface of her skin as she lifted the hand just a little as a test. A dark green smoky mist pulled from the woman's chest. Lifting her hand a little higher brought quickness to the stream. It clung to her hand, swirling gently like a slowly rotating storm cloud.

With the last wisp of foulness pulled from her chest, the woman took a deep breath, able to freely do so without restraint. Aiden reached both his hands over and carefully clasped them around Raven's hands where the dark energy was gathered. A golden hue sparked up, encompassing their hands and snuffing the energy out.

Aiden pulled his hands away and nodded his head to the door. "Thank you." Father Stevens spoke with relief and joy. "Thank you." He repeated himself, moving to the bedside to check on the woman. Aiden stepped out into the hall, giving his reluctant charge a smirk on the way by, motioning her for her to follow him.

"What happens to her now?" She asked as she made her way back out into the hall.

"Father Stevens will help her with what comes next. She has a long road of healing ahead of her, both mentally and spiritually." Aiden reached into his jacket pocket to grab his cell phone and check the time. "What about you? What have you decided?"

Raven looked back into the room. A wave of emotion came over her. The woman was awake, clinging to Father Steven's hand and sobbing softly with what little energy she had. It was hard to fathom the position this woman was now in. To wake up and find your husband's blood on your hands and his lifeless body on the floor. To face the days ahead knowing that, even though you weren't in control, the last thing he ever saw was your face. That he died thinking his wife was ending his life.

But despite it all, the woman was alive, thanks to Raven's abilities. The sense of dread had lifted with the removal of the corruption from the woman, making room for a feeling of pride. It felt good knowing she helped someone. "It's bittersweet. Sure, she's alive, but…"

"It won't always be like this. Sometimes it will be worse." Aiden spoke matter-of-factly in response.

She turned to him, eyes wide. "I thought you were trying to convince me I can do this, not convince me to just go home and hide?"

Aiden shrugged, putting his phone away. "I'm being honest."

Raven turned without a word, heading down the stairs and to the front door. "Well, be honest in the car."

"Taking you home?" He followed with a confident smirk to his face.

"Nah, I think I'm ready for my training montage." She called out, jumping off the last step to the porch, heading to the car.

Aiden paused, watching her as she went. "If only it was that easy."

Chapter Three

Raven stood within the darkened space between two houses. The faint light from a half moon and a street light down the block was all that gave highlights to the features around her. She stood in silence, watching a particular house across the street while waiting. Everyone in the neighborhood was fast asleep, no lights in windows to be seen, save for this one. The hues of an active television screen reflected off the window curtains.

It felt crazy standing there, decked out and ready for battle. Women's combat boots, a little on the fashionable side, because it would raise a brow or two if she started running around in military grade boots as Aiden wanted, so they were a compromise of sorts. Black boot cut jeans and a plain dark blue top clung to her slender, fit form. The ensemble was topped off with her lucky black jacket which concealed black leather harness straps holding sheathed daggers.

All there was, was the silence of the night and her thoughts. It had been almost five weeks since the accident. Time moved slowly, yet so fast. Days and evenings spent juggling family, training, and reading about various things like demons, angels and spells were all a blur. Yet everything was also crystal clear.

There was a peace in reflection, in the idea that everything felt so natural once it was decided not to ignore what had happened and move on. It all made sense, to her, anyway. For most humans, we grow up to know our parents, our family is our world. But as youth progresses, some find themselves bouncing and drifting from groups of friends or through cultural fads to try and find a place that feels right. Some never find that place and spend their whole lives feeling like outsiders. With this new perspective, she couldn't help but wonder, is it because they, too, are Nephilim? Or something else, altogether? Unfortunate beings that never learned who or what they really are, so they spend their lives just feeling out of place, no matter what?

"Heh…" She softly mumbled out to herself at the idea. Then again, there are a lot of people who feel that way, they couldn't all be something other than human, could they? Maybe some are just unlucky, or have other underlying psychological issues.

"Hmm?" Aiden questioned, peering to Raven as he stepped up next to her.

"Nothing." She whispered.

A police car made its way down the street. Two officers could be seen in the car as it rolled by. Both officers were looking forward, talking, and right at the moment they were making their way past the two dark clad people creeping in the darkness, the officer driving looked at his partner. The night shift patrol, but what was the point if they don't even look around?

"You have one hour until they come back by, you got this, right?" Aiden asked, watching Raven as she checked over jacket pockets and the straps to her dagger sheaths.

"Do I?" She looked to Aiden, smirking a little.

"You are going to be fine. " He offered confident assurance, looking to the house.

Raven nodded before stepping out from where she was lurking. "Yeah, I got this." A confidence came over her as she crossed the street and stepped into the yard of the home in question. She had never broken into a house before, so this was a new experience for her. It was important that she get in, unseen, to maintain the element of surprise.

First she checked the picture window that faced the street, peeking inside to the living room where the television was, and saw it was empty. She crept down the side of the house, glancing into the window of the empty dining room. Finally making her way around the back of the property, she peeked into the windows of the kitchen, which also appeared unoccupied. With the first floor looking to be in the clear, the back door handle was tested it. It was unlocked. She slipped into the house, being careful not to make any noise that wouldn't be dismissed.

"Almost…. time." A voice could be heard scratching out from the direction of the front of the house. An unsteady creaking and the soft thuds of someone coming down the stairs from the second flood accompanied the disturbing tone.

Raven stood next to the kitchen table, listening carefully to the noises of the house. The television, while on, was muted. A wheezing could be heard coming from the same direction as the voice. The positioning of things based on her recent glances into the windows was reviewed within her mind to determine how much time was left.

"Is someone there?" The voice called out. "I can smell you."

Raven's eyes widened a little. She carefully reached into her jacket pocket, brushing her fingers over three smooth stones before moving away from the table to the entry way. This now put her face to face with a woman in her forties. Her long blond hair was filthy and ragged. The floral print apron she was wearing was stained with blood and dirt. Her skin was pale and clammy looking, and there was darkness around her eyes.

"You don't belong here." The voice seemed to be coming from the woman, but her chapped and cracking lips didn't move.

"And you do?" Raven quipped back.

"Did he send you? Did the master send a little….pet to check on….me?" The voice questioned as the woman took a few steps forward. The closer it got, the more it grated on Raven's nerves. It sounded like a chain smoker with a hint of nails to the chalkboard overtones. When certain words were spoken, its tone would raise and stretch out.

"I wouldn't say pet." She thought quickly, responding with a smile, amusement to her voice.

"Pet, no… yes. You are right, Nephilim, not pet." It got even closer. Its steady shuffle through the dining room caused the china cabinet and the dishes displayed within to rattle.

Raven stood still, watching as it moved. It knew what she was, and hearing it indicate so brought a skip to her heart beat.

"Problem?" The voice scratched out.

Raven's smile quickly dropped and her overall tone turned more serious. "No." She pulled her hand from her pocket, dropping the three smooth black stones to the floor. As they bounced and clattered against the woodwork, the woman in front of Raven turned swiftly.

There it was. Attached to the woman's back was a demon. Raven just stared, freezing up. A gaunt creature that seemed to be roughly the same size and build of a six-year-old boy stared back. The demon's brownish skin looked raw and fleshy. Dangling legs, originally hidden by the woman's dress before she turned around, were disfigured.

There didn't appear to be a ribcage. Instead, there were holes with tentacles protruding out of them. The tentacles had forced their way into the woman's sides. Eyes of mahogany, a tone that encompassed the entirety of the eye, were positioned just above two slits that made up the nostrils of a torn off nose. The demon was filthy, dirt and dried blood could be seen on its body.

A crooked grin revealed jagged slimy teeth. "What….. is this?" It questioned, its head moving up from the direction of the three stones to Raven. "What??" It stepped forward. "What??" Another step and another, suddenly within arm's reach, its gaunt hands stretched out. It was close enough now to see the demon's features in full detail and get a good whiff of the stench wafting off its human host. Weeks of sweat, urine and fecal remnants accumulated over the body turned puppet as a result of not bathing.

A single word of demonic slipped past Raven's lips, followed up by a strong gag and dry heave. The three stones rose up and started rotating around the demon. It leaned forward, the human it was attached to leaning and bending backward as it did.

"Stop!" Raven demanded while taking a step back. The demon stopped advancing, hesitating. Its eyes slammed shut. The woman turned around, no longer walking backward, straightening up and jumping forward.

The demon was fueling the woman and she was able to move faster than a human normally could. She slammed Raven into the fridge, pinning her in place. The decorative magnets on the fridge and the notes they were holding fell off, clattering and drifting to the floor. With the act, the three black stones also fell to the floor. One of the tentacles dislodged from the woman's side. A foul smelling brown fluid sprayed out. It splattered to the fridge and over Raven's arm.

"Shit!" Raven blurted out. She struggled, pulling on her arms to try and get free. The woman kept going despite the struggle, and leaned in, opening her mouth wide, exposing stained teeth before biting down onto Raven's neck hard enough to break skin. The act brought an end to Raven's struggling as she let out a half scream.

The woman pulled away, giving Raven enough room to take action. Raven pushed her head back against the stainless steel fridge, then snapped it forward in a quick head butt, sending her forehead slamming into the woman's face. This caused her to let go, stumble back, and slip on the fluid that had sprayed all over a moment ago. Falling onto her rear with a bang and a snap of bone, the demon squealed out in pain.

Raven called out that single word of demonic once more, one hand raised in a motion to the three stones that came to life at her command. The stones moved into place, lifting from the floor to move around the demon in a circle and continue to move around the demon even as it struggled, forcing its host to stand and resume her advance.

Words in old world Latin started to pass through Raven's lips. Her tone was flooded with emotion, doubt, fear, and panic. Those were not the ideal combination to accompany the words learned from one of the many books Aiden had made her study. The demon wailed, spinning about and swatting at the stones before going after Raven. The loose tentacle lashed out and latched onto her neck directly over where the woman had bitten. Raven stopped reciting, grabbing at it frantically. "Get off me!" She growled out, ripping it away, but it was too late. The stones dropped to the ground and so did she.

The blackout only lasted a moment. Opening her eyes, Raven was greeted by the blank stare of the woman she had been trying to help. The body was on the floor, resting in a small pool of blood.

"Thank you, stupid Nephilim." The demon's voice scratched out. "A welcomed…. upgrade."

Raven's jacket had been removed, not a good sign, given the demon's choice of words. Her eyes rolled, darting over the rooster print window curtains and counters. She closed her eyes tight, trying to move, but every limb felt so heavy. A small, warm, slimy hand wrapped around her ankle, holding it in place. Another clasped the back of her calf. It pulled itself over her, letting our labored gasps as it did.

Hand over hand, it grappled over her body as it pulled itself slowly over her backside, getting into position.

"Open…. your eyes." It spoke right into her ear, a foul breath rolling past her nose, causing an already unsteady stomach to turn even more. Fleshy tentacles brushed over her arms and neck as they slithered into place. The ones along her sides pushed at the spaces between her ribs, but didn't attempt to penetrate just yet.

"I want you to know." It explained as Raven opened her eyes. It was on top of her, chest heaving with the difficulty it had breathing while pressed to her back, and leaning around to the side to look at her eye to eye.

"How stupid it was…how silly it is to think…" One of the tentacles dug in, ripping through skin and pushing into the muscles between the bones of her ribcage. The pain throbbed through her side, but the only reaction she allowed was a pained gasp. Full paralysis was ruled out since everything could still be felt, movement was just impossible. A cold sting filled that side of her chest, spreading as the extension lodged itself firmly in place. "…a being such as you could get anywhere reciting spells designed to be spoken by….humans." It reached down, pawing at her hair roughly. "..I'll make good…. use of you, my new host."

Raven closed her eyes, trying to calm her nerves and focus on the lessons she'd learned during training. A power was available to command and manifest in different forms. It could be felt stirring within, like a gentle scratching under the skin's surface that radiated throughout her whole body. A rushed build of pressure brought a throbbing ache to both hands. "Don't fight it…. Don't be scared! I smell the fear on you." Two more tentacles broke through her skin and writhed into place, bringing another wave of cold stinging through her side.

A half scream pushed past her lips as the pressure building within her body became unbearably painful just before its sudden release. The pressure pushing at every inch of her body was there, and then gone. The sensation of something trying to scratch its way out from under the skin lifted as her power flooded through her body. Slender fingers curled against the fluid she was laying in. "Heh… so, I can't use those spells? Good to know." She spoke in a dark, almost cocky tone. Her eyes flew open and straight into a glare at the demon, who was attempting to hijack himself a new body to leech off of. His eyes widened in confusion. The glare visually unnerved the demon as he stared at the dual black orbs as if staring into the abyss.

Raven shifted her body weight swiftly, rolling to the side. This caused the demon to fall off and the attachments to disengage. Her hand reached out to the sheath harness on the floor, pulling one of the daggers as she kept rolling by until she was flat on her back.

One of the tentacles lashed out, jabbing at her arm. An awful noise came from the demon as Raven slashed at the incoming appendage, severing it. The sound wasn't screeching as much as it was making random noises akin to screaming in a strange, scratching tone.

Raven got up, turning and kicking at the thing, sending it flying toward the front of stove. It slammed into it with a loud clang that brought an end to the awful noises it had been making. It was face down on the tile. She tilted her head slightly to better examine the demon's position as she gripped the dagger tightly. Raven stepped forward, being cautious just in case the thing was playing 'possum.

"Need…. to….." The demon gasped out, tentacles reaching in Raven's direction.

"Sorry…" Raven responded to the demon. "Not going to happen." She didn't let it speak another word. She dropped to one knee beside it and rammed the dagger in hand down into the back of its skull. The demon ceased to move, its extended tentacles falling to the floor just short of reaching their target.

She stared down at the demon a moment before pulling on the dagger. "Gross." she grumbled to herself as she roughly yanked it out, eyeing the blood and brain matter coating the rune covered blade.

She paused a moment to take in how it all felt. Dark energy, shadow energy was flowing through her. It flushed away the demon's influence and provided the strength she needed to push past the pain of injuries. It felt amazing, as if there were no limit to what she could do. She felt a level of exhilaration that, when trying to compare it to anything she ever felt before, she drew a blank.

It also felt terrifying, the desire to do it again. To kill something, anything else. The watering of her mouth as the thought of licking the blade and taste the blood of the kill entered her mind as naturally as the idea of tasting a new drink.

With a deep breath, shaken by her own thoughts and feelings, the black in her eyes receded as she forced the power back. Carefully, Raven stepped over the demon's body and the pooled blood to make her way to the woman on the floor, who hadn't made a peep through all of this. She crouched down, pressing two fingers to her clammy neck. There was no pulse.

"Sorry…" Even though it didn't seem that the woman was even breathing, she needed to be sure. As she looked over the human body, one thing was clear, there was no saving her. Peering through the tears in her clothing, Raven saw that the skin along her sides was bruised and marred and, in a spot or two, bits of bone were exposed through the muscle tissue. She had bled out when the demon jerked the tentacles from her sides.

Raven stood, reaching over to grab a towel off the counter. She used it to clean off the dagger. She picked up the leather harness from the floor, shook it off, and roughly wiped it clean before slipping it back on and sheathing the dagger. A glance to the clock on the wall showed her that the hour was almost up. She turned back to the demon's lifeless body. The smell it was emitting surprisingly cut through the already existing stench in the room. She collected her jacket and pulled it back on before kneeling next to the demon, and pulled a piece of black chalk from the pocket. The clink of the chalk hitting the checkered kitchen tile seemed louder than it actually was through the crushing late night silence.

She held the chalk to the slick surface of the floor a moment, deep in thought. It dawned on her that the chalk wouldn't work on the laminate tile. "Dummy…." She mumbled to herself, getting up to look around. She rifled through the drawers, looking for anything that could be written on. She discovered a note pad in the very last drawer, half buried under an assortment of random things like paper clips, rubber bands, pens and various odds and ends one usually finds in a 'catch all' drawer.

"Ok. I guess this will work," she said with a chuckle, setting the note pad down on the counter. With careful skill, she drew the chalk gingerly over the paper, marking it up. The black demonic symbols she drew were a stark contrast to the adorable kitten staring up at her from the paper, its paw held up with a red string around it with the phrase 'Don't Forget!' in cursive red text.

"Yeah, don't forget, chalk doesn't work on all surfaces Raven, duh." She kind of laughed at herself as she finished, leaving room for one more mark, then tucking the chalk away. She pulled the paper off the pad and headed over to the entry way to the kitchen. Bending down to scoop up the three stones, she caught sight of something sticking out from under the couch in the living room.

"Shit…"

She crammed the stones into her pocket and very gently set the paper on the dining room table on the way past it into the living room. She noticed something that couldn't have been seen from outside through the windows, family photos. Photos of the woman with her husband and two children. Raven looked over at the toy car that had gotten her attention, then to the time on the cable box.

She then looked up to the ceiling and over to the stairs. There was no time to overthink things. She made a quick dash to the top of the stairs and noticed blood smeared over the walls. A carpet runner was also stained with wet spots and there were scratches on some of the door frames. She needed to check the rooms, but time was running out. She pushed against the door of the first room, opening it and making her way in to take a look around. It appeared empty, but also showed signs of trouble. A teddy bear tea party was toppled over, the small pink child's play table and chairs on their sides. A plastic tea cup was crushed into the carpet as if someone heavy had stepped on it.

"Anyone in here?" She called out, taking a few more steps into the room. She looked over toward the other side of the bed and glanced into the closet, where all she found were clothes and toys.

Raven moved to the next room. Her hope that the family members in the photos got away, or were never here at all, was crushed as soon as she pushed the door open. Her senses were assaulted by the smell of rotting flesh. It was potent. Air tainted by a body left to decompose could only be compared to the smell of uncollected festering road kill on a smoldering day. She lifted the back of her hand to cover her nose. There were stains on the walls, blood and something else she couldn't identify, most likely the brown fluids from the demon she just killed. On the bed were the remains of the man from the pictures, face down in dried vomit and blood stained sheets. His clothes were shredded away, giving her a clear view of the holes along his sides. Discolored flesh showed entire chunks missing, as if something had been feasting on the body at some point. The stomach had been ripped open, leaving a mix of half eaten and nibbled-on organs pulled out and spilled over the edge of the bed to the floor.

The glimpse of a tiny pink shoe sticking past the corner of the bed brought tears to her eyes and a lump to her throat. She took a hesitant step forward, but it was enough to look past the bed to where a smaller body lay. A little girl, her tiny frame half curled on its side. She was a mess of dried blood mixed with patches of molding remains that had been eaten away to such severity that in some areas it had been stripped to the bones.

She could feel her knees buckle. She felt like she was about to break down into tears, but she had to push on. The sight hit too close to home. She had a little sister around the same age. This small girl could easily have been little Myra, this man could have been her Dad.

"Move." She growled to herself, pulling trembling fingers over her eyes to wipe away the tears. The room might as well have been filled with quicksand pulling her down as she pushed herself to keep moving and head back into the hallway. The bathroom and hall closet were void of any signs of life, leaving one kid unaccounted for and only one room left to check.

The last room. Each step she took toward the door was harder than the last and, with each one, she whispered 'please', begging to anyone or anything listening to make this last room be empty, because that would mean the other kid in the photo might be alive somewhere. She froze, hand clamped to the door handle, hesitating with the thought that it could also mean he met the same fate and might be in the attic or basement.

She shook the door as she tried the handle, and was met by a welcoming sound--the whimpering of a child. Even though it was obvious the door was locked, in her eagerness to make sure it wasn't a figment of a hopeful mind, she tried the door again.

"Hold on! Stay away from the door!" Raven called out. She took a few steps back, giving herself room, then dashed forward and delivered a swift kick to the door. The blow ripped it from the frame and it went falling to the side, hitting a wall. The boy, who looked around five, was huddled in the corner of his room, trembling. His clothes were dirty and his eyes were blindfolded. Raven took a sweeping glance around. No blood on the racecar themed walls, no blood on the kid, and she noticed a fresh, half-eaten sandwich, which was a sign that the demon was feeding him.

She took a deep breath, calming herself. It felt important to her that the child didn't hear the distress in her voice. She moved to the boy, stooping down and looking him over. "It's ok…" She whispered, surprised at being able to sound so calm. She gently placed her hand on his arm. It served a double purpose, to try and calm him, and to see if she could sense anything hiding within.

The boy said nothing, but did seem to calm with her assuring words. Sensing nothing out of the ordinary, she gently pulled at the cloth around his eyes, taking a peek to make sure it wasn't covering a hidden horror or two. Everything looked fine, but she left the cloth in place. He didn't need to see the blood smeared all over the hall outside his room.

"I'm going to get you out of here, ok?"

The child gave a nod as Raven picked him up, and she carried him out of the room and down the stairs.

"I need you to stay right here…" With great hesitation she set him down right next to the front door. "Just for a moment, ok? I promise, I'm going to get you out of here."

"Ok." He whimpered out with a tremble.

She moved back to the dining room, pulling out the black chalk again and moving to the 'don't forget' reminder note she'd previously prepared. The open space was quickly filled in with a final mark, which prompted them all to light up in a heated glow. Raven lifted it from the table and ran into the kitchen. She threw the paper down on the body of the demon. As the paper made contact, the body erupted in flames.

But was it good enough? She stepped to the counter, grabbing up the notepad, questioning whether what she'd just done was enough to bring the whole house down and destroy the evidence of what had gone on upstairs. Raven swiftly moved back into the dining room with the intention of whipping up another set of fire runes. She could hear the flames roaring in the kitchen as they covered the demon's body and started up the wooden cabinets. Looking to the small boy still waiting in fear, she shoved the notepad in her pocket. She felt the need to go all out. She pressed the black chalk to the wall and pulled it over faded patterned wall paper, quickly forming the same symbols that she'd used to start the fire that was already spreading. As she lifted the chalk from the wall, the marks started to glow with a heat. Flame rolled out from the runes, spreading like a spark to dry wild brush. Raven went back to the child, picking him up.

Without looking back, she opened the front door and ran down the steps, almost tripping on a loose board on the porch. She didn't let it slow her down, running through the yard to the side of the street. "Listen to me…" Raven explained, setting him down calmly and glancing over the little boy one more time. "Just stand right here, the police are coming. Ok? Just stand right here, you're going to be ok."

"Ok…" The boys tiny peep of a voice brought a small smile to her worried features. She looked down the street, then over to where Aiden was waiting. The expression on his face spoke loud and clear of worry and confusion about what exactly was going on. She rose, stepping away from the boy, and darted across the street.

"What the heck just happened?" Aiden questioned, showing no hesitation as he grabbed at the opening of her jacket to get a better look at the mess soaking her clothing.

"Hey, hey get off me…" She swatted at him. "There was a family." She nodded in the boy's direction. "He's alright. though."

Aiden pulled his hands away, looking over to the child. "The demon is gone, then?" He questioned, watching as the police came to a halt in front of the burning house. It had actually been a little more than an hour. Coffee and donuts were dropped as the officer in the passenger side came busting out of the car, scooping up the kid to move him out into the street, putting the patrol car between them and the house. Even though a full sized yard was between them, the officer didn't want to take any chances. The other officer followed suit and got out of the car while calling the incident in.

"Yeah…it's gone." Raven explained, pushing a few fingers against one the holes in her side that had already healed enough to not be life threatening. "Fun fact…." she glanced to him. "That Latin stuff didn't work for me."

"Well it's good to learn so you know what to listen for in case someone tries to use it on you." Aiden tried to find a bright side of sorts to the situation. "You understood everything it was saying, though? And the runes worked?"

Raven was silent a moment as she watched the little boy, holding back tears. She didn't understand why she was starting to cry at this point. Before it was because of the little girl, but now? Was it because of the whole experience, or was it fear and the reminder that she was half something not human? It was the demon half of her that allowed the understanding of every word the demon spoke. "Yeah, I understood what it was saying and the runes worked." She motioned to the fire. "As you can see."

Aiden turned just as she wiped the tears from her eyes. "You ok?"

"Yeah, I'm fine." She replied softly as she looked down the street. The sound of sirens could be heard in the distance and it wouldn't be too long before the emergency crews arrived. "Let's get out of here before someone spots us."

Without another word they both turned and headed to the alley, out of sight.

Chapter Four

Her wide brown eyes were focused on the door handle. The door before the child led to her big sister's room. Unlike her own or her brothers, nothing was attached to the door. No childish signs indicating whose room it was, though there were nicks and worn marks from tape once added and removed.

"Can I come in?" The small girl whispered in the tiniest voice she could, knowing if she was heard asking, she would be told no.

"Oh, I can? Thank you, thank you, I will!" She whispered on, reaching tiny hands up to the door knob and turning it ever so carefully. The door opened and the wee invader slipped in. One wall of the room was painted a medium purple, Violet Majesty, the sales man at the paint store called it. Cubed shelving was tiered along half the wall's length. The shelves were filled with books, comics, picture frames, music cds, video games and random things collected over the years. Myra's personal favorite, even though it didn't belong to her, was the baseball sized glass ball found at a flea market. Every time she saw it, she imagined the mix of colors was a whole galaxy preserved in glass. A colorful pin board with notes and photos pinned to it hung on the wall next to the computer desk. Clothes littered the floor, and a reading corner looked welcoming with paper lantern lighting hanging from the ceiling. Across from that was a few old milk crates filled with random computer and electronic related things.

Myra looked to the bed and at the sleeping lump buried under the array of mix and matched covers. Not a peep, not a word, she had to be careful. She tip-toed over to the chair in front of the computer, climbing atop it and stood there, looking around in admiration. She wanted to be just like Raven when she grew up. She turned on the chair, reaching over and pointing her fingers at the keyboard, poking at the air as if pushing the keys.

She then climbed down, scampering over to the lucky black jacket on the floor, pulling it up around her shoulders. She smiled real big, looking at the mirror and cuddling the jacket to herself. Her nose wrinkled a little, the jacket smelled funny. Clean, but not the way Mom makes clothes smell. Unknown to the girl was the fact that before the sun was up that morning, it was soaked in demon blood and being washed in a twenty-four hour Laundromat on the city's south side.

Curious brown eyes now fell on the black leather dagger sheaths on the floor in the closet. The girl stared at them, leaving the jacket where she found it, only to stop and turn as she heard movement in the bed. She bound forward, curly black hair bounced off her shoulders as she went. Tiny hands grabbed at the bed post as she climbed up on the bed to pounce on Raven.

"Wake up!"

Raven woke up with a jerk and a gasp. "Myra…." She mumbled out, pulling the blankets away from her face. "What are you doing?" She questioned, looking at the child with squinted eyes.

"Mama said…." The girl huffed. "…pancakes….and you have to come downstairs."

Raven stared at her little sister, the events from the night before rushing to the front of her mind. The thought of the small girl laying in a puddle of her own blood, half eaten away, made Raven's stomach turn. She sat up and reached over, pulling Myra into a tight hug.

"No hugs! Pancakes!" The girl protested before cuddling into her sister.

"Ok." Raven agreed with a chuckle, letting Myra go. "I'll be right down, save me some of the good stuff, alright?"

Myra started to crawl off the bed, answering before sliding down onto the floor. "Aright, if Jaden don't eat it all first!" The small girl went running off, calling out a warning to her brother. "Ja-den! Don't eat all the stuff!"

Raven eyed the door and then peered over to the sheaths on the floor. She sighed, rubbing the back of her head. Those things would need to go somewhere else. She got out of bed and proceeded with a quick swap of clothes. The weaponry in question was collected and crammed into her backpack before heading down stairs.

The large old house was tucked in the historic housing district along the river and had just the right setup so that standing just out of sight was easy. Approaching the oak wood framed entryway to the kitchen, she stood there a moment, watching everyone, thinking. Her Mom was working on a fresh stack of pancakes, her Dad was cleaning his glasses and the two youngest were having at the pancakes like they hadn't been fed in days.

It was always obvious Franklin wasn't her biological Father. However, he helped raise her as if he was. The question came to mind as she stood there, what exactly happened to her real Father? Since he was a demon, did he go back to hell? Maybe he was killed by a light Nephilim? Maybe it didn't matter. Dwelling on such a thing did seem counterproductive.

The same could be said when dwelling on the situation with her Mother. It was a train of dark thoughts she had started on many times, but always avoided. Was the tale of her father being in the army a lie to cover a darker truth, or was there some other form of deception on his part? It's not like she could flat out ask about it. Oh, hey, Mom, were you lying to me about my birth Father? Her gut instinct told her it was a subject better left untouched.

Why mar the memories and future times together with such things? Memories like this moment. Everyone was happy, sitting around the aged kitchen table. The kitchen nook windows faced the backyard and allowed plenty of sunlight into the kitchen. Along the windows, what was once a cushioned seating area was converted to a shelf to hold pots of herbs for cooking and a couple Gerbera daisy plants.

"MmmMmmMmm!" Jaden hummed out.

"Did you save me some?" Raven asked as she stepped around the corner into the kitchen, moving to the table. She hung the strap of her backpack on the corner of a chair before sitting down. Her attention went to the very empty container of 'the good stuff', as it was called in their house. Caramel and sea salt pancake spread, Grandma Jones' secret recipe, and there was none left.

"No! He ate. It. All!" Myra explained, raising her voice as she looked at Jaden, who was cramming the last bite into his mouth. The fluffy caramel mess was all over his lips.

"That's ok." Raven said with a laugh, getting a pancake and putting it on her plate.

"Just one?" The smooth voice of her dad drawled out curiously as he finally got his glasses clean and placed them back on his face.

"I'm not that hungry," was all the response Raven allowed as she started to eat her pancake slowly.

"We going to aunty Dee's house today to build forts!" Myra explained, mostly to Raven, but she kept raising her voice in excitement like maybe she was trying to tell the whole world as well.

"We *are* going, Myra." Their Mom walked over, putting down more pancakes on Raven's plate. "Kids, why don't you go upstairs and get ready, ok?" She continued, taking a seat at the table. Myra took another pancake into her hands and took off.

"Good luck." Jaden said, looking right at his older Sister before getting out of his chair and leaving. He was old enough to know what was up, anytime someone got singled out to remain at the table, a talking to was about to go down.

"Thanks…" Raven replied, less than enthusiastic.

"You know, you have me and your Mom pretty worried." Franklin spoke from the head of the table, a Fatherly tone to his voice.

"How so?" Raven questioned, taking a glance at him as she begrudgingly ate the now full stack of pancakes.

"You aren't eating as much as you normally do." He stated as he observed her behavior. "You're out late and, honestly, I don't even know when you get home— "

"She's here when we wake up." Raven's Mom interjected.

"Thank God for that." He followed and swiftly proceeded with asking. "What do you do all day?"

Raven looked her Dad right in the eyes. "Stuff?" She replied, poking at the pancakes with her fork.

"What kind of stuff?" Her Mom asked.

"Reading, hanging around with friends, playing video games." Raven replied, going back to eating. Learning how to kill demons, cast spells, and swing a sword…stuff, she thought to herself.

"I ran into your boss. I thought you were going back to work last week?" Her Dad asked with concern.

"I was…" Raven replied, taking the last bite off her plate. One thing she had never done to either of her parents was lie, and lies had been slipping past her lips often since the accident.

"I left a message for him, letting him know I was going to take one more week, that I had some stuff to finish sorting through." Yet, lying also seemed to come naturally to her, it's something that didn't escape her attention. Was it a demon thing? She wondered about that every time she lied and someone bought it. Demons and the Devil will both lie to get what they want, maybe it's just a trait they all posses. The silver tongued spinning of whatever 'truth' one wanted others to believe. "I guess he didn't get it, I'll swing by the shop and talk to him."

At this point, Raven's Mom was more or less pleased with the talk and headed out of the kitchen, glancing at her husband with a look that clearly read 'try to not be too hard on our daughter' as she went. "Well…." He started up again. "I guess that's ok. As I said, we're worried about you. You just haven't been yourself since the accident and—"

"I'm fine…." Raven assured him, and stood up, pulling the backpack strap off the wooden kitchen chair and up over her shoulder.

"Alright." He replied with a sigh, standing from his chair as well. "I have to head to the Church and take care of a few things before we head to Dee's house." He smiled, pulling a small stack of three envelopes from under a placemat and handing them to her. "We will talk about this later at dinner."

"Oh…ok…" She replied in confusion, taking the envelopes. Franklin gave Raven a hug and made his way out of the kitchen.

Left alone in the kitchen, she hesitantly opened the first envelope, reading over the letter inside. It was an acceptance letter for a University. They all were acceptance letters. She stood there, staring at the letter in silence. There was a time when going off to college was a possibility. She knew in her heart that the possibility ended the night of the accident. The problem was now how she would explain to her parents that she no longer wanted to attend school.

She shoved the envelopes into her bag and headed out the back door.

It was a bit of a walk to Aiden's house, a place that had become in many ways the center of Raven's world. She got there first thing in the morning for hand to hand combat training. Lunch was normally takeout of some kind, because neither of them could cook if their lives depended on it. The afternoon was spent reading and getting pop quizzes on different things, followed up by an evening of weapons combat training, which all led up to her first hunt.

He was pushing her, impressing at every turn that he had to, reminding her of what she was until it no longer felt insulting, just annoying to hear, making sure she could do certain things in a 'quick draw' fashion. She had to be quicker, faster and able to adapt to any and all situations. Any time she would ask if he would be this tough on a light Nephilim, he would answer with a pop quiz.

Hunting and assignments were her future, but these were things that couldn't be explained to family. For now, she felt like she had to 'handle' them, starting with the work situation. Thinking all this over as she walked, she eventually made it downtown to her place of employment, Court Street Computers and Electronics.

The faded brick building had bars over its windows and a small store front, with the majority of the building being used as a warehouse and work stations for repairing things. Raven made her way in and past the short aisles of custom built computers and small packaged merchandise. By the time she got to the counter, a man in his late twenties was coming out of the back. A mobile tablet in his hands had his attention and partially blocked the black and white print of a chimpanzee on his t-shirt.

As his greenish brown eyes glanced up, he did a double take, surprised to see her standing at the counter instead of a customer. "Hey, Raven!" He greeted her before looking over his shoulder and calling to the back happily. "Hey, Larry, guess who's here!"

"Hey, Hani." Raven chuckled, leaning against the counter, watching him.

"My favorite employee?" An older man answered as he came hurrying from the back. He was well dressed in slacks and a button down collar shirt. His brown hair showed his age with a graying hairline.

"You said I was your favorite." Hani looked at Larry, a bit surprised.

"When Raven isn't around, yes, you are my favorite." Larry nodded a single nod in affirmation. "You ready to come back to work?" He asked eagerly, looking at Raven in anticipation.

Hani looked to Raven, confused by what their boss had said. She shrugged a little at Hani before answering Larry. "Actually.... I was stopping by to ask if I could have another week or two. I'm still not feeling right and, well, I still don't have a car."

Larry's enthusiasm faded as he responded with a sincere understanding. "It's ok, you take all the time you need and when you're on your feet, your job is here waiting."

"Thanks, you really are the best boss." Raven smiled a little.

Hani looked down to the tablet in hand as he mumbled something in Hindi before turning and making his way into the back.

"What did he say?" Larry looked to Hani swiftly as he headed back to work, then looked back to Raven. "Seriously, I hate it when he does that."

Raven laughed a little. "I think he said he wants a raise, just give the guy one, already."

Larry stared at Raven in thought for a second. He lifted his hands and clapped them together. "This is why you need to come back to work."

Raven smiled, knowing Hani had said something completely different, but the guy did deserve a raise. "Soon, boss." She assured him in amusement. "I'm taking off….and taking this." Snatching up a candy bar, she turned, heading out.

"Alright, keep in touch!" Larry turned, heading into the back room as Raven made her way to the door. "Hey, Hani, let's talk about a raise." He called out as the door closed behind her.

That was one of the many little details of what she was that would take some getting used to. Knowing a language without being taught was kind of fun. Ever wonder what exactly people are saying when they are speaking another language? Sometimes it's just innocent chatter, other times, it's not.

The language thing wasn't all that had changed. Every time she walked down the street, as she was in that moment, there was always a reminder. A whisper or noise, a glimpse of something that might be suspicious, she could see things other humans couldn't. The most interesting so far was the ghost outside the old theater, a building steeped in local and national history. It had been a Vaudeville hotspot for about two decades, and hosted acts like The Marx Brothers. There were rumors about it being haunted by the woman who built it in 1912. Raven could see now that she was always there, no matter the time of day, standing outside the main entrance, watching everyone who walked past or entered. In death her spirit remained, and yet no one but Raven noticed her as she stood watch over her great accomplishment in silence.

Other ghosts and disjointed remnants of those who had come and gone weren't always seen and not heard. There was the ghost of a small child sitting on the porch of a house a few doors down from Aiden's house, and when Raven walked by, if she looked at her, the girl screamed. It made the first couple of morning walks to the house unsettling until she learned to just not look.

Raven let herself into the two story, grey shingled, blue trimmed house like she had day after day before. Unlike every day before this one, however, she found it empty. A note on the door that led to the basement simply read, "Be back soon, read some of the books I left on the desk."

Aiden's house was fairly plain. Pretty much everything had been gotten from second hand shops and there was barely anything in it. The walls needed to be repainted, and the plumbing had issues. It didn't feel like a home, it felt like a place that could be abandoned at any moment.

She headed to the basement, going straight to an old wooden desk. Three new books had been added to what had previously been stacked there. Sitting down, she glanced at the clock and pulled one of the books open.

This book was a new subject, druidism. Druids were typically humans who were born with a natural affinity to call on aspects of nature. They had spirit animals, could command the elements, and were far from neutral in the ongoing war between heaven and hell. They often got involved in the affairs of witches and warlocks or provided aid in hunting certain demons. Heavy into natural remedies and maintaining the balance, they have all but disappeared. A small order remains hidden, suspected to be somewhere in Ireland.

After spending almost the whole afternoon reading the basic history of druids, looking over accounts of spells and sets of runes, she had read the whole book. She pulled out a blank sheet of paper and grabbed a pen. Raven rapidly tapped the pen against the edge of the book that was laid out on the table. She wanted to try one of the runes, something simple that shouldn't get her in trouble.

The sound of the screen door at the back of the house opening and closing, followed by the sound of multiple footsteps upstairs broke that line of thought. Aiden appeared at the top of the stairs to the basement calling out, "Hey, come on up here." Raven set the pen down before heading up the stairs to find Aiden waiting with two people.

"Raven. This is Owen and Zaida," he explained, motioning to each person as he named them.

Owen had light auburn hair, brown eyes, fair skin and freckles lightly peppered the tops of his cheeks. He was wearing a pair of maroon and white sneakers that looked to have been around a while, jeans, and a brown leather jacket over a thin maroon hoodie. Resting within the naturally orange toned shaggy hair was a pair of simple brown steam punk style goggles. He looked kind of young and smiled wide at Raven.

Zaida was another story. No smile, rather she looked at Raven critically with warm, maple brown eyes. The black woman's hair was pulled to the side in a braid and she was dressed as if she was ready for combat. Black leather boots, pants and a sleeveless brown shirt were accented by a brown and black buckled suspender harness. The Enochian tattoos on her right arm were also an attention getter.

"She's shorter than I imagined," Owen pointed out, sliding over to Raven.

"It's nice to meet you?" Raven questioned, looking to Aiden.

"Owen is…." Aiden paused.

"Think of me as your second guardian." Owen placed his arm around Raven as if they were the best of friends.

"Second? Why do I need a second?" She looked at Owen, feeling mildly perturbed by his invasion of her personal space.

"Because you're a demon," Zaida answered bluntly with a bit of distaste to her Australian accented voice.

"Ok…" Raven looked at Zaida. "Why is miss cranky pants here?"

"Assignment, just needed a place to crash," Zaida explained and picked her bag up off the floor. "I'll find my own way to the guest room."

"Sure, Zaida that's fine," Aiden answered as she went.

Zaida made her way from the kitchen, side glaring at Raven on her way by. Raven eyed the woman right back, before eying Owen, who was still hanging on her.

"Whose idea was this?" She questioned.

"Mine." Aiden replied.

"Me and Aiden go way back," Owen piped up. "When he told me his new charge was of the shadows, I headed straight here."

"Owen can help in certain areas I can't. Plus, having two guardians has eased the counsel's concerns about you, for now, anyway," Aiden explained.

"Ok, then." Raven pulled away from Owen gently."If it's ok, I'm going to call it a day early and head home."

"Home?" Owen questioned. "You don't live here?"

Raven looked back and forth between the two.

"We haven't had that talk, yet." Aiden broke the awkward silence. "I suppose now is a good time." He sighed, motioning to the kitchen table.

Raven sat down, Owen right behind her. He pulled a chair out and spun it around so the back faced the table and sat down, straddling it.

"The farther into your training you go and the more assignments you get, the more dangerous it's going to be for your family," Aiden carefully explained.

"Other demons could follow you home," Owen pointed out.

"Or sense you inside as they pass by," Aiden added.

"They could even sense you live there, when you aren't home." Owen peered to Aiden.

"Doesn't even have to be demons, could be light Nephilim." Aiden peered back to Owen.

"Ok....ok I get it." Raven interrupted them both. "It's not safe for me to stay there."

"I already have one of the spare rooms set up for you. Whenever you are ready. Just not too much longer, ok?" Aiden offered with a bit of concern.

"Fine…." She mumbled. "Can I head out early?"

"Su—" Aiden started to reply, but Owen interrupted.

"No." He leaned forward, grinning. "I want to see where you're at. Training room in ten minutes." Owen then stood up, grabbed his bag, and headed up stairs.

Raven stared at Aiden, who stared right back before speaking. "I didn't say anything sooner because I know how close you are to your family. It's not going to be easy, I know it won't be the same. But you need to learn to rely on me and Owen now to keep you grounded and…"

"Human?" Raven finished for him.

"Just consider this and I'll leave it for you to handle…" He paused. "How much harder will it be, if one of them dies because you stayed in their lives?"

Aiden left the kitchen, leaving Raven to her thoughts. It wasn't something she wanted to think about. The idea of her family getting hurt, or worse, all as a result of her being around was nauseating. She stood from the table and hesitantly headed down to the basement so Owen could get an idea of what he was working with.

"Let's start slow." He nodded to her as she came down the stairs.

"Alright," she answered in a tone that reflected the burden still on her mind from the talk about her living arrangements.

Owen jumped up and down on the sparring mats, motioning her over. Excitement shone through his eyes. She glanced over the energetic red head and stepped onto the mat. As soon as she did, he dashed forward, throwing a punch that she caught without much effort. Having hold of his fist, she moved around to his back, twisting his arm and pushing him down to his knees.

He laughed wholeheartedly with the release of his arm. "You're strong and quick….but!" He stood, reaching up and pulling the goggles down into place. "That's not really what I want to see!" He turned, lifting his hands up, holding them open to each other. Bright golden light flooded into the space between them, arcing out sporadically like electricity. The light reflected off the goggle's dark lenses and lit up his excited grin.

She could feel the holy energy's warmth radiate against her skin. Something that should inspire feelings of safety, peace and tranquility made her feel like she was in danger. It felt painful to be near, causing her to back up swiftly and pull on her shadow energy, bringing a flooding of black to her eyes.

Seeing this, Owen pushed his hands out in her direction, letting the energy fly. He was expecting a show, a grand, up-close experience of shadow energy being released in some kind of protection. What he got was Raven doing a not so coordinated barrel roll out of the way and falling sideways onto the mats. The blast hit the basement wall, crackling, then dispersing.

"Owen, stop!" Aiden's voice boomed from the stairs as he flew down and right to Raven. "What are you doing? She's not ready for that!" He helped her up and glared at Owen intensely.

"I'm ok." Raven huffed. Her eyes cleared as she peered at Owen from behind Aiden, who had put himself in front of her.

Owen pulled the goggles back to the top of his head. "Obviously!"

"Her powers haven't manifested physically yet." Aiden turned and looked Raven over.

"Can I just go? I'm fine, he didn't know. No harm, no foul, right?" She just wanted to leave, feeling threatened by Owen.

"Yes, go ahead and go." Aiden looked from Raven to Owen, still angry.

"I'm really sorry, Raven," Owen offered apologetically.

"Hey, it's fine." She grabbed her jacket and took off up the stairs, leaving the two to, no doubt, argue over the rules Aiden was about to lay down. It was early enough stil, that if she ran, she could make it home in time to have dinner with the family. Out the back door she went, heading down the alley and across the main street of the city to head across town. Just when she was going to cross the multiple lanes of traffic, something pulled at her.

She made an attempt to ignore it, crossing the street with the intention of heading home, but it pulled again. She turned and looked up at the sky. There was a swirling of dark energy in the distance. Raven looked back in the direction that would take her home, but then started off toward the disturbance.

She ran over the bridge that crossed the river before darting into a residential area. She kept glancing to the sky and followed whatever was pulling on her, making sure it was still there. The closer she got, the more intense the pull became.

It was right over the museum, a swirling of dark red smoke that kicked up a bit of a breeze that rustled through the trees and put a haze over what little lighting there was. The museum was set back from the road, tucked into the start of a small wooded area that made up the property that once belonged to one of the state's long dead governors. During the day it made for a breath-taking sight. The small garden between the museum building and historic home was kept up with flowers during the summer and housed an old fountain and other relics from the city's past. At night, however, despite lighting, the area could hold a different mood.

She caught a glimpse of something creeping out of the small wooded area behind the museum. It was roughly 6 feet tall, but its height wasn't what would get someone's attention. It had no eyes. The demon's skin was a rusted crimson tone and sectioned out in a way that it looked like it was pieced together from different sized remnants of hard leather. It had thin lips and no nose or ears. A tattered brown sleeveless over vest served as a cover that extended down to about the thighs and was tied off at the waist. Finger and toe nails looked sharp enough to rend flesh. The demon hadn't noticed her yet or, if he had, he wasn't doing anything about her arrival.

"Hel—help me." A voice rasped out through the darkness of the area.

She turned and gasped a little in surprise. A man was on the ground, reaching out for her, struggling to ask for help again. His jogging clothes were covered in blood and his hand was clutching his bloody stomach. She took a quick glance around to make sure there wasn't another of these demons nearby and then she moved to the man, dropping to one knee.

"Hold still," she whispered, looking over his wounds. It looked like something had raked its claws through his stomach, ripping him clean open.

"Please…" The man whispered.

"I'm going to get you out of here." Raven started to reach for her cell phone, becoming very still, her eyes looking down to the man who suddenly looked terrified.

A heated breath rolled over Raven's neck. She pulled her hand slowly from her inner jacket pocket, moving in preparation to make a grab at the sheathed daggers under her jacket. The breath hovered from the back of her neck to the side of her face. She kept her eyes on the jogger until her hand reached a blade's handle.

A slight turn put her uncomfortably close to the demon's mouth. The demon tilted its head, breathing steadily at her. A guttural soppy squishing sound came from its throat. Thin lips parted, exposing a round appendage about three inches across. It was lined with curved, sharp teeth, and had another opening in the center. The appendage pushed past the demon's lips, heading right at Raven's face.

She drew her dagger as quickly as she could and slashed out. The blade clanked against teeth as her other hand pushed at the demon. The demon pushed right back, causing her to fall, slipping a little on blood. Her attention snapped to the jogger. He was dead, his blood soaked hand fallen away from the damage to his gut he'd been trying to hold closed.

The demon pushed Raven again, looming as she fell back even more, elbows hitting the sidewalk and preventing her from going all the way down. It reached down and she stabbed at its hand. The thing didn't even flinch and pulled his hand away from the blade. Leaning forward, the appendage extended further, emitting a wet clicking.

Whatever was going on came to an end as the blade of a sword came slamming through the demon's skull and out of its mouth. The tip of the blade burned with holy light and stopped an inch from Raven's face, blood dripping off of it.

Raven leaned back, eyes blackening over as they averted from the energy radiating off the blade. It was yanked out, allowing the demon to fall over. The tip of the blade quickly returned to being pointed right at her, which suggested she could easily be next.

"You still with me, Raven?" Zaida questioned urgently.

"Yes." Replied Raven as she got up, noticing that Zaida's eyes were no longer a warm brown, but a stunning mix of amber hues.

With Raven's confirmation Zaida spun, swinging the sword wide at one of the demons rushing up from behind. Golden energy flared from the weapon as it cut through flesh and organs, disemboweling it. Discolored innards splashed to the sidewalk.

Raven backed up and into a demon. It lashed out, claws slicing over her cheek. She turned to face it, taking up a defensive stance as the demon engaged her. It lifted its claw, suggesting the intention to either slice or grab. She got in a side step and managed to jab the dagger into the demon's side. She yanked, ripping through leathery flesh and bringing the demon to its hands and knees.

No hesitation, no opportunity was given for it to do anything else. A spinning roundhouse kick to the jaw sent it flying back with an audible crack. Her boot was pressed down to the demon and used to roll it over. She leaned down, jamming the dagger into the demon's heart.

"We need to get inside," Zaida called to Raven. "If we don't stop the source, they will just keep coming!"

Raven looked at Zaida just as she was pushing the door to the museum open and slipping inside. It wasn't locked and the alarm wasn't going off, which was a red flag, from her perspective. She took a quick glance around to make sure the area was clear, then she went after Zaida, calling out, "Hey! Slow down!"

Zaida stopped, turning to Raven. "What?"

"Don't just go rushing in, stop and think about this."

The light Nephilim narrowed her eyes at Raven a little, who motioned her hand out in a wide gesture to the empty area of the museum lobby. The main lighting was off and the secondary lighting was dimmed.

"This place closes up at five, yet the door is unlocked and the alarm is deactivated. Kind of odd, don't you think?" Raven looked at the nearest security camera, pointing her dagger at the cut wires. "That is clearly not normal."

Zaida gave a small nod to Raven, looking down the hall next to her. Her eyes darted over the statues that could easily provide cover. "You know this place? Ok… it's either a trap or someone came back after hours to work." She looked at the open door at the back of the lobby that led to a hall where the lights were on.

"Or the day time staff never got a chance to close up," Raven mused.

"What's back there?" Zaida nodded at the door, taking a few steps as she looked into the room adjacent to the lobby. It contained a large wooden desk, an old grandfather clock, a baby buggy, a rocking chair, and a china cabinet filled with things. Some of the items on the desk were knocked over, including an inkwell. The black ink ran off the side of the table and onto the carpet. "Looks like a struggle went on in there." She motioned into the room.

Raven looked into the room with the desk, her eyes darting over the scattered things. "Sure does," she agreed, looking at the door. "I think it's the office and where they store things not on display."

"You sure?"

"Yeah." Raven started to the door. "The same hall loops around to the other side of the building."

"You feel anything?" Zaida asked, following behind her.

"Kind of..." Raven mumbled hesitantly.

"Hey, hold up." Zaida grabbed Raven's arm and turned her around. "You looking at me? I can't tell with those black eyes of yours."

Raven's brows rose. "I'm looking at you."

"I'm having a hard time trusting you. It took a lot of will power not to run you through out there. You understand?"

Raven gave a simple slow nod.

"We have an advantage here if we work together, so focus. All I can sense is the demonic energy funneling out of this place. What do you feel?" Zaida asked firmly, looking around to make sure no one or thing was coming up behind them.

Raven took a deep breath and looked down the hall. She focused and listened, allowing her hand to rest on the door frame.

"It's like a pulse," Raven whispered. "And a scratching, like something is trying to claw its way through a door." She then pointed to the middle door with her dagger. "In there."

Zaida stepped past Raven, holding her hand back to her. "I'll go first."

Raven tilted her head, following Zaida. "Careful," she whispered.

Zaida grasped the handle of the curator's door and pulled down slowly in an attempt to make as little noise as possible. Someone could be heard on the other side of the door. They went back and forth from mumbling inaudibly to talking as if someone was in the room with them. Zaida glanced back at Raven just before pushing the door open.

The room was filled with all the things needed to clean, repair and restore items of historic value, but other than that, seemed to be empty. The floor was covered in blood, a mix of puddles and smears that streaked over the floor and through another doorway. Zaida moved to the secondary door, and Raven went to the opened package resting on the floor. It was addressed to the museum with a return label placing the package's origin somewhere in Europe. Raven crouched down, using the tip of her drawn dagger to lift the box and peek inside.

"There is no more to give!" A man's voice came from the room adjacent to the room Raven and Zaida were in.

Zaida motioned to Raven to follow before she stepped into the next room. Filing cabinets and storage lined one wall, and a work station with cleaning tools and restoration supplies lined the other. Above the cabinets was a large taxidermied bird with its wings spread open. A man was sitting on the floor, shirtless, his legs tucked under himself, blood stains on his khakis. Several museum employees were on the floor, laid out to form a circle of sorts around an old clay urn. Covered in strange markings, it had a wide brimmed opening and the stopper was set next to it.

Raven stepped in right behind Zaida. The man on the floor stood to look at them. His chest and arms were carved up in demonic summoning symbols, and a singular mark was carved into his forehead. His carving tool was a box cutter firmly held in his hand. By the looks of the bodies it was also used on them. Their arms had been slit open horizontally from their wrists to the folds in their arms.

"He's possessed." Zaida reached into her pocket and pulled out three white stones. Raven recognized them immediately. While shadow stones would assist in the practice of dark magic spells or even directing one's natural born powers, moonstones did the same for light Nephilim. She tossed them to the ground at the man's feet, which immediately drew his hazed eyes down in their direction.

Raven stayed back as Zaida lifted her free hand and started chanting in old Latin the rites of an exorcism. The three white stones rose, spinning and moving in a circle around the possessed man.

He threw his head back and laughed. "Children!" He sneered out, looking back and forth between the two. "Child of heaven, child of hell, playing together?" He started at Zaida, and his carved features were zapped by holy energy as he touched one of the stones rotating around him. The zap caused him to scream and recoil. Zaida kept going, speaking calm and clear. Raven slid behind her and headed over to the urn to get a better look.

"How unfortunate." The man coughed, his head jerking to the side to look at Raven. "Shadows should not play in the sun." He jumped, levitating swiftly to the ceiling and away from the white stones. The ceiling tiles cracked under the impact sending pieces and dust falling to the floor. "No matter, I'll kill you both just the same."

His taunts were ignored. Zaida held steady to her words while Raven carefully inspected the markings on the clay urn. The man started to roar and thrash against the ceiling, his back contorting.

Whispers stirred up around the urn, mumblings, an array of sounds that to the human mind would translate into gibberish and indefinable noise. It drew Raven's attention away from the exorcism, pulling everything around her out of focus.

"You should be helping him." The words were easily understood through the haze of muttering. Raven stood and backed away until her heels bumped into one of the bodies on the floor.

"Zaida, hurry up." She pushed a hand into her pocket, grasping at the shadow stones she kept within.

The man crawled with his back to the ceiling and then dropped in front of Zaida despite the stone's holy zaps. His movement was a blur as he grabbed her and slammed her into the cement block wall that made up the main structure of the building, sending her to the floor. Her sword clanged to the floor and the white stones went tumbling. Zaida wasn't moving.

Raven started toward Zaida and the possessed curator intercepted her. He rammed into her and drove her to the wall as she dropped her dagger. His forearm pressed against her chest at near crushing strength to pin her in place. His opposing hand lifted the bloody box cutter up in front of her face. The human body being possessed wasn't all that was pressed against her. The demon itself was pushing its presence on her. The back of his bloody hand brushed her bangs away roughly and pressed the box cutter's blade to her forehead lightly, teasing at what was about to happen.

"I'm going to kill you," Raven growled out in demonic.

Her choice of language brought a grin to the man's face. "No, I'm going to posses you." His eyes were locked on hers as he taunted. "And then we will finish the summoning."

He pushed the blade into her skin, drawing blood. Raven's lips parted, letting out a short gasp at the sting of pain. She looked at Zaida, who was showing no signs of movement. The creature dragged the blade horizontally along her forehead and pulled down, beginning to carve a symbol into her skin. Raven tensed, gritting her teeth. Blood trickled down her face, over her lips and chin as she was cut. Her breath became uneasy, and with each movement of the blade she pulled on the shadow energy within and tried to focus a push back on the demonic presence. Just when she was going to start screaming for Zaida to get up, the man's meticulous carving stopped as his hand suddenly stilled. He lifted the blade away slightly as his hand started to shake.

The weight of the demon's presence lifted off Raven, giving her back her stolen mobility. She grabbed his arm, pushing it away and causing him to drop the box cutter. She reached back swiftly, pulling her other dagger and thrusting it at his chest in a quick, fluid movement. He took a step back, grabbing at the dagger sticking out of his chest with both hands. Confusion painted his features, unable to understand how Raven had managed to push past the influence of his presence to stab him.

She pulled her shadow stones out, tossing them down at the man's feet. They didn't hit the floor, however, halfway down they pulled up in levitation and started to circle around the possessed curator. He fell to his knees, pulling the blade from his chest and tossing it aside. With a wheezed cough, blood splattered to his lips. Raven stooped down, picking up the dagger she'd dropped when he pinned her to the wall. Not taking her eyes off him, she stepped over a body to get to him and leaned down next to his ear. "I told you I was going to kill you," she whispered darkly. His hand rose to grab her, only to be caught at the wrist. She squeezed hard, then pulled her dagger up and drove it into him. She held it there a moment before she pulled it out and released her hold. A sharp, strained gasp pushed past his lips and his eyes cleared up. The man's carved up body collapsed, half landing onto the corpse of a co-worker.

Raven looked at the urn and narrowed her eyes. A demonic aura was still pouring out. "It…can't be that simple. Can it?" She questioned as she picked up the urn's lid. She held the lid over the opening, and the red, smoke-like substance billowed up, rising past the lid and her hand. She gently lowered the lid into place, allowing it to settle and seal the urn with a roll of dark hues around the seam and over the urns markings. She looked up, able to sense the disturbance over the museum dissipating.

"Raven?" Zaida spoke softly as she pulled herself to her feet, lifting her sword from the floor as she did. "Are you with me?" She questioned just as softly. Her free hand was held out toward the fallen white stones, and they rose up and flew into her grasp. All the while she watched Raven leaning over the dark artifact responsible for the carnage around them.

Raven picked up her other dagger and reached back under her jacket, sheathing them both with a gentle click. The black in her eyes receded as she mimicked Zaida's actions. Her hand raised, the three shadow stones lifted and moved to her grasp. "Are you with me?" A small smirk pulled at her lips.

Zaida pocketed her stones, smirking back at Raven. "Yes."

"Good." She tucked away the shadow stones and looked down at the urn.

Zaida held her sword up, and the metal blade became engulfed in golden hues, then as they faded, so did the blade. She clipped the hilt to her belt and her own gaze fell to the urn.

"We probably shouldn't leave that here," Raven calmly pointed out.

"Probably not." Zaida answered and stepped over, picking it up.

They both looked around, their minds and hearts in the same place. They had stopped whatever was in the urn, but there had still been a loss of life that night. Zaida handed the urn to Raven without a second thought. Raven watched carefully, finding herself studying her new friend. The light Nephilim went to each body, lowering her head and saying a small prayer over them.

She turned back to Raven, taking the urn from her. "Let's get out of here."

"Right behind you."

The two took their leave like bandits. The bodies of the demons outside were missing, and all that remained was the pierces of tattered cloth they had been wearing, a detail that wasn't questioned as their quick pace brought them around the back of the property, to Zaida's car. She moved to the trunk, popping it open and reaching in for an old wooden box. It looked like it had seen better days, and was carved with angelic markings. She placed the urn carefully inside. "This will keep it hidden until I can get it to the proper people."

"Was this your assignment?"

"Mmhmm, thanks for the hand." Zaida closed the trunk of the car and turned to Raven. "Want me to give you a ride home?"

"Nah, I'll walk. Gives me time to think."
"Alright, just be careful." Zaida moved to the driver's side door and watched as Raven took off walking down the street.

She didn't make it far, maybe a block or two, before a pair of headlights came up behind her. "Oi, hold up." Zaida called out. "Want to go with me to grab a few beers?"

"What would you say, if I said I've never had a beer?" Raven turned, facing the car and lifting a hand to shield her eyes.

"I'd say, you're about to have your first one. Come on, get in!"

With a slight glance in the direction she had been headed; Raven got into the car. For several blocks, neither of them spoke. The silence was interrupted briefly by police sirens and then by Zaida. "I saw a place downtown when I was scoping out the area." She glanced over as they drove. "You did good back there."

"Thanks…I think?"

"I'm giving you a compliment girl, take it." Zaida chuckled.

"I killed a man, not sure how that can be seen as good." Raven looked over, unsure what to think of her choice of words.

"I get what you mean. We do this to protect innocent people, but it's going to happen. You can't let it get to you, though….it looks like you're handling it alright."

"Sure." She shrugged and looked out the window as they pulled into a small lot outside of a liquor store. The red glow of oversized letters across the front of the building illuminated the dash of the car.

"Stay here, I'll just be a second." Zaida got out and headed inside.

While she waited, Raven pulled her phone out. A missed call from home and a text notification from Hani brought on feelings of guilt. She crammed the phone back into her pocket. Guilt turned to frustration, even anger, over the fact she missed another family dinner and had been dodging her friends.

Zaida hopped back into the car, setting a brown paper sack into Raven's lap. "This is your city, where's a good place to hang out?"

"Eh…head up this street here and take a left on the main road. It will take us back in the direction of Aiden's house, but you want to keep going past the hospital. You'll see the park sign."

"Sounds good, tell me…" Zaida pulled from the parking lot, heading off down the street as instructed. "What's it like? Being…you know?"

"Still not used to it. It's been a lot, real fast and heavy. Sometimes I wish everything could slow down, but at the same time I feel if it did, I would have too much time to think about it and it would bother me more."

"Working away your troubles, so to speak?" Zaida questioned thoughtfully.

"I suppose. Over thinking it just seems like a waste of time, it's not going to change how things are."

"That's a good attitude to have, better than the one I had." She pulled into the park and gave a quick glance around before she parked and got out, grabbing the paper sack. "Over there looks good." Raven got out of the car, following Zaida as she made her way past the playground equipment to a bench near a lamp post overlooking the river. Once there, she opened the paper sack and pulled out a beer, offering it to Raven.

"What kind of attitude did you have?" She lifted it to her nose and took a sniff before taking a sip. Both brows rose at the sharp, full flavor of the alcoholic beverage being consumed for the first time.

"A shitty one." Zaida replied with a huff and sat down next to her.

"Can I ask what your awakening was like?"

Zaida was silent a moment, taking a deep draw from the bottle in her hand. "The Blue Mountains." She leaned back into the bench, eyes focused on the lights from across the way reflecting off the river.

"That a place?"

"Yeah." She fondly recalled. "It's a place near where I grew up. Breathtaking, beautiful, a place that before my awakening I thought was the closest thing man could get to paradise."

"Wow…"

"Mountains as far as the eye can see with cliffs rising from a sea of trees, and there is a

125

formation that, through an early morning fog, looks like a castle." She took another heavy drink from her bottle. "My Mum and Dad took me and my brothers up there often to go climbing and exploring. After Dad passed, I went to one of his favorite cliffs. I sat for hours, just me and my thoughts. When I stood to climb back down…" She took a deep breath and shook her head. "I fell."

"Shit…." Raven cringed.

"That's exactly what I thought just before I blacked out." Zaida laughed. "I woke up in some crazy black and white room and, six years later, here I am." She raised the bottle to her lips and knocked back the rest of its contents.

"You've been doing this for six years?"

"Luckily I've lived this long, thanks to my guardian--or unluckily, depending on how you look at it." Zaida got another beer, glancing at Raven.

"Is Owen your guardian?"

"No…." She looked down at her bottle in thought. "Her name was Sophie, she died two years ago. I refused a new guardian."

"I'm sorry," Raven offered apologetically, feeling like an ass even though she couldn't have known.

"Don't be." Zaida finished off her beer and tapped the bottle to the bench. "They really got you following the same rules as us heavenly half-breeds?" She changed the subject a bit quickly, not wanting to get into too much more detail about her personal affairs.

"And then some made up just for me it seems." She paused a moment. "Some of the rules seem a bit archaic. Yeah, some of them are pretty simple and coincided with the teachings of the Bible, I get those. But no sex? Come on….really?"

Zaida smirked. "We are holy beings. Angels have rules; they don't have the freedoms humans do. The rules are in place to keep us from temptation and make sure we stay on the righteous path."

"It just seems unusual, maybe unfair? Your life is destroyed and then on top of you get handed a list of rules that include such an asinine thing. Sex is strictly prohibited. You aren't a nun or a priest and me? I'm no angel, biologically speaking, that is."

Zaida couldn't help but laugh. "While I guess I can agree that some of the rules should hold no weight on your handling, but for those they are designed for, they are imperative. Did Aiden not explain this to you?" She peered at Raven.

"No…. he told me to just follow the rules and not worry about it."

"He should have told you, it's not like it's a big secret." She reached into the bag, getting another beer and looked up at the sky.

"What?" Raven questioned before taking the last drink from her own bottle.

"Just as an angel can fall from grace, so can a light Nephilim."

Chapter Five

The rumbling of thunder rolled through the dismal sky. A drizzle had come and gone through the morning, into the afternoon. Raven sat in the basement, browsing over a new set of books Owen had come up with. Page turn after page turn revealed nothing more than a different perspective on material she had already learned. She read each page anyway.

Page turn after page turn also brought a familiarity to the noises that were now quite noticeable around the area. It became a symphony of previously inaudible sounds and mumbled whispers. The pages stilled as her attention shifted to the dark corners of the basement. Her fingertips pulled along the edge of the book and teased at the corner of the page in curiosity. Each page turn appeared to bring whatever she was hearing more into focus.

The page was lifted, but the sound was lost to another rumbling of thunder and the sound of shoes rushing down the stairs. She pulled her fingers away and allowed the page to fall back into place as Aiden hastily made his way to her. In his hand was what looked like a manila envelope, but the paper it was made from was the color of tree bark. Two words were written on it in Enochian.

"What's this?" Raven asked as Aiden placed the envelope down on top of the book she was reading.

"I don't know if you're ready for this." He explained.

"Is this from the Oracle?"

"Yes." He replied. It was clear by the tone of his voice that the envelope's arrival had him on edge.

"From what you told me about this Oracle and how she doesn't just write anyone's name down, it feels like I won the lottery, somehow."

"That's debatable. I'm still swallowing the fact that she divined your name." Aiden paused. "My Father even suggested it was a mistake."

"He hates me that much?" Raven chuckled, but wasn't surprised.

"Well…. yes. Don't take it personally, it's not who you are, it's what you are." He half peered away in thought. "Mocking him probably didn't help."

Raven opened the envelope and pulled out the contents. Inside were several photos, dossiers and newspaper clippings. She glanced at Aiden as she started to look over the contents. "Wait," she mumbled, and stopped the initial glance over of the files. "Really…. her?" She raised the single sheet of paper with a photo clipped to it and turned it to show Aiden.

"This was her assignment." Aiden explained, softening his tone. "Actually, she was the third person assigned to the job. The first two were killed. Each time, the group in question moved to an unknown location and, by the time Megan found them again, things had progressed past the point of just trying to prevent their plans from happening."

"Because they had already started them," Raven interjected, setting the paper down and flipping back to a set of reports about missing girls.

"Yes." He motioned a finger at the reports. "Someone in the group was here in Illinois for some time, getting a head start on the next phase. The pattern of the abductions started as far north as Rockford, then goes through Chicago, and tapers off down around Watseka. Megan was sent to infiltrate the group, using spells and an old demon charm to mask her true nature. She managed to get the details of the girls being held against their will to us before she was exposed. We're still not sure what happened, and that's where you come in."

Raven gave an absent nod, flipping the papers back to the information on the 'group', as Aiden called them. "You need someone on your side that can infiltrate without charms and spells."

"Exactly."

"So, what do I have to do?" Raven asked.

Aiden had a deadpan expression as he replied. "Convince them you're one of the four spawn of Mephisto."

"You're joking, right?" Raven questioned as she laughed. "This isn't the time for kidding around."

Aiden just stared at her, offering not a single word as he held the stoic expression. Her laughter was normally something that Aiden welcomed, but not this time.

"The Oracle has spoken. This is what you have to do. Convince these people you're the one they are looking for, locate those girls, get them out, and stop them from summoning Mephisto from hell," he explained rather seriously.

"You're fucking serious?" Raven blurted out. Aiden's expression didn't change. She lifted the envelope and turned it upside down, allowing a metal medallion to slide out into her hand. It was about three inches in diameter and riddled with demonic markings. "And, this?"

Aiden looked at the medallion warily. "According to Megan's last report, they use those in some ceremony that kind of calls out to dark Nephilim in order to gather them to an unknown location, where they weed out who fits the profile of being Mephisto's spawn. The ceremony can only be done during a full moon."

"If they use this…." She lifted the medallion to get a closer look at the markings as she spoke. "How is it going to help me?"

"You're going to use the medallion to, I guess you could say, intercept the 'signal' and make sure you get the vision they send out."

Raven lowered the medallion, but didn't take her attention from it. The girls were taken from a fairly specific range. Megan had been in the same town Raven was in the night of her death. Too many coincidences. "You would think at this point, I wouldn't be surprised at the news of a cult in the area."

"You'll get used to it." He paused and looked from the medallion to her. "This goes down tonight."

"Tonight?" Raven looked at him quickly.

"Tonight's the full moon. Let's not overthink it, though. We need to start prepping for the spell," Aiden explained and headed to the supply cabinet.

Raven watched him as he went, her brows furrowing at a thought. "Um…Aiden? I'm going to do this, so don't misunderstand what I'm about to say, because I'm not sure how to say it." She paused as Aiden turned to face her. "I don't know how much longer I can lie to my family, and I know you said I should move out, but…"

Aiden set down what he had already gathered up, and proceeded cautiously. "You have to, Raven, you have held out long enough. After tonight and this assignment, it will be even more dangerous for you to be around your family because you *will* be on an arch demon's shit list."

"You know how close we are as a family. I don't know how to just leave."

"Tell them half of the truth. You got an offer to live with a friend," he offered, understanding the difficulty she was facing.

Her eyes narrowed at Aiden ever so slightly. "You know, for someone descended from holy beings, lies seem to come awfully easy for you."

Aiden laughed. "Yeah, I guess it just comes with the territory, despite that." He turned away from her once more and re-gathered the things they would need. "Help me get these things upstairs."

Raven took the envelope with the medallion as she stood and helped get the supplies gathered. It was a curious collection of chalks, salts, rocks and herbs. They headed up into the second story of the house and into the bedroom he'd previously mentioned as having been prepared for her.

The room reflected the rest of the house. It needed work. A simple wrought iron bed with canopy framework, but no canopy, was made up with white and green bedding. There was a desk with a drawer missing and curtain rods resting next to the windows, waiting to be put up.

The floor rug was rolled up and set aside so a protective circle could be formed around where Raven would be laying. Aiden guided her through drawing out a complex formation of runes and markings that would link the medallion to whoever was holding it. Several sticks of chalk later, night had taken over the sky.

"Alright, what's the plan?" Raven asked as she finished the last rune.

"A form of astral projection is the plan," Aiden explained.

"That sounds kind of unpleasant."

"Maybe? According to Megan's notes, the cult's ritual calls to dark Nephilim and pulls them into a state of astral projection, and while they are in that state, they are somehow convinced to head to a particular location." He sat down just outside the circle and leaned against the bed.

"Must be some experience," she mused out loud. "Is this acting as their awakening? I didn't see anything about that in the file."

"Good question. I didn't see anything, either." Aiden tapped at the floor within the circle. "Only one way to find out."

Raven sat in the center of the circle, focusing on the medallion while she fidgeted with it in her hands. "Now that we have this all setup, I'm having doubts. This is so dumb…."

"Yeah." He agreed all too quickly as he set an empty mug down on his knee. One by one, he opened four small jars, taking a pinch or two of their contents and adding them to the mug. There were a variety of colors and textures of dried plants, and a powder that might be cinnamon. "I've got to admit this is pretty dumb. However…." He smiled at her. "You're going to be doing a lot of dumb things in the days to come, for all the right reasons. This is just the first of many." As Aiden finished, he offered up the mug.

An awful smell wafted from the mug as Raven accepted it. Despite the scrunching of her nose and disgust that overtook her features, she managed to take a few decent swallows. As soon as she pulled the edge of the mug from her lips, she began to gag, which was followed by a dry heave. "I had hoped that last pinch was cinnamon. What was it?" Her free hand moved to her stomach. The taste was worse than the smell. It was like vomit mixed with sour and spice, with a very green aftertaste.

"You don't want to know."

"You can tell me later." She offered the mug back.

"Go on, then, lay down," he instructed, taking the mug and shoving it aside on the floor.

"Now remember, use all your senses. All of them...." His tone was stern as he spoke. He lifted the medallion and held it up over Raven. "You can't think like a human through this, so listen to your other instincts."

"Alright." A soft reply slipped past her lips as she looked at the object in his hands. "Ready."

Aiden lowered the medallion, placing it on Raven's chest. He then gently reached over and lifted her hands, folding them over it. The contact of her skin to the cold metal surface brought a slight fiery glow to its markings.

"Just close your eyes, let yourself fall asleep," he whispered.

She took a deep breath and nodded a little to him. She could feel the dark energy emitting from the medallion as her hands rested on it. Plopping into bed, closing her eyes, and going to sleep had always been easy for her. She was never the kind of person who was kept awake by worry and thought. But as she closed her eyes, she couldn't help but wonder what her family was doing. They were probably already at the theater right now. That was the plan for the night. The movie of choice wasn't of interest to her, it was more for the kids. Being there to spend time with the family was important. She had agreed to go, and didn't even call to say she couldn't make it.

Was the potion even working?

She opened her eyes to ask Aiden for her phone so she could send a text to let her family know she wasn't going to make it. At least, she thought she did. All she saw was a black nothingness. Her body felt weightless, as if she was floating, unless she tried to move, and then it felt like she was being weighed down to the point of immobility. She had felt something like this before on the night of the accident, right before waking up on the operating table, the sensation of existing in a void of nothing.

That feeling was soon accompanied by sound, the echoes of car horns blaring and tires squealing tapering off into an encroaching tapping. Something was wrong. She felt panicked and wanted to wake up as she lost herself to human emotion. The sound got

137

closer just before a sharp sting of something sliced through her arm. She parted her lips and gasped, but that brought on an inability to breathe. Each attempt to take a breath was countered by the air being forced from her lungs.

An overwhelming heat flooded the space around her, encompassing her being. The darkness abound ignited into a blazing onslaught of flames. Thick sharp claws dug into her arms from behind. Flesh tore as the claws pulled through her skin and dug in to latch on like hooks.

"Is it you?" A voice questioned from behind right before Raven was yanked backward.

After being pulled back several feet, she heard a snapping, like a thick stick being broke in half. She was released, sending her into a disorienting tumble into dew covered grass. She could breathe and could move again but remained still on her hands and knees, clutching the grass while taking deep breaths through coughing.

Her head lowered with a tremble, sweat dampened hair fell over scratched arms and tips of grass poked gently at her face. The sound of a constant wind passed through the area, yet no wind could be felt. The smell of fresh rain was heavy on the air, mixed with a hint of burning wood.

The sound of cicadas in the distance came into focus, and Raven opened her eyes as she stood. A pain and pull in her arm muscles brought a wince to her eyes. A tremble came to wet, dirtied fingers as they lifted to the claw marks. A few claws were sticking out of her arm. She let out a sharp gasp of surprise at the sight of it. Carefully, she plucked them out and tossed them aside. Each claw's removal brought a strain to her breath and tension to her form.

An overwhelming feeling of being uncomfortable crept in. Exposed toes curled into the grass and felt the damp soil beneath them. As she lowered her hands to her sides, she tugged at the unfamiliar cloth. A dress of the softest black fabric she had ever felt clung to her form in a simple design that flared out at the hips. The dress had thin straps and the bottom was tattered and uneven.

The sound of the cicadas got a little louder. She looked around the field and up at the clouds in the sky, which were starting to darken, as if a storm was blowing in. Then, out of the corner of her eye, she noticed a tree that hadn't been there a moment before.

Some of the things about her less than desirable half came to mind. Shadow demons, their many tricks and traits, this should be her domain and playground. Focus. Concentration. Determination. Anything that could be forced into existence here would be a help, like maybe shoes or pants…but nothing presented itself.

The sound of the cicadas became distant again. Turning in the grass, she faced the direction it sounded like it was coming from, and took off running through the field. She made it a good distance before a child's voice called out, causing Raven to slide to a halt. "Hey!" Bare feet pushed down into the dirt as she spun to see who was yelling. With that turn, everything changed in a blink of an eye.

Instead of a field, she was in the middle of the aisle in a church, and her bare feet met with plush, wet carpet. The faintest sound of running water flowing and hitting the wet floor could be heard. She took a few steps forward, looking around. The water noise was due to a constant flow from the bowls being held by angel statues near the entrances.

The antique white walls were lined with stained glass windows, each one framed off with decorative molding that had golden accents. The colors from the sun shining through the windows made the wooden pews look like they had been stained with splotches of color. The ceiling arched up into a rounded point with the altar area carved out of the structure like a dome. Along the top of the dome-like nook was a line of alcoves, each holding a statue.

She turned around, noticing the dirty footprints she had left as she walked.

"This isn't right." Raven spoke out loud and turned to face the altar. The cream tone of the carpet was darkening to blood red. A sense of urgency pushed her to head to the exit. The rapid flapping of feathered wings filled the church, echoing through the empty space of worship. Each step she took changed the texture beneath her feet. Wet carpet started to feel slimy and hard. It felt like she could slip, forcing her into a slower, more careful pace. As she pushed the doors open and stepped through, she did slip, but caught herself on a bathroom sink.

"Is it you?" She heard the words again, this time darker and closer.

Confusion quickly set in as she steadied herself and stood straight. A bathroom mirror put her face to face with herself. Her heart stopped as she reached up, gently pressing fingertips against the corner of her eye.

The brilliant green eyes she was known for were engulfed by the void that is a trait of a shadow demon powering up. Her fingernails were thickened, blackened and pointed. Her attention moved to her ears, and saw that they held a slight point which stuck out from under her thick black hair. Was this what she really looked like, or how she would look one day?

She understood that the more she used her power, the less human she would become over time. She gently reached up and pulled some hair back to get a better look. It was a brief viewing, as the mirror fogged up.

The sound of soap thumping against porcelain made Raven flinch and turn to face the shower. A full blast of water pushing through the shower head wavered as the flow was being interrupted by whoever was in there rinsing off. She took a step closer and pulled the shower curtain back.

There was indeed a man in the shower, however, the interruption to the water flow wasn't because he was rinsing off. Something was extending, in a way, growing out of the broken showerhead. About a dozen of them had reached out toward the man. They reminded her of crab legs, however, these were smoother and colored in hues of black and brown with subtle hints of a sickly green. Each one was about half an inch thick and looked to be sectioned into joints every two inches or so.

They went through his hand that had been raised in a moment of surprise and a desperate attempt to stop them, then right into his chest. A mixture of surprise and pain was frozen on his face. His head was tilted back, his mouth was open as if he had been screaming, but there was no sound. Blood ran down the front of his chest, staining the bottom of the tub. Raven tilted her head, stepping closer to observe the strange, still scene. He, and whatever was attacking him, wasn't moving, but the water was still running.

The lights flickered, and for that second she could hear the man's screaming. It echoed through the bathroom, drowning out the sound of water. Some of the hard bone-like tentacles extended further, and they ripped through the man's chest and protruded out his back. Blood splattered to the tub and over the sea foam green wall. and dripped off the sharp pointed ends as the lights flickered again.

Another burst of screaming. Now the half that had remained sticking into his chest had broken out of the side of his neck and mouth.

The light flickered again, this time unaccompanied by the scream. The man's eyes were still wide open and they moved to look at her instead of the ceiling.

The lights flickered. Entranced by what she was witnessing, she didn't notice. The claws had gone through his chest, out of his back, and began to extend in her direction. With each flickering of the light, the claws coming out of his mouth and neck extended to a point only inches from her face. She snapped out of it and stepped back quickly. Bloody tips that extended out of the victim's back brushed against her hair in the process. She reached back and grabbed at the bathroom door handle just as everything sped up.

Like someone turning a light switch on and off quickly, the lights flickered and flashed, each fraction of darkness bringing them closer. Raven winced, closing her eyes tight as she pulled the door open and slipped out. It closed behind her. The sound of the things thumping into the door could be heard as she fell on her ass into a pile of some powdery substance.

143

She opened her eyes quickly, relieved to be anywhere but in that bathroom. She lifted her hands to look at them. They were covered in whatever she had landed in. Ashes of a grayish color were falling from the sky like snow and blanketing the ground.

The ash was all over her legs and had powdered the dress she was wearing. Raven stood up and immediately tried to brush herself off. She felt grimy and unclean, but her efforts were in vain. A swipe of her hand over her arm caused the blood spatters to smear, mixing it with the ash on her hand. They were only on one arm, leaving her to assume it came from the man in the shower.

"Watch where you're going!" Someone demanded as they bumped into her.

"Watch where I'm going?" She questioned as she looked up and over in the direction the voice came from. She was standing still, he was moving, who should watch where who was going?

There was a line of people formed in between two tall brick walls that stretched upward into a void of nothingness. Ash gently drifted down from above at a slow but steady pace. The ground wasn't the only thing it was accumulated on. Everyone in the line was completely covered from head to toe.

Raven started walking alongside the line that had stopped moving. A mix of people from all walks of life, from all over the world, all stood waiting. The majority looked forward, some glanced around and a few were caught in a looped action.

A man in a business suit with his briefcase in hand kept checking his watch. One woman kept looking at the person behind her and asking what time the in-flight movie started. There was a child who kept checking his pockets, each time looking disappointed to find them empty. As she started to pass a man mumbling about not seeing something coming, her attention was pulled in another direction.

"I don't belong here!!" A woman screeched out.

Raven came to a halt, turning to look at the woman, who was running as fast as she could. This one wasn't covered in ash, aside from the flake or two that may have clung to her as it fell from the sky. She was in a yellow containment suit which hindered mobility, but she still managed to move. As soon as she saw Raven, the woman ran right to her.

"You aren't like them! Right?" She huffed and puffed, pointing to the line of ash covered people. "I don't belong here!" She screamed frantically, grabbing at Raven's shoulders. "Tell them! Tell them I do— "A violent cough interrupted her mid-sentence, blood splattering all over the lower half of the protective face shield of the suit. "Oh, God!" She cried out, tears coming to her fear- filled eyes as she grabbed at the front of the suit. "Help me, please!"

Raven tensed up as she was released, and the woman screamed for help practically right in her face. "Them, who are you talking about?" She leaned to the side to look past the woman and see if anyone was following her. The line stretched on as far as she could see, and nothing was coming.

The woman coughed again, stumbling forward, crying out. "No!"
Raven turned her attention back to the woman as she screamed and fell to the ground, more blood splattering on the protective shield. She took a few hesitant steps toward the woman with the intention of pulling the head cover off the suit to try and see if something was inside. She abandoned those plans as she heard a melodic humming of sorts coming from the front of the line.

Stillness overcame her, a calm that couldn't be explained. Any anxiety felt over what was going on, the uncertainty and tinge of fear in the back of her mind, all melted away. Raven left the dying woman's side and followed the sound toward to the front of the line.

The closer she got, the safer she felt.

The glow of flames came into focus first. Three beings in black and red robes turned from abstract blurs to defined prominent figures. The hoods covered all but their lower faces, which were heavily disfigured with burn scars. Raven stood in front of them, the humming starting to sound more like hymns. At first she couldn't understand everything they were saying but, slowly, bits and pieces started to make sense.

"Burn…the flames….the flames of your Father"

One of the long sectioned things from the shower head earlier came zooming out of the flames and plunged right through Raven's right thigh. It slammed her into the ground, pinning her in place, blood splattering on impact. She didn't even flinch. It registered in her mind that something had impaled her and that there should be pain, but she felt nothing.

"Gather and burn…" The humming and strange tongues of the hymn continued.

Another barb slammed through her left shoulder and kept going until it hit stone a few feet behind her. A burning pain crept up where her shoulder was impaled. Heat rose up from behind, illuminating the poorly lit area. She could see a silhouette of herself, projected by the flames now crawling up her back. The sight was a little sobering. She grabbed and pulled on the boned tentacle sticking through her shoulder in an attempt to remove it.

"Come home…." The words were not part of the ongoing hymn, but from another source right behind her. Rough, gravelly, but warm and inviting at the same time. Efforts to remove the thing from her shoulder stopped as her grip loosened.

"Give in…. come home…" Whatever it was wrapped its arms around Raven, holding her gently. The heat it was generating was on the brink of being overwhelming and brought intensity to the lull of feeling safe and content.

"Ok." Her head lowered as she finally spoke.

"On the hundred and second road…Be amongst the dead in three days…."

The relaxed state of her being lasted a mere moment before it shifted, tension returning over the sight of something thick and black forming around her legs. It billowed and danced up from the ground under her. Like ink consuming water, the black mass spread from a dense core to spastic wispy extensions.

"Calm yourself." The unseen being holding her urged. "I can help you, I can teach you to control it." Raven's eyes started to flutter as the voice tried to sooth her. All that she heard was the strange melodic hymn. The only thing she felt was being let go and that feeling of falling as everything went dark.

Raven jerked awake, taking a deep breath as if she had been under water, holding it for a minute too long. Aiden stood over her with a gun pointed at her head. "Calm down!" He pleaded. "Raven, just calm down!" His tone, the fear in his eyes and the gun weren't exactly things that would contribute to her calming down. Her eyes rolled to look past him toward the ceiling, however, it was hard for Aiden to tell since they were completely black. For all he knew, she was just staring at him.

The ceiling was billowing with a black smoky looking mass. In some spots it had started to roll down the walls and creep along the floors in Aiden's direction.

"I'm trying, put the gun down!" Raven replied, eyeing the gun.

Aiden tensed even more than he already was and took a step back, his aim unwavering. "Don't speak like that! Where did you learn that? I can't stand it!" He yelled at her. "Raven, stop!"

Raven's fingers curled around the medallion resting on her chest. She was speaking a tongue that was anything but human. She understood this much, but wouldn't have realized it if he hadn't pointed it out, which only drove deeper at her fears and anxiety. She shoved the medallion away, sending it clattering and rolling under the bed. She took a chance despite knowing that the slightest movement could cause Aiden to shoot. She closed her eyes and rolled out of the circle. The mess of looming shadow reacted violently, swirling chaotically as she screamed. Her whole body felt like it was being torn apart as the spell broke.

"Raven!! Don't make me shoot you!!" He yelled out again, tears coming to his eyes.

Convinced he was going to shoot, she curled up, pulling her arms over her head. Slowly, all of the shadow energy billowing around the room thinned and faded away. The sound of the gun's safety being clicked on brought a soft sigh of relief from Raven.

There was an awkward silence as Aiden made his way over and sat down next to her. With one leg stretched out and the other propped up, he placed his arm over his knee, taking deep breaths to calm his nerves. The gun was still in his hand, hidden along the other side of his leg where she couldn't see it.

Aiden looked down at Raven, who was still curled up in a ball. What do you say to someone you were just threatening to kill? What do you say to someone you had started to see as more than a charge, started to see as a friend and you were about to put them down like a rabid dog? He looked away, unable to find the courage needed to utter a single word.

She wouldn't stop trembling. He could hear her breath shake.

He set the gun down as carefully as possible as not to make any noise. Being cautious with his movements, not wanting to upset her any further, he laid down in front of her. He allowed a moment to pass before he reached over and gently tugged on her arm. Brilliant greens rolled open, peering at him through thick black hair. Another tug pulled her into his arms and he simply held her in silence.

Chapter Six

Wracked with guilt and worry, Aiden refused to leave Raven's side. He knew she hadn't been ready for what happened. He watched her sleep the day away, questioning his worth as a guardian. Was it a mistake to so brashly volunteer to do the job? He was sure he'd had enough experience to handle anything. He had been guardian to a number of Nephilim through the ages. There was no formula or pattern that could be followed, and he couldn't look back to any of the difficulties of past assignments for reference or guidelines, not because of the fact that she was born of darkness, but because he had never felt the need to point a gun at his charge.

Owen eventually joined him in the silent waiting. The way he carried himself, Aiden could tell he was also stricken with guilt. He was supposed to be there to help, but had gone with Zaida for what was only supposed to be a day that had turned into three. Within Owen's mind he was thinking that maybe if he had stayed, the events of last night would have turned out differently. He could have offered a calm to the situation, maybe a solution other than a gun, anything. Owen felt like he had failed them both.

Raven opened her eyes half way and peered over at the two of them. They had dozed off in their patient wait for her to wake. She looked at Aiden fully. The panic in his voice resonated within her mind along with the vivid recollection of him aiming a gun at her. The memory stirred a thought, a disturbing idea—to crawl from the bed and kill him.

In a fluid movement her bare feet were out from under the covers and gently landing on the floor. Her eyes remained on Aiden as she moved forward, managing to be quiet enough that she was able to get right in front of him. The act in itself inspired excitement and fueled the dark thought. Where was his gun? Her hand curled into a half fist, imagining how it would feel to hold the weapon and press the barrel to his forehead. Would he scream in a panic as he did last night while begging for his life?

She could almost see crimson fluid and fleshy bits of brain matter decorating the dingy white wall behind Aiden's head in a splattered array as she allowed her mind to explore the dark urge. It brought the slightest hint of a smile to otherwise emotionless features. A fraction of a snore from Owen broke her train of thought. What little smile she had faded as she looked over at him.

She turned away and headed out of the room. Her stomach burned with a hunger that hadn't been felt in some time. It felt like the brief distance between the upstairs bedroom and the kitchen was a journey across an endless landscape.

She invaded the fridge. Whatever was left over from Zaida's cooking she scooped onto a plate and shoved it into the microwave. She also went through the take out containers. She attacked a practically uneaten order of orange chicken. Her slender fingers dipped into the cold, gooey chunks, pulling them out and shoving them into her mouth.

"I...could order something fresh." Owen hesitantly offered with amusement in his voice, making his presence known. He had managed to approach the kitchen unnoticed during Raven's search for food.

Her response came in the form of a shake of her head as she sat at the table and kept chowing down the tangy chicken. "Ok." Owen answered, keeping an upbeat attitude. He took the plate from the microwave and placed it down on the table near her, along with a fork. Watching intently as he sat down next to her, he said nothing as she finished eating what was in the container in her hand. There was barely a pause as she set it down and pulled the plate over. Sticky fingers snatched up the fork and she kept eating.

"Raven, you're kind of worrying me, you ok?" Owen asked calmly.

There was a slight distance in her eyes as she looked at him before catching sight of Aiden making an attempt to hover near the door to listen in. Her eyes looked in his direction. "He was going to shoot me." Her voice rasped out tiredly.

"Raven, I'm so sorry, I..."

Owen lifted a hand to stop Aiden without looking away from Raven. "This is the main reason I'm here." He kept calm, a demeanor she didn't think the energetic, carefree guy was capable of. "All the knowledge Aiden has of shadow demons was acquired from books, field reports and fireside stories. I, on the other hand, have had the misfortune of two encounters."

"Misfortune?" Raven pulled her glaring gaze away from Aiden to look at Owen questioningly.

"The passages provided to you were not exaggerated. Shadow demons can be chaotic, with, at times, no rhyme or reason to their actions other than the gratification of the destruction, suffering and pain caused by what they have done." He glanced over at Aiden to make sure he had no objections or thoughts to add.

Met with silence, he continued. "Based on what Aiden described, you manifested a lot of your power, quickly."

"Like a river breaking through a dam." Aiden added.

"Too much, too soon, but not your fault." Owen assured. "What happened last night? Can you tell us?" The more Owen spoke, the more he showed that he did have a hidden serious side.

"I think Mephisto was there." Her eyes averted to the table as she recalled. "There was some kind of sing-humming. I was told where to go….and something held me from behind and said it would help me. I looked down and…" She trailed off.

"He forced your powers to the surface." A hint of anger came to Owen's voice.

"Mephisto is forcing these people into their awakening and convincing them that they are his kids?" Aiden questioned.

"Looks like it. We know Megan wasn't and he still claimed she was." Owen reached over and poked Raven. "Hey."

"Huh?" She looked back up.

"Where are you supposed to go?" He questioned curiously.

"Amongst the dead on the hundred and second road."

"Ok…so we need to figure out where the hundred and second road was put down in America is?" Aiden chimed in, ready to figure it out.

"Or in the world?" Owen asked, pulling out his cell phone to start an internet search.

"No…" Raven looked back and forth between the two of them in disbelief. "You guys hit your heads or something?"

Owen grinned. "There she is…. Ok, miss smarty pants, let's hear it."

"It's not literal. The hundred and second road….route 102, which there is a cemetery inside the Kankakee River State Park that the highway goes right through." Raven stood from the table, stretching out, the distant look in her eyes having faded. "I have to be there in three days, I imagine around the same time we did the spell."

"Then we have a lot of planning to do and details to go over." Aiden slid right into serious mode.

"Or how about we take the rest of the day and tomorrow to just relax?" Owen looked at Aiden. "Let's process this and give Raven some time to recover."

"I like Owen's idea better." She glanced at Aiden. "I'm going to shower and then rack up your credit card bill by ordering lots of take out."

"Ok…." Aiden conceded without a fight.

Time came and went, consumed by sleep and mindless television watching. Her preparation was a brief 'go get 'em tiger' speech, which Raven thought lightly on as she drove down the highway. "*We decided the best plan is no plan! The less you know, the better you'll be able to convince the cult you're new at this and need them. So go get 'em, tiger, save those girls and stop Mephisto!*" Those were the words of the non-plan presented by Owen, and she was surprised Aiden was ok with it. Most likely still feeling guilty, Aiden was also helpful in coming up with a cover story for her prolonged absence to avoid a missing persons report being filed by her parents.

It was late and the park was closed, yet upon arrival there were cars parked near the cemetery. That

NephilimNovels.com
nephilimnovels@gmail.com

Nephilim House of Mephisto

After a car accident that should have taken her life, Raven awakens to a revelation and a peculiar choice that turns her world upside down. She learns that an ongoing war between angels and demons has been playing out for centuries, and the world of man is the battlefield. She is tasked with stopping the arch demon Mephisto's plans, a task that leads to becoming mixed up with a dangerous cult. But lives are at stake and this ill-prepared hero in the making will have to make sacrifices to get the job done, as a new and unexpected chapter in her life begins.

 /nephilimnovels

 /nephilimnovels

 /thenephilimnovels

nephilimnovels. **t**

doesn't look odd at all. Did the park ranger not notice? She couldn't help but laugh a little as she drove by, heading to another area that would also lead to where she was headed.

She knew the park pretty well, having been to the old settler's cemetery a few times over the years, or at least gone past it. There were two ways to get there. One way was quick, which seemed to be the way others had chosen, given they were parked closest to it. The other way gave more cover and distance for observing before approaching.

She got out of the car, heading to a covered bridge that went over a small creek and into the forest. The trees overhead were separated enough to allow light from the full moon to bathe the bike path. It was a brief walk before she went off the path and into an open stretch of grass. The thick brush and heavy weaving of trees made it feel like she was headed down a dark tunnel with no light on the other end to follow. Memory and trust that she was walking in a straight line were all she had to rely on as she went. She took each step carefully, not wanting to snap any twigs or trip over a rock.

The sound of something moving through the brush brought temptation. If she allowed her power to stir and take hold she might be able to see through the darkness, but she couldn't take the chance that one of the Nephilim ahead may be able to sense the flux of power.

It was a deer, nothing to worry about. Maybe it was a raccoon, no reason to be scared, right? Fear set in as it felt like something brushed past her leg, accompanied by the sound of soft panting.

A flame ahead cut through the darkness. Raven kept going until she was just outside the reach of the campfire's glow. There were several people there talking and laughing. But were they there for the same reason, or was this just a group of friends out having a party?

"I set my foster parents on fire." One of the girls explained with a little too much amusement.

She was in the right place. The two girls and three guys gathered around the fire were all half demon, just like her. A strange nervousness set in as she continued to eavesdrop.

One of the older looking guys laughed. "Man, I wish I could have set my step-father on fire. He was a no good drug addict. If he hadn't overdosed, I'd go do just that."

"I'd help you!" The girl cheerfully added.

"Hey." Raven spoke out calmly as she approached the group, not wanting to stay back too long and get caught listening.

"We got a late comer," the second girl pointed out with a bit of a drunken attitude, taking a decent swig from a bottle of whiskey.

"What's your name, hon?" One of the guys asked and hopped down off the wooden fencing that enclosed the cemetery.

"Alex." Raven replied. There was no way she was giving anyone her real full name during this ordeal.

"Well, Alex!" He said as if announcing her to the group. His arm slide around her and he escorted her over to the others. "Welcome to the party, this is--" His introductions were interrupted as another person approached.

The entire group turned, showing a mix of reactions as their focus was drawn to a figure in a black and red hooded cultist robe. It stopped just inside the light of the fire. "Good evening, boys and girls." The sultry voice of a man came from under the hood. He pulled his pale hands from behind his back and tugged the hood down.

Attractive was a good word to use, despite a few odd features. His lips were a bluish grey, the same coloring that comes with a lack of oxygen. Sprawling from his temples and across the hairline of his forehead was splotchy discoloration that stained pale skin the same color. Eyes of icy pale blue darted over each of the gathered Nephilim.

"You are all here because you had a series of dreams, all leading to your awakening and bringing you one step closer to your real family." His words were like music to everyone's ears, except for Raven, who glanced around, checking everyone's reaction.

The girl with the bottle had dark circles under her eyes and looked a bit on the thin side. As she lifted the bottle to take another drink as she listened, her sleeve pulled back, revealing heroin scars on her arm. The younger girl was dressed in a fashion that suggested she came from money. A prim and properness radiated off her designer dressed form.

The guy who said he would have liked to set his stepfather on fire had a gang tattoo on his neck, and a zigzagged pattern shaved through his hair on one side. The one who greeted her when she arrived was wearing a football jersey from one of the local high schools. He kind of held that confidence a sports player held, and was clearly a team leader and motivator. The third guy was a wallflower. He said nothing as he hung back and observed, waiting to see what happened, with his hands crammed into the pockets of his hooded sweater.

They all wanted this, they needed it.

Maybe the girl with the bottle saw this as a chance to start over and get clean while putting whatever, or whoever, drove her to doing drugs far behind her. The guy with the fancy buzz job to his hair, maybe it was a way out of gang violence. Perhaps it was time for the shy wall flower to be someone else. The sports player and the girl? You would think just by looking at them their lives were great, but since they were here, maybe not so much.

The man in the robe motioned to them. "As you were told a few nights ago, you are all half demon. A truth you accepted." He took a smooth step closer, looking at each person evenly. "What was not mentioned, is that one of you is the missing child of my master."

Everyone now exchanged glances, mumbling to each other. "But we can all go home with you, right?" The individual in the sports jacket, who took the initiative when Raven got there, took it again. "You won't leave us all behind?"

"Oh, no, you were told if you came, you would be taken home. That still stands." He motioned his hands. "Now line up for me, face the fire, just a quick little test and we can get going, ok?"

There was some hesitation from a few, but they all complied, lining up. Six in total, standing straight and looking forward. The man walked along behind them, stopping at the opposite end from where Raven was positioned.

Something moved in the forest, drawing her attention to the trees. Slowly, six large black hell hounds crept into view. They were built like wolves, but larger, stockier, and furless. Their eyes were a deep crimson and their black skin looked a bit like suede. Each one had some kind of deformity or affliction. The hellhound in front of her, parts of its spine protruded through the skin and there were scar-like patches on his body.

Raven tensed and leaned forward ever so slightly to glance down at the line of people. They all looked oblivious to the new arrivals. The robed man stepped behind the young girl at the end of the line, leaning in and whispering past curly blond hair to her ear, his long, thin, dirty blond hair covering his facial expression as he did. The girl, being at best thirteen years old, looked so confused by whatever he said. He stepped to the second, leaning in and whispering. The guy reached up under the hood of his sweater and rubbed his temple, as if whatever was whispered had pained him.

The man in the robes adopted a neutral expression on his face as he stepped behind each remaining potential recruit, whispering. The third person was the girl with the attitude and bottle of booze. She grinned with excitement in response, looking toward the others that had been previously spoken to and those who remained. The fourth person kept looking forward as he was whispered to, not even a blink of a reaction. The fifth, the one who made the man promise everyone would be going tonight regardless, nodded upon hearing the whisper.

Raven looked at the hellhound standing in front of her as the man in the robes stepped up behind her. The hellhound looked at her as if she was dinner.

"You can see them, can't you?" He whispered to her, his chest gently brushing against her shoulder. Raven gave a slight nod. "Then turn and embrace me, save yourself from the fate of the others." His sultry tone turned darker as he spoke in the same demonic tongue in which he'd spoken to the others.

Each one was told to turn around, and none of them did.

Raven turned as the man stepped back and opened his arms. Uncertainty brought hesitation. Embrace him, or warn the others? Her hesitation brought a faint worry to his expression as the hellhounds started snarling and growling. A quick step forward closed the gap between the two and she wrapped her arms around him, burying her face in his chest. There was no desire to see the hellhounds do what she suspected they were there for.

He sighed with relief, wrapping his arms around her, and he lowered his forehead down to rest it against top of her head. "It's ok, I got you." He whispered gently. "You're going home."

"What the fuck?" The girl with the bottle of booze stepped out of line as everyone turned. Her free hand raised in anger. "The fu— "Her outburst was cut off as the hellhounds revealed themselves. They lunged in attack, going after each person. The girl with the attitude went down flat on her back. the bottle in her hand clanging against the ground as it was dropped. She screamed as the beast held her down with large, heated paws and clamped down on her neck, nearly crushing it before ripping away a mouthful of flesh. Blood sprayed out over the hellhounds face as her main artery was torn open by his large, sharp teeth. The guy closest to Raven, along with the thirteen-year-old girl, both went down with a scream. The other two were quick enough to run, leading the hounds on a chase.

"Alex, was it?" The man spoke out, unfolding his arms from around her and placing his hands on her shoulders. "I'm Lucas." He paused. "I need you to let go now, and look at me."

Raven did as he asked and stepped back, looking up at him. His hands remained on her shoulders as he looked her right in the eyes. "Are you scared?"

"Yes" Raven answered quickly, barely able to hear over the screams.

"That is a human emotion, I need you to overcome it and look at what's going on." He demanded harshly, moving behind her, hands still on her. She was forced to turn and look.

The girl with the bottle was staring blankly up in Raven's direction. The hellhound that had her pinned had his blood soaked muzzle buried in her abdomen. Chunks of the girl's insides were being torn out and consumed as if the beast was plagued with a never-ending hunger.

Raven tried to step back, only to be held firmly still. She was so tense it almost hurt. She wanted to scream, to cry for it to stop, but nothing came out. "Watch. Are you human or demon?" Lucas questioned in a condescending manor.

The thirteen year old girl was trying to crawl away. The hellhound attacking her was playing with his food. The back teeth of his strong jaw had crushed through the bone of her leg and ripped it open. Every time she managed a foot or two of distance, he would stalk over and growl while pulling her back. Flames erupted over the girl's hands, twisting out uncontrolled. The hellhound clamped onto her other leg, lifting and shaking her like a dog would a toy before throwing her back toward the camp.

The hellhound pounced after her tumbling, frail body, pinning her down and latching onto an arm. A rapid head shake ripped it clear off. The sound of the girl's bone crunching and snapping made Raven feel sick. An end to the girl's screams and suffering came with the hellhound chomping down into her stomach.

"Alex…help me…." Raven tried to remain calm as she looked down at the boy calling out the false name she had given. It was the guy who welcomed her, who wanted to make sure everyone was going to get a better life.

The hellhound hadn't bitten into him yet and was just holding him down. There were burns on his cheek and mouth from the demonic hound's paw. "Please!" He begged, his fingers grasping at the edge of her jeans.

"It's your call, Alex." Lucas spoke soothingly and let Raven go, remaining right behind her.

Raven looked over at the two people already being eaten. A scream echoed from the distance, giving a good indication that one of the runners had been caught. Her eyes darted over the blood soaked grass and mangled bodies before looking back at the boy pleading for his life.

She closed her eyes, listening to the hounds lapping up blood and tender flesh in their near frenzied gorging. "Alex!" the guy managed to shout out as the hound started to push a smoldering paw firmly against his mouth. Raven opened her eyes and gave a simple nod to the hellhound. The guy screamed as sharp teeth latched onto the soft flesh of his cheek and ripped it away, exposing bone and teeth.

The hound that was there, no doubt, to eat her joined in, sinking his maw down into a thigh. Blood splattered up over Raven's clothing. The boy screamed frantically, reaching for her pant leg. One of the other hounds padded over, grabbing the hand and completely ripping it off.

Numbness crept through her as she watched. The three hounds kept ripping through the lifeless corpse, sending a splattering of blood and flesh everywhere. Another unearthly howl echoed in the distance. The hounds broke from their feast and lifted their heads, returning the call before running off.

Lucas turned as someone else approached. Fixated on the man laying dead at her feet, Raven didn't bother to look.

"This one?" A new voice spoke out.

"Yes." Lucas answered, holding out a set of keys and a cell phone that he'd lifted from Raven's pocket while she was watching the carnage unfold. "Make sure nothing is left and bring her car to the house." After passing off cleanup duty, Lucas moved back to Raven.

"Alex." He took her arm gently. "We have to leave, now."

Raven nodded at him absently and allowed him to escort her through the forest to the parking lot she opted not to park in earlier. There were people in hooded black robes getting out of a van. Lucas didn't acknowledge them, however, as he led her to the side of the highway, determined to get her out of there quickly. He was being protective, and tried to usher her into the back of a car before she saw the blood smeared all over the road, but it was hard not to notice. An eerie thought came with the sight; someone driving down the highway wouldn't be able to tell the difference between this and the remains of a deer plowed down by a semi truck.

"At least you're wearing all black. If we can't get the blood out, it may at least be hard to see." Lucas mused out loud as he settled into the car. "Then again, we can just send someone to buy you all new clothes."

Raven sat there staring at her lap, unsure of what to say or do. Step one was well underway, infiltrate the cult. But she felt naïve, in a way. While she fully understood that violence would be a possibility at some point, it never crossed her mind that she would start the assignment watching people get eaten alive.

"Alex, are you alright?" Lucas asked with a concern that came off half feigned.

"Where are we going?" Raven asked, looking up from her blood splattered jeans to look out the car window. They were moving away from Kankakee, that much was clear.

"The Collins estate." Lucas explained. "It's in the town just ahead. You'll be safe there. Many of its citizens are loyal to your Father."

His words struck a chord. Mephisto wasn't her Father, but she had to pretend he was. "How many?" She questioned, looking over at him.

"A couple hundred. It's impressive, actually. Not many of these sects loyal to the cause survived the cleansing of the 1870s."

"Cleansing?" Raven questioned.

"During the witch hunts and trials, while everyone was wrapped up in the frenzy," he explained with mild amusement, "While they were pointing fingers and burning people alive, angels descended to the earth, targeting those loyal to various forces."

"Well, wasn't that nice of them…" Raven replied sarcastically, looking back out the window.

"They certainly thought so." Lucas still sounded amused as he commented.

A silence settled over the car for the remainder of the trip. They drove into town and into the residential area, off to what would be considered the edge of town. Amongst some older historical houses near a creek, there was a black gate blocking off a paved cobblestone path that went off into a wooded area. The driver of the car reached his hand out the window to one of the stone structures the gate was attached to. Raven leaned forward a little, acting like she was trying to look down the path. In truth she was trying to see how he was opening the gate. Was it a keycard? Just a button? Unfortunately, it was too dark to tell.

Down at the end of the path stood a large two and a half story Victorian style home that could pass as a miniature mansion. The front porch was open rail, with a rounded sitting area on one end. There was a carriage house and the main road stretched back behind the house. The driver of the car, however, didn't go around back. He pulled up the circle drive and went about opening the car doors for the two.

Lucas got out first and straightened out his robe. "Alex? You coming?" He inquired, peering at her lack of movement.

"Huh? Yeah…." Getting out of the car, she looked at the driver apologetically. "Sorry, I think I got blood on the seats."

The classically dressed chauffeur simply tipped his hat to her.

As the two approached the house, Lucas offered some advice, possibly a warning. "Alex…" His sultry tone crept out. "Much will be expected from you." He stopped on the porch, looking at her. "If it becomes too much and you need help while you adjust, come to me before your Father."

Raven listened, a little surprised. Was he being kind, or did he have an alternative motive? Great, not even in the door and things were already becoming more complicated. She managed a small smile. "Alright, thank you."

Lucas opened the door, allowing her to step inside first. The decor was a bit on the lavish side. The wooden entry hall floor was covered in an antique area rug and above them was an old chandelier. A period appropriate waiting settee was placed against the wall across from the staircase.

"Welcome home, Alex." Lucas spoke as he looked up at the staircase with expectation.

Raven suddenly felt crowded, even though it was just her and Lucas standing there. Three young men came rushing down the stairs. "Is this finally it?" One questioned. "Do you see that around her?" Another asked with excitement.

She took a step back, resisting the urge to look around herself to see what he was talking about.

"Boys." Lucas greeted them. "May I introduce your sister, Alex."

"I'm Graver." The heavier set male had a southern twang to his voice. He was in a black leather trench coat, torn up jeans and a t-shirt for a heavy metal band. His brown hair was long, to his shoulders. He looked to be in his mid twenties and was easily the tallest one there, standing at about five foot eleven.

"I'm Austin." He was a slender young man with red hair that contrasted beige skin. Cutter's scars were scattered up and down his arms in different lengths. A t-shirt left that detail exposed, and was paired with baggy jeans.

"Jason." The youngest, so it seemed, maybe seventeen at best. A black silk bathrobe was wrapped around his fit body and tied off loosely. A show off, as he made his name known, a molten hue flashed over his brown eyes.

"I don't see it." Austin admitted, looking at Graver.

Graver grinned darkly. "The energy around her, I ain't seen nothing like it."

"Ok, just take a step back!" Raven backed up.

"You can get to know her later." A woman spoke up, sauntering from the entry way that led to the rest of the house. "If she's staying, that is."

"Mara." Lucas addressed the woman, placing a hand on Raven's shoulder. Mara was a tall, slender drink of exotic goodness that had a radiance about her. There was a confidence to all her movements, from walking to turning her head. Dark hair barely touched exposed, sun kissed shoulders, and her dress looked like it was made of fine silk.

"He wants to see her now, Lucas." Mara explained, a hint of an accent rolled off her tongue and tickled the senses. Piercing olive colored eyes settled on Raven, unimpressed.

Lucas took notice of Mara's composure. His pale hand lifted and waved at the woman in a dismissive fashion. "Fine, I'll take her." He then nudged Raven along, giving her no time to have a say in the matter and, in the same respect, giving Mara no room to insist on him doing it.

They went through the entryway leading to the rest of the house, which took them into the dining room. There was a door to the living room, the kitchen, and a set of double doors. It was through those two doors they went, which led to a place once intended for entertainment and dancing. The hall stretched along the back of the house. Arched windows that overlooked a terrace and garden lined the exterior wall. The first half of the area had a wooden floor, the other half was polished marble, perfect for a grand ballroom dance. At the far end there was a balcony overlooking the area, where once upon a time honored guests would sit to dine and gossip.

On the main floor just under that sat an altar. Obviously not part of the original design of the room, the structure was carved from black stone. Ornate gothic era designs adorned the corners. Along the base, the phrase 'from the fire we rise, to the fire we return' was carved out in an older style of writing.

"Brandon?" Lucas called out as they started down a red carpet runner to a man standing with his back turned.

"No." A single word was spoken, which brought Raven to pull away from Lucas and stop. The voice was just like the one she heard during the astral projection. Dark, rough, and gravelly, yet deceptively warm and inviting. The sound of it pulled on her senses as a heat started to rise within the room. Lucas let Raven go, stepping aside to silently observe.

The figure before the altar turned, looking right at Raven as if she was the only one there. "Don't be afraid." In his thirties, he was well dressed in black slacks and a tucked in black button up shirt. His dark hair was combed back and had the lightest peppering of grey along the sides. The features of his eyes were striking. Around the pupil were hues of light golden amber that faded into darker amber tones and held a faint glow to them.

"What do the humans call you, child?" He remained where he was and allowed Raven to move toward him.

"Alex. My name is Alex." She answered, approaching him with caution.

"For now, that is what I will call you." He paused. "You may call me Father when I am in control of this one, otherwise address me as Brandon."

"When you're controlling him?" She could start to sense the demonic presence as they spoke. It was almost suffocating to be near.

"My true form can't come into the world until a ritual is performed and you…" His hand reached up, brushing two fingers against her left brow. "…my daughter of shadow, open a portal for me to step through."

Raven gasped. A searing heat shot through her skull like a bad migraine. "What did you do?" She questioned his actions in a pained tone, roughly pressing her fingers to where he touched her.

"Relax. I just gave one of your developing abilities a push." The dark tone of his voice remained calm and soothing. "I said I would help you. Didn't I?"

Raven's vision started to blur with the pain, but it only lasted for a few seconds. As the blurriness cleared up, she could see something behind Brandon. It was a portal, wavering in and out of flux, the edges dancing about chaotically. Right in front of it stood a demon.

Mephisto. One of the arch demons of Hell. An impressive sight to behold, his strong features stood tall. A destructive being whose appearance gave the impression that his very essence was a raging fire being contained by cracking hardened skin that allowed glimpses of the destructive force caged within. The deep maroon features twisted into charcoal tones from his elbows to his hands and from his calves to his feet. The four fingers of each hand and his three toed feet were tipped with sharpened claws. The entirety of his eyes radiated with the heated glow of a being who wanted to destroy everything and rule over what little might survive his rage.

A thick reptilian like tail extended from the back of his form and was lined with black horn-like spikes that ran up its length, up his back, over his head, and down over his forehead, tapering off at the bridge of his nose. While they started on the tail a decent size, by the time they got to his forehead they were just less than half an inch long. A large set of leathery wings were folded closed. Topping his being off was a set of horns. The large, thick features extended from his forehead and arched back along his skull before they curled forward with the points stopping just below his jaw line.

"You're lying." Raven blurted out. It didn't cross her mind that calling an arch demon on his lies may not be the wisest idea. Getting closer was also not the best idea ever, but she did.

"You see him?" Lucas asked with excitement, also moving past the inhabited Brandon to stand next to her.

"Here but not here." She mumbled, glancing at the Mephisto controlled Brandon as he moved to stand next them.

"My disciples will finish the ritual, allowing you to fully manifest the portal." He explained, watching Raven intently. "Once they have done this, the link between Hell and Earth will be established, allowing you to finish pulling me through, at which point, I can call in my army."

"You're stuck? How did that happen?"

"I don't want you to concern yourself over such things." A cooing of words was accompanied by a hand resting on her shoulder "I will see you again soon." Brandon's eye color changed to a normal brown and he started to fall to his knees. Raven half caught him, preventing a full fall to the floor. Lucas stepped around, helping her to lower Brandon's trembling form into a seated position.

"Mephisto is gone?" Raven questioned, taken by surprise as Brandon grasped at her arm tightly.

"For now...." Brandon spoke with exhaustion. "He is so pleased you are here."

She looked down at his hand on her arm, tensing. The simple gesture reminding her of the way the hellhound ripped that guy's hand off as he grasped at her back at the cemetery. Lucas looked back and forth between the two, sighing. "You both have had a rough evening, haven't you?"

Brandon nodded, managing a smile for Raven. "It is good to meet you, Alex. My home is yours. Anything you need, we will provide."

"Do I get to kill her?" Mara asked as she came bursting in a second too late to hear Brandon's welcome. Her confident strut into the grand hall came with the obnoxious tapping of high heels. Her eyes filled with anger at seeing Brandon holding onto another woman, even if it was innocent.

Lucas stood from his crouched position next to the two on the floor, spinning around and grabbing Mara's throat before she could get any closer. He lifted her off the ground several inches. "I tire of your pathetic insecurities and uncouth jealousy toward every woman who comes into this house. You will gain no favor by acting in such a way toward your master's daughter. Do you understand me?"

"Y-y-yes." She coughed out, grasping at his wrists with pampered nails as he squeezed on her throat.

"Do you?" He snarled back, letting Mara go.

Mara fell to her feet and ran to Brandon's side. Lucas bared his fangs at the woman, causing her to jump a little. He laughed in amusement, looking upon her as if looking at simple minded child. "Come along, Alex." His amusement showed in his voice as he reached down toward Raven and helped her up.

"Nice to meet you, Mara." Raven said with as much sincerity as she could muster. As Lucas pulled her away, she managed to glance back and see that the out of phase visage of Mephisto was gone.

She was led up the stairs and down the hall to one of the bedrooms in the back of the house. "Get some rest. Someone will come for you in the morning." Lucas offered briefly, opening the door for her.

"Alright." She smiled at him, stepping into the room. Once the door closed, she barely made an effort to look around before plopping down on the bed. Getting to sleep wouldn't be easy. Her mind was in overdrive, going over everything she'd seen and learned that night. Thoughts kept drifting back to the five people at the graveyard. She allowed it to happen, and even gave that hellhound the order to proceed.

"What have I done?" She whispered to herself, closing her eyes tight.

Chapter Seven

"Good morning, mistress Alex, time to get up!" Mara's voice rang out in a cheerful contrast to the tone presented the evening before. Thick velvet curtains were pulled open in a sweeping motion, allowing the morning sun to flood into the room.

Raven sat up, watching the woman bustle about the room. A mix of paper boutique and decorated plastic shopping bags were on the floor. "What's all this?"

"You came here with literally nothing but the clothes on your back. I took the liberty of acquiring you some things. I hope they are to your liking." Mara explained with a smile.

Sliding out of bed, Raven took a glance over the woman's personal choice of attire. A two toned blue laced dress was accented with a silver necklace and hoop earrings. Dread set in just as she leaned over a boutique bag and pulled away pink tissue paper. Within the bag were several pairs of black jeans. Her brows furrowed as she inspected another bag's contents. It looked as if Mara went to her house back in Kankakee and looked through her closet.

"How did you know what to buy?" She questioned suspiciously.

"It's one of my many talents." Mara bragged. "I can look a person in the eye for mere seconds and glean who they are, their likes, dislikes, desires and…other helpful insights."

"You're a demon, too?" Raven asked with a smooth, casual tone, taking a brush from the bag and pulling it through her hair.

"Human, for now, that is." Mara spoke almost regretfully.

"For now?" Raven peered at Mara curiously.

"Your Father has promised me and Brandon that we will one day be more, by his blessing." Mara gave small pause before turning. "I should check on breakfast, please, when you are ready, come on down."

"Ok, thanks." Raven watched her go and as soon the door clicked shut she checked for her cell phone. It was gone. So much for checking in and letting the guys know she made it in ok. She turned about, looking around the room. The walls were covered in lavish dark red velvet Victorian patterned wall paper. The bed was queen sized with a four poster frame and was generously made with fine silk bedding and maybe one too many pillows. A dresser between two windows was made of rich mahogany with a large mirror. An old fashioned wooden framed fainting couch was placed in front of the fireplace. There was also a walk in closet and a private bath.

"Whoa," she whispered to herself as she peered into the bathroom, which was almost large enough to be a livable room itself. Raven stripped off her blood stained clothes for a quick shower. She found a bathrobe hanging on the wall and pulled it on, then picked the brush back up on the way out to the bedroom. Raven gasped and jerked as she was instantly startled, and instinctively threw the brush.

Sitting outside the bathroom door was the hellhound from the previous evening, the one with parts of his spine protruding through his skin and who she assumed would have eaten her if she hadn't understood what Lucas had said. He remained non-hostile, even as the brush bounced off his face. It let out a small groan and its muzzle lifted a little with a growled woof.

Raven kneeled down, gently reaching out to the demonic beast. He allowed her to brush her fingers over the top of his head. It felt just as it looked, like soft suede covered the demon's features. She leaned a little to the side as she looked over his body. A few patches of skin had fur missing and looked like dried leather.

"Do you have a name?"

The hellhound stood and tilted its head at her while moving closer. He lifted his heated paw and placed it on her knee. It was not hot enough to burn, but hot enough to notice. The hell born creature would make a good heating pad. He leaned in, sniffing before nuzzling the side of her face.

He didn't speak, which she was grateful for, because a talking evil dog might have been just one thing too much to accept. A strange sense of simply knowing came to Raven. She was safe, it intended no harm, which, given no fingers were lost when she touched him, the feeling made sense. Loyalty by choice, he would stay by her side until she no longer desired the companionship or her life expired. His name came to her tongue with a compulsion to speak. "Atreus." It was the closest variation able to be spoken by the human tongue and it was accepted. Her hand gently ran over his muzzle and down the side of his face and neck before she stood to get dressed.

Once dressed, she made her way downstairs, leaving Atreus in the bedroom. With that unexplainable understanding at play, she thought that the people that originally summoned him didn't need to know of the vowed allegiance between the two, or that his compliance become known.

Everyone was already eating, but by the looks of it, not for long. The dining room table held a spread of breakfast items. The walls and décor maintained the old Victorian theme throughout the rest of the house. From the carpets to the chandeliers, everything felt fit for royalty, even the plates everyone was eating from.

"Morning, Alex, sit down and help yourself." Graver spoke with a smile between greedy bites of bacon.

Raven sat down in the empty chair and made a few selections. Brandon, Mara and Lucas were nowhere to be seen, which drew her curiosity. "Where are the others?"

"Around." Austin replied.

"Brandon and Mara will join us soon. Lucas won't be around until later tonight." Graver explained a little further.

"Oh, ok." Raven took a few bites, trying to figure out how to navigate the start of an investigative conversation. "Lucas kind of mentioned I'm coming in late on all this." She motioned her fork in a circle at them. "Craziness."

"It does seem crazy, doesn't it?" Jason questioned.

"Yet here you are, safe with us." Graver spoke up. "It feels right, doesn't it?"

"Like I'm finally home where I belong." Raven smiled and continued to eat, despite the thought making her want to throw up.

"And we're going to take good care of you, show you what it means to be a demon and get you ready." Graver continued.

"I…kind of have questions, if I can ask them?" Her eyes darted over each of them.

"I don't see why not, what you want to know?" Austin questioned.

"Everyone in the house but Brandon and Mara…. demons?"

"Lucas is a vampire." Jason pointed out.

She stared at Jason, setting her fork down as she acted like she just learned vampires were a thing. "What?" Truth be told, she had already read about them to some degree.

"You shouldn't be so surprised, demons and angels are real…." Austin sneered out. "….so is most of everything else. The real world isn't what it's portrayed to be."

"Austin." Graver shot a glare in Austin's direction, shaking his head subtly.
"It's just…. wow, ok, so vampires are real. But what is one doing helping demons?"

"Vampires were human once, their loyalties from that life sometimes cross over when they are turned. Lucas has been loyal to the Collins family for generations." Graver explained openly.

"And the Collins family is loyal to Mephisto?" Raven glanced around the table. "To us?"

"Not all of them. There was a divide in the family. Some of them no longer wish to be involved and they headed out of town, out of state, even." Jason spoke with slight hesitation.

Raven nodded, picking her fork back up to take a few more bites. "What about you guys? You're not all from around here, are you?" It couldn't be helped, she found herself half staring at the scars along Austin's arms.

"Nah." Jason tapped his fingers to the table.

"Problem, Alex?" Austin asked while staring at her. It was almost unnerving.

"Huh? No?"

"You just keep looking at me funny, so I thought I would ask. We're family, no secrets here. So if something's bugging you, spit it out." Austin continued apprehensively.

"What happened to your arms?" She softly asked, regretting doing so as the words came out of her mouth.

"This?" He raised an arm. "This could be you."

"Austin." Graver gave him a look that meant he should mind what he said.

"Well, it could." Austin kept his eyes on Raven, weighing her every movement and word. "I never made it to the gathering. My parents had me committed when they found out I was cutting myself."

"Why would you do such a thing?" Raven was visibly unnerved as she questioned him, and it wasn't part of her ruse.

"It felt…" He held his arms up, looking at the scars, and closed his hands into fists. "Like something was scratching me. I knew in my gut that the answer was in the dreams I was having, but I couldn't stand it anymore. The scratching eventually turned into a burning. I thought I was losing it when I thought I saw fire under my skin. I got the idea to give it a way out."

Raven absent mindedly wrapped a hand around her arm as he told his story. The mention of a scratching under the skin was something she experienced herself, but it never got so bad that she felt the need to start slicing herself open. "So, you cut yourself."

"Each time I got some relief, but it always built back up."

"That's….really shitty. I'm sorry, Austin." Raven looked away a little.

"It won't happen to her." Jason spoke up. "Because she has her brothers to help her through the change. Right, Austin?" The tacked on question held firmness to it.

"Of course." Austin released his fists and lowered his arms.

"I think for now we should continue to leave the past where it belongs." Jason continued. "We have a happier future ahead of us now, let's focus on that."

"Agreed." Graver stood from his seat. "I think breakfast is over."

"Yeap, I got a…meeting." Jason spoke a bit oddly as he stood and took off.

"Oh, hey, Graver? Do you know what happened to my cell phone?"

Austin looked at Raven. "I burned it."

"What?" She looked at him swiftly.

"You have no reason to call anyone." Graver's tone became a bit cold as he spoke. "Everyone you need is here. Don't think of the people and life you left behind, it will make everything easier. Trust me."

The thought to ask what happened to the car was tossed right out the window, given Graver's reaction. She didn't want to push the issue too much, but also not seem too willing to accept anything and everything being said.

Everyone parted ways for the afternoon, giving her a chance to explore the house. Maybe she could locate those missing girls, or a phone. She started by meandering around the first floor. She wandered into the library, obviously not a place you'd stash a bunch of missing girls, but there might be a secret door leading to a suitable holding area. The book collection was an impressive mix of fiction and older tomes, occult in nature. It started to become fun, pulling books out here and there and feigning interest if she thought someone was coming, while all the while hoping that the book she pulled out would be the one that opened the secret entrance to the hidden cave or room.

Disappointed in not finding a hidden room, she headed to the second floor to explore. The door to the attic was unlocked. This was a sign that either no one was stashed there, or they were over confident that no one would get into the house and all the way up to the attic without being seen.

The attic was full of keepsakes and belongings of members of the Collins family, no doubt dating back to the construction of the house. Old sepia toned family photos, documents and hand written letters. An old dresser had random things crammed into it. There was an old sewing machine and a bed frame, rims off an old car, a stack of cardboard boxes and a couple of old trunks.

The woodwork on the ceiling was just as interesting as some of the things abandoned to the attic. Someone's handiwork was still visible and active. Demonic runes lined every piece of wood and support beam. The energy from their activity was faint, but present. A strange mobile was hanging in one corner. Its black strings had bones, dried herbs, feathers and thin round slabs of crystals hanging from it.

Raven sat on one of the old trunks, looking out the round attic window, watching everyone in the gardens. It was oddly enthralling, despite being, at times, disturbing. Jason was having a grand old time. It started with a frolic, the two girls with him appearing excited at small playful displays of power. A spark of flame here and a spark there. They ran through the maze of bushes and landscaping, leading him on a chase. His movement and body language was more like that of a predator than that a teenage boy chasing tail.

Cornered near the middle of the gardens, they stood there a moment, watching him, listening. Just as Raven started to wonder what was being said, one of the girls reached up to the straps of her dress and carefully pulled them off her shoulders and allowed the garment to fall away, exposing herself fully to him. The second girl looked unsure, maybe shy, as she did the same.

Carefully, they both lowered themselves down to the grass and settled on their backs. Jason stepped forward, hovering over them. The girl who was eager to undress spread her legs, welcoming him. Raven's curiosity fueled enthrallment wavered a little as she noticed something disturbing about the girl. There were burns on her inner thigh. Jason looked at the other girl, who still had her legs closed together. He moved to her, kneeling before her and reaching to her knees. She started to smile, almost grin with excitement as he pulled her legs apart. He ran a hand over her inner thigh, smooth and unharmed.

It was like coming across a horrible accident. You know you should look away, you tell yourself you should, but you gawk as you make your way past. Raven found herself watching with morbid curiosity. Jason held his hand up, putting on a bit of a show as a light coating of flame came to his hand. He then lowered it down to the girl's thigh again, caressing it.

Her head tilted back as she screamed, the heat of the flame burning her soft, smooth skin.

Raven forced herself to look away, pulling her own legs together tightly with a cringe, just imagining how painful that would be. She looked over at Austin, who was working with Brandon to try and control his flames. She focused on that, trying to get her mind away from what her other pretend brother was doing. Brandon presented a fatherly demeanor in his guidance and attempts to keep the half fire demon in control. But Austin was clearly holding on to some anger issues surrounding the events of his awakening, which influenced his abilities.

While it was mildly interesting watching Austin try to form controlled spheres of fire, her curiosity drew her attention back to the middle of the garden. Jason was on top of the girl he had burned, a pleasured grin on her face. The other girl they were with watched on, gently playing with herself.

"Ok, well, that's enough of that." She whispered to herself, hastily getting up and away from the window. She headed out of the attic, abandoning her little session of spying to go check on the basement. As she made it down to the main floor, she was surprised to find a full staff of people in the kitchen, cooking up a storm and blocking access to the basement door.

Deciding it might be best to head to the garden and take part in whatever lesson was underway, she turned and tripped over something, her hand slamming to the wall as she steadied herself. As soon as her hand slammed to the wall she felt a wave of demonic energy wash over her. It was oozing off the walls like an open wound.

She looked at her hand pressed firmly against the wall of the old Victorian home. The energy flowing through it was terrifying, yet at the same time, welcoming and exciting. It plucked at her demonic nature, catering to it. With a clank of noise, she looked back toward the dining room. For a flash of a moment it looked like the room was covered in flames, with small fire demons hopping around. They were roughly a foot tall, colored of charcoal and flame, and they were ripping a man to shreds with their claws and teeth.

The moment that came with Raven's hand remaining on the wall too long now ended with a gasp and her pulling the hand away, turning and backing up as she looked around the dining room.

"Alex." Brandon's voice came from behind her. "Is everything ok?"

Raven turned around, looking at Brandon, caught off guard by his sudden appearance after whatever it was she just saw. "I thought I saw something." She softly explained, looking past him as Austin walked by, heading for the stairs.

Brandon didn't look surprised as he looked behind Raven and then motioned for her to follow. "Come with me, please."

Careful not to touch the walls, or anything, for that matter, she followed him through the hall to the main foyer and to the sliding wooden doors that led to the small library. Brandon made his way inside, barely motioning to a chair as he sat down. "How did you sleep last night?" He asked thoughtfully, watching her intently.

"Alright, I think the bed is the softest I have ever slept in." She explained, sitting down in the chair across from him. "You have a lovely home."

He smiled at her, leaning his elbow to the arm of the chair in a relaxed posture. "It has its…charms, doesn't it?"

"If that is what you want to call it, sure." Raven replied without much thought. "What's wrong with it? Is it haunted?"

"No. What you felt is the demonic force of your Father radiating through the house." Brandon started, his eyes glued to Raven as he explained. "It's for the benefit of you and your brothers. The energy feeds your true nature, it will help you grow." He leaned forward slowly, his eyes darting over Raven's face, a bit of awe coming to his expression. "It's nothing to be afraid of."

"I'm not afraid." Raven assured him, though it was a lie. The idea that the house itself was a demonic energy hot spot feeding her demon side frightened her. "What is it doing to the humans who come in here, like the people in the kitchen?"

"Does it matter?" He questioned, testing as he stood, moving over to a small section of the shelves that housed a selection of whiskey and brandy.

Raven hesitated, catching the trick question. "Maybe, maybe not?" She paused. "If it drives them mad and in a moment of confusion they mention something to the wrong person, it could cause problems."

Brandon nodded, picking up the bottles in front of him as if inspecting them, but as he did he placed them on the shelf instead of the tray they were sitting on. "I suppose it would." He glanced over his shoulder at Raven. "You are scared, Alex." He proceeded bluntly. "Through our connection, I saw what your father saw when he called to you during the full moon."

Raven watched him from her chair, eyeing each bottle as it was set back down. Brandon turned around, the old deco tray in hand. The thin metal framework was attached to a mirrored bottom. Its design wasn't meant for carrying things, but for placement to protect the surface of furniture. "Don't be afraid." He urged, walking over to her and standing in front of her, holding the tray so the mirror faced her.

She hesitantly leaned forward, looking at herself in the mirror. Touching the wall was the equivalent of touching a live wire. Through it, she couldn't feel what she had felt in the past just before the shadows flooded her system. The blackened color to her eyes was evidence of such happening. Brandon allowed her to stare a moment before he spoke again. "Alex, talk to me." He encouraged, lowering the mirror.

"What have you done to me?" Her expression twisted as the mirror was lowered. Flawlessly, she played off the distress she was feeling over the revelation that the house would affect her in such a way, and played along as someone who was learning about these things for the first time.

"I have done nothing. This is what you are, why you have come here." He set the mirror on the chair next to him.

"I changed my mind, I don't want this." She shook her head, gripping the arms of the chair, acting like she was preparing to make an exit.

Brandon held his hand out for her to wait. "You could just leave, but what has been started cannot be stopped. You can do this the hard way…" He explained with a cold edge to his voice. "….run off and suffer on your own until your very abilities have driven you mad, or stay here where we can help you."

195

Raven stared at him in silence, gently loosening her grip to the arms of the chair. Brandon stepped closer. "We can help you, you just need to let go of your fear like you did last night and trust me, trust us, Alex. Please." He held his hand out to her.

Raven lifted her hand, reaching out and taking his. As Brandon accepted her hand, he squeezed gently. She could feel the heat of Mephisto flowing through his body, a willing avatar. She wondered how much of him really was human, to be able to sustain such a connection.

Later that evening as the sun set, cars started showing up. People in black hooded robes were filling the grand hall. Raven and her three 'brothers' stood up in the balcony, draped in black and red robes that were a little more elaborate than the ones Lucas had been seen in, indicating their importance.

Mara had fawned over her, helping to prepare her for the big night. It was hard to tell if it was genuine, or not. A full body message, milk bath and curling her hair all felt like she was being prepared to attend an award show, but at this show, once she walked the red carpet, she would be awarded a false title and full roster of a flame loving cult.

Was this why some people in small towns had the mentality to keep outsiders out, because there were dirty little secrets like these that they don't want exposed? She recalled the night of the accident, when she arrived at the bar to install the stereo, there had been people walking down the alley that gave her a 'you don't belong here' glare. Could those people be in this crowd, or had they simply been eyeing her as a stranger that could have been up to no good?

"Penny for your thoughts?" Graver whispered, noticing the look of concentration on her face.

"Just thinking about everyone down there, what it must take to keep such a following secret." She whispered back.

"It's not easy, we've had a local detective on us a couple of times." He paused the whispering, seeing Brandon enter the hall. "Shhh…it's going to start."

Everyone raised their hoods and Brandon took his place at the altar. "Tonight we gather to celebrate the recovery of the lost. You were promised that this would be the year of our master's arrival. Salvation and a place in the new world that together we will forge through fire and sacrifice is upon us."

Brandon looked over the crowd. "You offered your loyalty."

"We accepted the flame." The entire crowd responded.

"You were asked for sacrifice."

"We offered the purity of our daughters." The entire crowd responded. Raven's mind went straight to questioning the circumstances surrounding the missing girls. Were they reported missing ahead of time to help cover what was going on? A string of spread out missing person reports was less likely to be connected than a dozen all filed at the same time. However, these girls didn't all come from the same area, leading to the conclusion that not everyone gathered here lived in town.

"From the fire we rise…." Brandon called out.

"To the fire we return." The entire crowd responded.

"Come, receive Mephisto's blessing."

Brandon cut his hand, allowing blood to pool within the cupped palm. One by one, the cultists approached the altar and lowered themselves down to one knee. Each time, Brandon ran his thumb over the cut on his hand and pulled it over their left brow.

After the blessing ceremony, Raven and the others were escorted down from the balcony and lined up on either side of the altar. There was a moment of awkward silence before a man was dragged into the hall. His hands were pulled behind his back in cuffs, his clothes were slightly dirty, and there were a few cuts on the side of his face. Two robed followers forced him to his knees and remained there, holding him from behind.

"Before the festivities begin, we must take care of a matter that will prove most difficult to some of you gathered here." Lucas explained. "This man…." Lucas pointed at the beer bellied, middle aged man. "Has betrayed us. He was working with that girl to try and end everything we have built here."

The crowd remained silent. Some held a mixture of expressions on what little of their faces could be seen through the shadow of their hooded robes. Disappointment, sadness, disgust and worry.

"But, we are stronger now." He paced, motioning to Raven. "All four of our Lord Mephisto's children are here, completing the circle." Raven stayed still, eyeing Lucas.

"This man will stand trial and face punishment for his betrayal." Lucas spoke on the matter further. "Alex, would you please step forward?" Raven's stomach turned. There had been no mention of having to do anything other than stand there. She took a few steps forward, looking at the man in question as Lucas kept talking. "He stands before you, accused of conspiring with a soldier of heaven to destroy Mephisto's human host and dismantle this very congregation. How do you plead, Oswald?"

Oswald looked up at Raven as if looking at an entity he was unworthy of being around. "I promise you, on the lives and honor of my family that have served your Father for generations, I didn't do it. Please, you have to believe me!" He begged emotionally, his fear getting the better of him.

Raven stared at Oswald, unsure of what to do. She felt panicked. Here was a man that, for all she knew, was only guilty of being unfortunate enough to be born into a family that was part of a cult. She then looked at the crowd, which was waiting in anticipation. Some people were looking at the accused with such hatred that she was sure they would be pleased with a death sentence.

Raven glanced back to Brandon and was able to see the out of phase visage of Mephisto behind him, fangs exposed with a grin. His fiery eyes focused on her, waiting in anticipation to see what she would do. Her slender fingers reached up, pulling the hood of her robe down.

"Is that your final plea? You didn't do it?" Her voice rang out, smooth, dark, calming, and alluring in its own right. She allowed her darker instincts to guide her actions.

"Y-yes." Oswald answered.

A symphony of whispers danced around her as Oswald answered. She moved forward, closing the gap between them and leaning down, tilting her head to him ever so slightly. Austin, Graver and Jason all glanced at each other in confusion, but watched on. Her eyes fell closed and she took slow, steady breaths as her mind cleared. Someone in the crowd gasped as her pale lips parted, letting out a low hiss of a whispered word or two.

"What?" Oswald questioned, looking at Raven.

The hisses and drawn out raspy sounds swirling around Raven started to become clear and make sense. Whispers of Oswald, who didn't betray anyone here. As a matter of fact, he was loyal to the core. He even offered up his own daughter for the ritual and killed his wife in the process. Glimpses flashed through her mind; Oswald's wife begging and pleading to not take their only child, the struggle over a sleeping girl, and the baseball bat from the garage that he used to cave his wife's skull in to stop her from calling the police.

Raven swiftly stood up straight, her eyes opening. Oswald leaned back in terror, bumping into the two robed men who hadn't moved. He was now facing an evil that wasn't there a moment ago as Raven's eyes had been consumed by black. "He's guilty." Raven spoke without hesitation, flat out lying. The cult may not have been betrayed, but he brutally murdered his wife and offered his child up to be killed as well. He was guilty of something and she wanted to punish him.

"No! She's lying! I didn't do it!! I didn't!" One of the men holding Oswald let him go long enough to pull a leather strap from his robe and fasten it over his mouth to silence him.

"Oswald Brunswick, you have been found guilty. As punishment, you and your family will be stripped of your positions." Through the sentencing, Oswald tried desperately to plead and argue through

the leather strap. "Furthermore, you will be purged."
The man started to scream against the strap and
struggle in the bindings as the men behind him moved
away.

Raven blinked, looking at Brandon
questioningly. Just as she did, Austin spoke with
excitement. "Purge him, Alex."

Graver glared at Austin and made his way to
Raven. "It's ok." He whispered and stood beside her.
"Like this." His arm reached over her shoulder,
extending out to Oswald. Fingers spread, palm facing
the floor, he allowed flames to engulf his whole hand.

He kept his voice at a whisper. "You can do
it."

She looked at Graver, hesitant to do anything.
Looking back at Oswald, she lifted her fist just under
Graver's. Shadow energy could be felt just under the
skin, clawing to get out. Trembling fingers unfolded
and spread. Thick black shadow energy swirled into
existence around her hand, resembling ink pouring
into water, just like the last time it manifested. It
moved around her hand in a spastic, billowy dance.
She tried to pull back, but Graver's free hand pressed
against her back.

"Breathe." He whispered. "Breathe and focus
your intentions…. we're going to kill him, Alex."

Graver settled his palm on top of Raven's
hand, curling his fingers down in between hers. The
shadow and flame mingled, twisting and melding

together. He guided Raven's hand until her palm pressed against Oswald's forehead.

Dark thoughts crept through her mind. She wanted Oswald to suffer. The thought of his actions drove at her, which influenced the manifested shadows. They seeped into Oswald's forehead, causing him to scream. Flames consumed his body, prompting Graver to let Raven's hand go. She pulled her hand away, looking at the shadow dancing around it. All the while, a follower or two silently and casually made their way to the windows, opening them.

Oswald's screams rang through the hall unmuffled as the leather strap covering his mouth burned away. The flames cut through clothes and flesh, bringing it to burn, bubble, and char as he fell over in a sickening thump against the marble floor. Thick smoke billowed up toward the ceiling. His screams began to subside as the flames kept burning away at his body.

The smell of burning flesh was heavy in the grand hall and was flowing out the windows, filling the night air. Raven look at the burning corpse, pulling her hand out of sight. It smelled like someone was cooking out on the grill. For a moment she forgot the fact that she was surrounded by a demon worshiping cult. A room full of people, yet all there was, was her and the burning corpse of a man she helped kill. The deafening silence in the room, only interrupted by the gentle crackling of flame devouring flesh, fed the illusion of such. Her mind raced. She should be feeling something. Panic? Fear? But just like the night before, as she stood staring at the bodies left mangled and half devoured by hellhounds, she felt nothing.

Raven slowly looked up, her eyes darting over the crowd as they stared at her like a herd of sheep. They were all human, but they didn't seem so. Most had blank expressions on their faces. Some of them had an unnerving glint in their eyes. Others barely held back grins of excitement.

Graver placed his hand on her shoulder, looking over the crowd as Jason and Austin stepped up to her opposite side. A quick glance to either side of herself gave a glimpse of her false brothers looking upon the crowd with authority. There was a strange energy to the air, an unavoidable presence of dominance exuded from the three dark Nephilim at her sides. The crowd lowered themselves to their knees and bowed their heads.

The situation felt more bizarre by the second as Brandon walked back to the front of the altar and stood in front of her. He looked like a proud father as he reached down to her still form and pulled the hood of her robe back up into place. No one in the crowd was speaking or moving, not a sound was being made as Jason and Austin stepped away from the altar and headed down the red carpet runner.

With a slight nudge of Graver's hand, Raven followed, his hand slipping away from her shoulder as she started to walk, and he was right behind her. The four of them left the grand hall and made their way into the main foyer of the house.

"Well done, Alex." Austin clapped his hands together gently as he turned around to face her as she made her way into the foyer.

"You truly are our sister." Jason grinned devilishly as he looked at her and Graver.

"That was….." She paused, hesitating as she pulled the hood of her robe off again. Now that she was away from the crowd she felt a surge of emotions and thoughts. She was anxious and wasn't sure why, and right alongside that feeling, she was excited and even happy. "Intense." Raven turned and looked back toward the doors of the grand hall. "What are they doing in there now?"

Graver chuckled as if amused by her curiosity. "They will perform a small ritual in your name." He placed his hand on her shoulder again, gently turning her back around. "After that, some of the more important followers will remain as honored guests for dinner and…additional activities."

"Additional?" Raven questioned.

"They are here to serve us, in all the ways we see fit." Jason replied, settling down in a chair with a grin.

"Oh…" Raven spoke the single word softly, eyeing Jason and trying not to think about what she saw him doing earlier in the day.

"Do you want me to select one of the men for you?" Jason asked casually. His question caused Austin to shake his head before slinking up the stairs to be alone.

"Or maybe she would prefer to study with me." Graver wrapped his arm around Raven.

Raven found amusement in the situation, however, she was more curious as to what kind of ritual was being performed in her name, as it had been put. "I…. kind of want to see what is going on, back there." She motioned back toward the grand hall.

"I have a better idea." Austin called out as he came back down the stairs with a package of cigarettes in hand. "Take your robes off." He encouraged, heading for the front door.

Graver pulled his arm away from Raven, pulling his robe off to reveal his clothes beneath before he slipped past her to follow Austin. Jason reluctantly stood, pulling his robe off and heading out the door as he smoothed out his button up silk shirt. Curiosity got the better of her, and as she pulled her robe off, Austin called out in a hushed tone. "Hurry up!"

She hurried out the front door, jumping off the last three steps of the porch. The four of them zig zagged between the cars and headed into the woods that lined the property. Jason brought a flame to his hand to light the way, and they kept up a steady pace as they walked a man made path.

"So, Alex, got any hobbies?" Graver asked curiously as they walked.

"Do comic books and video games count?" She replied with a question, keeping an eye on where she walked as they pushed past some branches.

"Sure they do." Jason replied, kicking a rock out of the way.

"Which video game is your favorite?" Austin asked, glancing back at her through the darkness.

"I don't really have a favorite. " Raven replied. "You?"

"Anything first person shooter, I'm all over." Austin explained.

"What about you, Jason?" Raven asked, taking the opportunity to get to know them.

"I used to ride dirt bikes." He responded, slowing down the pace a little. "Big rock up here, be careful."

"Used to?" Raven side stepped the rock, glancing back at Graver to make sure he did the same.

"Haven't found the time lately." Jason answered her with a hint of disappointment to his voice.

"At least you could ride again if you wanted to." Graver spoke up. "Every time I pick up a guitar, I start a fire."

"Talk about…lighting up the stage?" Raven teased Graver with the pun.

Graver laughed. "Good one, too bad it's a one stop trick. Once the guitar is gone, no more show."

Pushing past another set of branches and sliding past a few more bushes, they came to a decent sized stream of water. The area was secluded, surrounded by trees on all sides. There was a small break wall across the stream that served as a dam, and it looked like it was a few years past needing to be replaced.

The parting of the woods from the stream gave a window to the night sky. A blanketing of black, untainted by city lights and generously covered in stars. Raven couldn't help but stop and look up at them as they made their arrival.

"It's nice out here, quiet." Austin spoke light heartedly. He kept his eyes on Raven as he pulled a cigarette from its package and held it up. Lifting his opposing hand, he snapped his fingers together to strike up a flame to light it with. The flame was more controlled than he expected. He shook his hand, putting the flame out and repeated the act before lighting his cigarette.

Raven looked at Austin, catching a series of silent glances between the three. "Ok, what's going on?"

"Nothing." Graver explained carefully. "Come on, sit." He motioned for her to join them as the three settled down. Raven narrowed her eyes at them once they all had their backs turned to look out over the water. Nothing? So much glancing over nothing? She knew better, but held her tongue and sat down next to Graver.

Austin took a drag off his cigarette, letting the smoke out slowly to the side. The menthol infused smoke swirled around as a light breeze pushed through it, quickening its dispersal and eventual fading from sight.

The water's gentle flow past them added to the calm as they sat watching the stars. The simplicity of it was perfect. For that fraction of time within the larger scheme of it all, they were simply four people enjoying the night sky.

As Austin took the last drag off his cigarette, he flicked it toward the water, sending it off with a spiral of flame that reflected off the water and burned the butt away to nothing before it even neared the water's surface.

"Last night, did Father explain our purpose?" Graver broke the silence, questioning calmly as he glanced from the stars to Raven for a second.

"Briefly. He mainly talked about how I need to complete the portal." Raven replied, keeping her eyes on the stars.

"Once you do that, Father can step out of hell and join us. The next phase can begin." Graver continued, looking at Jason and Austin.

Raven thought a moment before looking at Graver. "What exactly is the next phase?" She proceeded with caution, recalling Mephisto's mention of bringing an army through the portal.

"The fun part." Austin spoke up excitedly.

"The part you need to be ready for." Jason interjected.

"Ready for what?" Raven leaned forward a little to look at Jason and Austin.

"Once Father comes through." Graver started to explain, leaning back on his hands and looking back up to the sky. "The town will be purged of anyone not loyal, or able to be controlled. From there, the world as we know it will burn, and a new world run by demons will be born out of the ashes."

"No pressure or anything…. But all this is dependent on you growing strong enough to open that portal." Jason pointed out with a chuckle.

"Yeah…" Raven chuckled, looking at the water. "No pressure." She mumbled, indeed feeling pressured as she was reminded of the gravity of the situation.

"It's a lot to take in, we understand that." Graver placed his hand on her arm. "Does the idea upset you?" He questioned in a tone that wasn't easy to determine whether it was concern or suspicion.

Raven nodded a little. "A little, not too much? It's confusing." Raven looked at the three of them, who were all watching her. "I…never really knew what to do with myself. My whole life, I just felt out of place."

"Square peg in a round hole." Austin commented with understanding in his voice.

"Exactly, yes." Raven's eyes darted to Austin as he lit another cigarette. "It feels wrong to be told that you're going to do something so horrible. But at the same time, it feels right." Raven paused, wanting to be careful of what she said. She knew she was treading dangerously, picking and choosing what to include in her act, things that were based off of how she really felt. "Like, for the first time in my life, I feel like I'm doing what I'm supposed to be doing. I feel like this is where I was supposed to be, all along."

Graver squeezed her arm. "There is going to be a conflict in thoughts and emotions." He motioned his opposing hand over toward Jason and Austin. "We all went through it. Two personalities. The human conscience battling a part of you locked away your whole life. You're becoming someone new. But trust, Alex, that you aren't doing this alone."

"We got your back, sis." Jason spoke up with a smile.

"Thanks." Raven managed a smile. "So, what was that before, the looks you were giving each other?"

"Since we are only half demon, our powers are linked to our emotions. There is something about being around you that makes me feel calm." Austin explained between puffs off his cigarette.

"We should get back." Graver suggested before anything else could be said as he stood, stretching out. "She's not supposed to be this far from the house."

"I'm not?" Raven questioned, standing herself and brushing off her jeans.

"Nope!" Jason explained in devilish amusement as he got up, heading to the path that got them there.

"We broke the rules?" Raven looked at Graver.

"What kind of demons would we be, if we didn't?" Jason turned around, walking backward a moment as he asked.

"It's not like we're going to get punished. We can do no wrong in Father's eyes." Graver pointed out, motioning for Raven to follow Austin and Jason.

Raven chuckled, following their lead. Once again, Graver was right behind her as they walked through the woods. Was it to make sure she couldn't run off, or a protective formation to have her in between them? The trip back to the house seemed shorter than the trip away from it. The four of them made their way back into the house, where they found their robes missing and replaced by Lucas.

He stood there, arms folded and looking at the four of them with a small smirk on his discolored lips. "I see some sibling bonding has taken place."

The four of them exchanged glances, half grinning.

The vampire gave pause and held his hand out to the stairs. "While you were out, I arranged for some evening entertainment."

"The girls are in my room?" Jason asked, making a dash for the stairs.

"Yes, master Jason, they await your company." Lucas replied casually.

Austin shrugged, looking at Raven before heading up the stairs. "Don't do anything you don't want to, Alex!"

Raven didn't put much thought into Austin's comment and smiled a little at Lucas before she headed up the stairs. On point, Graver headed up right behind her and hovered outside his bedroom door until she was safely in her room. She leaned against the closed door a moment, taking in a deep breath. In her mind, everything was going smoothly, she just needed to figure out this portal situation.

She turned around, letting out a startled half scream. Even though Lucas had said he arranged entertainment, she had thought he meant for Jason. The man standing next to her bed told another story.

He was standing there in silence, waiting for her arrival. He had black hair that had a slight curl to it, and brown eyes. His toned, sun kissed frame was draped in a red velvet robe. As soon as she had turned, he pulled the robe open, exposing himself fully to her. There was a pattern of runes over his chest, drawn on in a slick red ink. He held his alluring posture, waiting for her command.

Austin and Graver came rushing up from behind. "Alex, you ok?" Graver asked as the two made it to the door, pulling it open. His question was swiftly followed up with him stepping back and covering his eyes. "Ahh! I did not need to see that!"

"I'm still debating if I needed to see that." Raven shyly admitted, staring at the man despite suggesting she didn't want to see so much of him.

The man simply stood there, as if the conversation at hand didn't faze him. Raven turned around, looking at Austin and Graver. "I don't want that…him….I mean." She turned around to the man. "I really appreciate the…offer." She hesitated, feeling tempted. "But I had a long day, and just want to sleep."

"Then I will lay next to you and hold you, if it pleases you." The man offered, keeping his eyes on Raven.

"Alone…. I want to sleep alone." She glanced at Austin as he stepped into the room and held his hand out to the man.

"Come along, you can spend the night with me." Austin motioned his fingers as he spoke.

"As you wish." The man walked to Austin, taking his hand, and the two headed out of the room.

As they went, Graver peered inside. "All clear?"

Raven stood there a moment. "Looks like it."

"Excellent." He bowed his head. "Goodnight, Alex."

"Good night, Graver."

She watched as he pulled the door closed. As soon as it clicked shut, she covered her mouth with both hands to stop herself from grinning as her mind immediately started to wander over what she just passed up. It's not every day an underwear model without his underwear simply offers himself up like that. She took a step toward the door, pondering going to Austin's room and asking if she could have the sex slave back. Instead, she opted for a shower and sleep.

But sleep wouldn't come, no matter how hard she tried. A cluster of things plagued her mind. Letting those five people die at the state park, the 'purging' of Oswald, and the chat with the boys afterwards. This was all for the greater good though....right? Oswald killed his wife and handed over his own child to be sacrificed. He was the enemy and a casualty of war. That was something that couldn't be forgotten, that this was just a battle in one big war between good and evil.

She slid out of bed. The demonic energy of the house clawed at her already raw nerves and the more she thought about the things she had done, the more it felt crowded, even in the empty room.

Dark grey cotton pajama bottoms and a sleep shirt were decent enough, so the thought of getting dressed was dismissed. Creeping out of the room, she made her way out of the house and out the back door, being careful not to make any noise.

Raven wandered around until she found a small clearing located in the middle of the gardens. A stone bench wasn't the most ideal of seats, but it was better than the ground. The air was crisp and cool. Being on the edge of town, the sky was clear and untainted by street lights, allowing the stars to be seen.

She allowed her mind to wander over the events of the evening, the interaction between herself and her three 'brothers'. They were so quick to accept her and treat her as one of their own, chatting about trivial things in a fashion that made it feel, in some sick way, like she was just returning home after a long trip.

"What are you doing up so late?" Lucas questioned as he entered the clearing.

Raven jumped a little, startled by his sudden appearance. "I couldn't sleep."

He made his way over and sat next to her. "Something bothering you?"

"A lot of things, I would say." Her eyes darted over the blood on his shirt.

"I'm right here. You don't have to keep it to yourself. You can trust me."

She looked down, her fingers curling around the edge of the bench. If only it was that easy to just start rambling off everything that was bothering her. But her words had to be chosen wisely. "Ever since I started seeing things differently, feeling things...." She started slowly, carefully mixing some truth and presenting it with the lie of this assignment.

"Awakening as a half demon?" Lucas questioned as she paused.

"Yeah." She quickly glanced at him, then away. "It's been confusing. Everything feels like it's going so fast. It's a lot to take in all at once." She looked at him, feeling some form of relief at being able to say these things. "But at the same time, through the confusion and even fear, questioning if it's all even real...I feel like this is right. Like, somehow I knew all along, subconsciously, you know?"

Lucas smiled, his eyes meeting hers. "Give me an example. Think of a time from when you were younger that would fit that statement, the confusing thoughts and not fitting in."

Raven peered up in thought. "I was nine, I think? I was sitting in church, listening to my step-Father speak."

"He's a man of God?" Amusement filled his voice at the thought of a holy man raising a half demon.

"Yeah. He is one of the parishioners that speak every Sunday after the priest's sermon." She paused a second, recalling that day. "I found myself thinking, while he stood there and talked about heaven, that it was a waste of time. Me being in that place was a waste of time and that everyone around me…." She fell silent, unsure if the thought should be finished out loud.

"It's ok, Alex, I won't judge you." He assured softly.

"Worthless ash…it felt like everyone around me was ash. I couldn't come up with a reason why I thought these things."

"A pretty confusing thought for a nine year old to have." He commented.

"Right?" She chuckled a little. "I dunno, just little things here and there, I guess." She gently led

the conversation in a different direction. "But now…
I don't even know what I am, or really who I am,
anymore." There was honesty to the words she spoke
as she looked away from him.

"Well, I can say, you aren't like your brothers,
Alex." He spoke to Raven, lifting a hand up to reach
out to her. Thinking better of it, he instead pushed
thin, dirty blond strands from his face.

"Oh, you noticed?" She replied with a bit of
sass to her tone.

"Not just your powers. Your human half is
still intact, leaving an innocence in you that they
lack." He explained as Raven looked back at him.
"Even after you declared him guilty, you looked at
Brandon questioningly when he said to kill Oswald."

"I had no idea what he meant by purge, it
could have meant anything, like, banish him from the
house or something." She explained, following up
with trying to get an answer to something that was
bothering her. "But since you mention it, why is my
power different? Why not fire, like my brothers?"

Lucas raised his chin slightly at her question.
"Your brothers asked Mephisto the same thing." He
paused, being careful with his wording. "Fire is not
the only thing Mephisto reigns over, he forged you
each exactly how you were needed. But the difference
is more than that, I saw it." He paused, giving in to
his urges, reaching over to run his fingers down her
arm gently. "The others have been with Mephisto for

so long that they no longer doubt his word and freely follow their darker instincts. Your journey to your true self may not be as easy, with the final ritual happening soon."

Raven looked down at his hand, a slight tingling running up her spine. "Soon?"

"A week, maybe two. Mephisto will tell us when it is time. I imagine not too much longer." He leaned down toward her, taking in her scent and purposely brushing his cheek against hers.

"Are you smelling me?" She pulled back, eyeing him carefully.

"Sorry." He leaned away, smiling. "Something about you is just so…" His darkened tongue ran over his fangs as his eyes narrowed.

Raven eyed those fangs before leaning over to him and sniffing back.

"What are *you* doing?" He laughed out as amusement twinkled in his pale blue eyes.

"See how random and odd that is?" She laughed, and he laughed with her and then leaned over, pulling her into a gentle kiss.

Raven froze, feeling his cool, stained lips on hers. She didn't want to like it, and tried to convince herself it wasn't that great. But she leaned into the kiss, closing her eyes. Before pulling away, Lucas ran the tip of his tongue over Raven's lips.

"Wow…." She whispered, opening her eyes. "That was umm---"She fell silent, pulling a hand up to shield her eyes as a series of bright lights flashed through the area. "What is that?"

Lucas sounded confused and concerned as his hand squeezed her a little. "I don't see anything, Alex. But I hear something." Letting go, he stood quickly.

The sound of people running nearby could be heard. Lucas showed no hesitation in putting himself between Raven and the two uninvited guests that came barreling around the corner of the clearing.

It was a man and a woman. He appeared Asian in origin, with several holy symbols tattooed on his neck. Katana in hand, he took a stance as if he was readying for an attack next to his partner. A bow and quiver was strapped to her back, and the black woman looked ready to have at anyone or anything standing in the way.

"Alex, run to the house, warn your brothers that light Nephilim have breached the property," Lucas hissed out, baring his fangs at the two.

"Lilly, if you will?" The man spoke, raising his sword a little.

"My pleasure, Haru!" She replied, opening her fist and dropping three white stones.

The stones zoomed through the air, starting their rotation around Raven. Haru brought his sword down to the ground, sending a blast of golden light at Lucas. As it impacted, it sent the vampire flying through the bushes and crashing into something on the other side. Haru gave chase as his partner stepped closer to Raven, holding her palm out and chanting in Latin.

Raven laughed a little. "You can't exorcise me, this is my body and you're making a mistake." She whispered out. "You need to leave and have your guardian check in with—"

A severe pain ripped through Raven's chest. She cringed and gasped, clutching at it. This caused the light Nephilim to boldly step closer, reaching into her pocket and drawing a dagger lined in Enochian runes.

Just as Lilly raised it with the intention of plunging it into Raven's chest, Raven moved out of the way. Lilly kept at it, slashing mercilessly. Raven backed up as quickly as she could, letting out a gasped half scream as the holy blade sliced through her skin. Lilly suddenly backed off, calling for the stones once more.

Despite the pain, Raven kept moving and snatched one of the moonstones from the air as they zipped around back into their place of rotation. Eyes filling with darkness, her hand was engulfed in shadows as it closed around the stone. The chanting of old holy dialect resumed and halted just as swiftly as that closed fist went swinging at Lilly's face.

The woman's head snapped to the side as she went stumbling and tripping over the bench, then falling flat on her rear end. Raven didn't let up, as soon as Lilly pulled a hand from her bloodied nose, the dust that was once the moonstone was tossed at wide brown eyes.

"Listen to me." Raven hissed as she moved in and crouched over the blinded woman, grasping her arms tight. "I'm working wi---"She was cut off again, this time by an arrow slamming into the back of her shoulder.

"Shit!" Raven let Lilly go and backed away. She turned quickly about to look in the direction the arrow would have come from, and was met by another arrow zipping through the air. Her movement helped avoid a direct hit, instead, it nicked the side of her face. She got out of the shooters line of sight, putting her back against the bushes.

"Atreus!" Raven called out, and the hellhound responded with a ghastly howl that echoed from the depths. He came around the corner, flames swirling about as his being crossed into the world. She lifted her hand, motioning in the direction the arrows were coming from, prompting Atreus to take off on the hunt.

The sounds of Lucas and Haru fighting could be heard through the bushes, as well as a third person heading to the clearing. Raven reached back and pulled the arrow out. "You know." Pain could be heard in her voice as the arrow was tossed aside. "You know it's kind of dumb, you guys attacking this place."

"It's what we do." Lilly replied, getting to her feet, glancing in the direction of a scream in the distance. Atreus was now having a late night snack.

"Dumb?" Raven mocked Lilly with a chuckle before rushing forward and tackling her.

The two went tumbling to the ground. Lilly managed to grab her dagger, thrusting it blindly as Raven pressed a palm to the light Nephilim's forehead. Dark energy seeped from her hand into the woman's skull. She screamed, slashing the blood soaked dagger at Raven's arm to try and get her away.

"Alex!" Graver called out in a panic. He tried to make sense of what he was seeing as he ran into the clearing.

The skin along Lilly's forehead started to darken with decay as golden energy sparked out around the two chaotically. Graver ran over and wrapped his arms around Raven protectively, lifting her off Lilly. He turned, putting his back to Lilly and putting himself between the holy energy and the girl he knew as sister.

Jason came around the corner into the clearing, eyes ablaze in molten tones. He stalked right up to Lilly and thrust his hands out at her. A spiraling of flames poured out of his palms, covering the woman. Her continued screams were cut off as he slammed his boot down onto her face.

Lucas made his way to the clearing, blood soaking his mouth and chin. His shirt was torn and splattered with blood. He started walking toward Graver and Raven, but stopped when Jason intercepted him.

"Let her go." Jason demanded.

Graver set Raven down, pressing a hand against the gash in her side.

The black of Raven's eyes receded as she looked at the burning body. Questions came to mind, like why had light Nephilim been dispatched to this location? Or were they drawn here by the demonic presence looming over the property?

"How bad is it?" Jason asked, pulling the sleep shirt away from Raven's shoulder to inspect the arrow wound.

"I'm fine." Raven tried to assure them, but she was ignored as they continued to fuss over her.

"Deep, I can't tell if she started healing, will she? Is that one of her abilities?" Graver questioned, growing more concerned.

"I don't know." Jason grumbled, looking around.

"She should." Lucas offered, keeping his distance. They all looked like they probably needed medical attention. Cuts and holy burns were present on all three men.

Spotting the dagger on the ground, Jason plucked it up, cleaning it off on his pant leg before inspecting the engraving. "It's a blessed blade." He explained, looking at Graver with a growl. "Get her inside."

Graver pulled his hand from the wound, scooping Raven up again. As they headed to the house, she passed out. The last thing she heard was the sound of Austin saying the house was clear for entry.

Chapter Eight

Things were tense in the days following the attack. Raven woke to find people hovering, and not going away. Someone was always just outside the door, standing guard. Her wounds had healed, but she could barely remember what happened between the attack and waking up. There was a vague recollection of intense pain as someone held her down, and a soothing voice speaking to her, but she couldn't remember what was said.

Paranoia was thick in the air. Brandon and Lucas were both convinced it couldn't be a coincidence that light Nephilim attacked on the same night they announced Raven's arrival. This, from what she gathered, put everyone to the task of questioning those who had gathered that night.

As time dragged on, Raven eventually found distraction in an offering of comic books to read. Atreus hadn't left her side, and sat next to her on the bed, looking over the pages intently as she read to him, pointing out different characters and giving brief commentary and history.

"Don't you two look kind of adorable?" Graver interrupted as he stood in the doorway.

"How long have you been standing there?" Raven looked up and over her shoulder.

"Long enough." He made his way in and sat down next to her, glancing at the hellhound. "How are you feeling?"

"Better." The comics in hand were folded closed as she answered. "Have you guys been avoiding me, because I didn't tell you about him?" She looked at Atreus, reaching over and petting him. She knew he wasn't the reason why, but felt it was an innocent enough thought that might pull at Graver's heart strings…. if he had any.

"Oh, Sister…" Graver's tone saddened. "No…."

Raven held back a grin, keeping a confused expression on her face. There was an excitement and satisfaction that came with such deceptions being believed. "I don't understand why, then. I feel like I'm being punished."

"Protected." Graver explained. "We got so wrapped up in trying to figure out if there was another spy in the ranks and trying to get answers that we neglected you, and I'm sorry."

Raven nodded, reaching up and pushing her fingers over her eyes as if pushing away tears. "I understand, I guess. We just seemed like we were really bonding during the gathering, talking and joking around, that I really thought maybe— "

"Hey, none of that. It's your human half getting the better of you." He ate the act up and tried to comfort her. "Which is to be expected."

"But you guys are fine, how do you do it?"

"Not much left of us is human." He paused. "Maybe we shouldn't discuss it."

"No, it's ok. I'm curious, how did you 'lose' your humanity?"

"Mother was rarely home, working double shifts to make ends meet. My Step-Father? Couldn't hold a job, but could hold a liquor bottle. One night he pushed my little sister down the stairs. Her neck snapped and the drunken fool kept kicking her body, telling her to stop faking it. I know that was the night I lost it, my humanity, that is. I could feel it just slip away, and I didn't care." He recalled with an eerie calm, as if the events had stirred not a shred of emotion. "After the funeral, I killed him and left."

"Was this before or after your awakening?" She asked, pretending she was no longer upset.

"After, Lucas and Brandon were staying a county over and I hadn't moved in with them yet."

"Because you wanted to protect your sister." It made sense now why Graver was so protective, more so than the others, trying to buffer Austin's sharp tongue in the beginning and being quick to help her purge Oswald.

"Yes. I won't fail you as I did her, though."

Raven eyed him. The sentiment was rather human. She kept the thought to herself. "Thanks." She looked back at the comics in her lap in thought.

"I need to ask you something, Alex." Graver reached over, taking the stack of comics to inspect as he spoke.

"Huh?"

"How did you know Oswald was guilty? You did something, what was it?"

"I, uh…" Raven kept her eyes on him. She was caught off guard, honestly not sure how she knew to do what she did. "…Don't really know. When he answered me, I started hearing things." She paused. "Wow….that sounds insane to say."

He laughed. "Go on…."

"From there, it was just instinct. Leaning closer just felt like the thing to do. I saw flashes of Oswald talking to some girl about killing Brandon and then those words just spilled out." Her eyes widened a little as she continued to act a mixture of confused and surprised.

"I'll admit, most of my studies have been in necromancy and the dark arts. I should have spent more time reading up on other demons." He spoke with a hint of regret. "But I did do some quick reading last night on shadows."

"Why didn't you just ask Father?"

Graver shrugged. "We have to do some things ourselves, but perhaps we both can speak with him later. For now, it turns out opening portals isn't the only thing you can do. There is much to explore." He smiled. "I think that little trick of yours could be helpful."

"I'd say so." She chuckled.

"Are you feeling up to trying that again? Right now?"

Raven's eyes looked over at Atreus. The hellhound had fallen asleep during the conversation and was drooling on her pillow. "Sure, looks like I lost my reading buddy for now, so why not?"

"Come on." Graver took her hand, helping her stand, even though it wasn't needed. He guided her into the hall, motioning the guards to follow. He led her downstairs and out through the garden to the guest house at the back of the property. The door wasn't locked and the place was empty, with no furniture or signs anyone lived there. There was a set of stairs that led to a second floor loft, and under the stairs was a door. Graver knocked on the door, and after a moment it creaked open, revealing another set of stairs leading down.

"Alex." Lucas smiled. "Feeling better, I see?"

"Yes, thank you."

"She's going to help." Graver explained with authority to Lucas.

"As you wish, Master Graver." Lucas half bowed, his eyes unwavering from Raven's face before he turned and led them down into the cellar.

It was cold and damp. The old stone walls were covered in dried blood, scratches, and burn marks. Chained to the wall was a young man, his head lowered. Cloths of white and blue were stained with his own blood. His shirt was torn open, exposing his chest. His pale skin was littered with burn marks and cuts. His unwashed hair looked to have been pulled out in some spots as part of his torture.

"What's going on?" Raven questioned, looking at Jason as he teased a hand of flame back and forth in front of the man's chest.

"Trying to get information out of him." Lucas walked to a multicolored lawn chair and took a seat to observe.

"Lucas says the blade that bitch attacked you with was designed to use against demons who wield shadow as you do." Graver rested his hand on Raven's back, gently nudging her to get a little closer.

"Which means they knew you were here, and we want to know how." Jason said in anger, grabbing the man's arm. The flames from his hand ate through the light Nephilim's shirt sleeve and burned his skin. He pulled his hand back as his victim lifted his head, waking with a scream.

Raven stepped closer, looking him over. Her mind raced over possibilities. Perhaps Lucent sent them to take her out. Then again, maybe, just maybe they were watching the place and sensed her mixed in with all the fire demons. "Hi." She greeted the prisoner, smiling a little. "I'd ask how you are, but it doesn't look like you're having the best day ever, here."

Jason laughed, hovering near the prisoner, keeping himself positioned that, if need be, he could get between the two. The man looked at Raven, taking deep breaths to push past the pain. With ire in his eyes, he glared at her.

"I don't think he likes me." Raven looked at Jason. "Has he said anything?"

"Not much." Jason replied.

She took another close look. "Did he pee himself?" She questioned in disgust and then sighed. "Will you talk to me?"

The prisoner looked to be on his last leg, hanging there with his knees planted to the blood and urine stained dirt floor. "No. You're wasting your time…just kill me." The man on the wall tiredly rasped out.

Raven became still, her eyes settling on the prisoner's. The whispers stirred up, fluttering about. With a careful step forward, she leaned in to listen. Jason lifted his hand ever so gently between the two, glaring at the prisoner in warning.

It came in a quick burst. Flashes of a sunny day, an old tattered plaid blanket in the grass, the taste of cherry pie and the feeling of a heated caress. Raven tensed and gasped, stepping away.

"What was that?" Graver questioned quickly.

"I don't know…I think he's blocking me?"
Raven took a deep breath, still able to taste the sweet
cool, cherry filling on her tongue and feel the
sensation of someone trailing their fingers up her leg.
"It's different from last time."

"Keep trying, Alex." Lucas encouraged.

She leaned back toward the man, listening to
the whispers. A name stood out amongst the rasps,
hisses, and half spoken phrases. It came with flashes
of events that had nothing to do with invading the
estate and a glimpse that sparked an idea. Moving
away, she turned to Graver and motioned her thumb
toward the stairs. "Can I talk to you over here?"

The two stepped aside, dropping their voices
to a whisper. "I think he's purposely focusing on
anything but what we want to know."

"Shit." Graver sighed.

"I got an idea, though. You trust me, right?"

"Yes, I do." He assured, placing a hand on her
shoulder.

"Ok…wait right here." Raven smiled and took
off.

"Where is she going?" Jason questioned with
a bored yawn, poking at the prisoner idly with a
heated finger. "Did she get anything?"

"No. She'll be right back, though." Graver
shrugged and sat in the other lawn chair.

"Think it's smart to push her like that, Lucas?" Jason questioned protectively, eyeing the vampire with suspicion.

"She is spawned from Mephisto, just as you, she's strong enough to handle anything." Lucas answered with confidence.

The prisoner laughed, shaking his head at what he was hearing. Jason prodded at him viscously with his fingers, burning holes into his arm. "What's so funny, huh?" The prisoner said nothing, gritting his teeth under the sting of flames eating dots into his skin.

"I want to make sure there are no more surprises." Lucas assured them both. "If one of you were to die, we would have to start over and wait for you to reincarnate, a cycle the devout are eager to see an end to."

"As long as it's not her, let us die." Graver looked at Lucas. "Once the portal is open, we can return, just the same."

"Hmmm." Lucas clasped his hands together. "I see you did some reading outside the realm of necromancy. Master Graver, how did you find it?"

"Enlightening." Graver replied bluntly.

"Here we go." Raven called out cheerfully as she came back into the basement moments later. "I figured." She lifted a mug with a spoon sticking out of it. "Maybe he would be more willing to just talk if he was fed. I imagine you're starving?"

The prisoner looked at the mug, wetting his lips at the hearty aroma coming from it as Raven got closer. Catching himself, he looked away. "Hey…." Raven spoke out softly, a kindness to her voice. "I made it myself, homemade stew." She stirred the mug and lifted the spoon and tipped it, allowing the thick rich gravy to pour off, chunks of beef and carrots tumbling out. He looked over warily.

"Look at it this way, you asked us to just kill you." She shrugged. "This could be poisoned." Lucas grinned ear to ear, leaning forward in his seat. Her choice of words got everyone's attention. The prisoner hesitantly opened his mouth. Raven gave no hesitation in stepping closer, scooping a decent amount from the mug and spooning it into his mouth.

His eyes closed, savoring the explosion of flavor on his parched tongue. She steadily spooned mouthful after mouthful to him, feeding him like a wounded bird. "You like it?" She questioned with a smile."

"Y-yes, thank you." He replied with hesitation and confusion at the kindness he was being shown by a demon. "It's not poisoned, it tastes fine and I'm not getting sick." He rasped out in disappointment.

"No…it's not poisoned." Raven assured him.

Jason, Lucas and Graver exchanged glances, confused themselves about what exactly was going on. "Is she really going to get him to talk by feeding him?" Jason whispered in disbelief that the man they just spent days torturing said thank you.

"It *is* made from a particular cut of meat, though." She lifted the overflowing spoon up and put it in the man's mouth and slowly pulled it out. "Leg of Liam." Raven announced, her voice falling into a darker, more sinister tone.

The man choked half way through swallowing, gagging and spitting out what he could. "You---"He gagged out. "Vile!" He heaved, coughing as tears flooded to his eyes. "Monster!"

Lucas and Graver stood from the lawn chairs to get closer so quickly that one chair fell over. "Who…is Liam?" Jason questioned.

Raven watched the man, sobbing and trying to force himself to throw up, his face stricken with horror. "What did you say?"

"Demon bitch!" He screamed out, his answer stirring the whispers once more. This time they spoke more clearly than the last. She saw flashes of the man before her, spying on the property and witnessing Raven bringing shadow to her fingers. Words were whispered into jumbled sentences that told broken tales of plans to avenge Megan's death and no knowledge of Raven's assignment to the house.

She turned to the three, a bit of a dark grin to her face. Seeing the looks of thrill and excitement on their faces only fueled her own. "He tried to block me the first time by focusing on his lover."

237

"Beautifully done." Lucas praised, looking at the man who had been driven to a mental breakdown under the impression he had just eaten his boyfriend. Raven turned, looking back at the prisoner. The results of her deceit brought on a feeling of elation and she wanted more, she wanted to cause him more pain and hear him scream. "Can I finish him?"

"Yes." Graver said with pride and excitement to his voice.

Raven moved back to the prisoner, raising the mug still in hand and hitting it against the wall right next to his face. He winced, crying out as it broke, pieces of the mug and stew falling on his shoulder. She lifted the jagged edge up to his face, hovering it over his eyes. His breath quickened to near panting as he closed his eyes. Either way, he was dead, be it by her hand or the others. This way, she got to explore her impulses and put a swifter end to his suffering.

The jagged end of the gravy coated mug was pulled down over his cheek before she pulled it back and rammed it into his chest. His eyes flew open with a startled scream. A gasped deep breath pushed past chapped lips as she twisted the mug and pushed in. The light in his eyes went out with one last gasped breath.

She let the handle of the mug go, leaving it sticking out of him. The urge she'd previously resisted was now given into. She pressed her fingers into one of the wounds on the man's chest, coating them with blood. Raven examined them for mere seconds before lifting them to her lips and darting her tongue over the blood.

"How does it taste?" Lucas inquired softly.

"Kind of sweet." She replied contently, her eyes focused on the prisoner. A swirling of shadow kicked up around her feet as she became very still.

"Alex." Graver spoke to Raven, who didn't respond, since it wasn't really her name. He stepped forward, grabbing her arm gently. "Hey!"

Raven turned, looking up at Graver. Her eyes were blackened over, prompting him look over to Jason in a 'are you seeing this?' fashion. "Alex?" Graver spoke again.

"Huh?" She replied, the shadow influence dominating her eyes receding, as did the shadows swirling around her.

"How about we go play one of those games with Austin?" Graver suggested warmly, letting her arm go.

Raven glanced at Jason and Lucas, finding the suggestion a bit random. "Which one?"

Jason headed up the stairs, taking the lead. "I forget what he said, it's the fourth in the series, though."

She followed, but this time Graver stayed behind. She wanted to know why, but reluctantly held her tongue and followed Jason to the house.

Chapter Nine

As tensions died down, free movement around the house was possible again. Getting outside was another matter. If someone wasn't available to play guardsman, she was told to stay inside. Any opportunity to leave alone was thwarted every time. Brandon always offered distractions by way of saying there was something more important to do, such as practice using her abilities, discussing Mephisto's plans, and spending time with the boys.

The basement door was another opportunity lost several times over, until one early morning. It was usually kept locked, and while she imagined several times how easy it would be to just kick it down, she knew that wouldn't exactly have been subtle. Cultists whose duty was to tend the kitchen and house chores weren't due in yet, and finding the basement door open by an inch or two didn't go unnoticed. It was a gamble, she could go down there and come face to face with whoever unlocked the door, or no one at all because someone left it open by accident.

Raven carefully pushed on the door, holding her breath and hoping that it didn't creak like most wooden doors in old houses do. Slipping through carefully, she headed down the stairs. It was nicer than she expected. She'd imagined because of the houses' age that the basement would look more like the one in the guest house. The floor had concrete poured at some point and the walls had been bricked over. There was a door on one wall that sectioned the area off at about half the length of the house.

The area that remained had an old Hoosier cabinet, more boxes of things the family had collected over the years, an old banana seat bicycle, a freezer, and a clothes washer and dryer. There was also Graver, who hadn't noticed she was there watching him.

"What are you doing?"

"Alex!" Graver jumped, startled as he dug around in a cabinet. "Are you alone?"

"Yeah." She jumped off the last step as she finished coming down the stairs, keeping a close eye on him. "What you doing?"

"Looking for something."

Raven looked around. This had been the one area of the house she hadn't been able to investigate, though, at first glance, aside from the door, there didn't appear to be much to see. "Looking for what?" She replied, noticing the shotguns on the other side of the cabinet, propped up in the corner created where the cabinet met the wall.

"Ingredients." He said shortly, getting frustrated.

"Did you check the supplies in the altar room?" She got closer; eyeing what was in the cabinets. They looked different than the supplies she'd just mentioned. She noticed a jar of claws, dead spiders, a bottle of black ash, and many odds and ends that looked like something out of a twisted fairytale.

"What I need isn't up there, nothing really potent is." He explained and pulled out a small jar.

Stepping up right next to him, she peered at the paper he had. "You're going to do a spell?"

"No, you are."

Raven blinked. "When were you going to tell me this?"

He sighed, growing more frustrated. "When I was sure I have all the things that are needed. I didn't want to ask you until I was completely sure it could even be done."

"Whoa, calm down. Take a deep breath and start over. What kind of spell, what do you need?" She glanced at the door on the back wall as the sound of metal scraping against stone came from behind it.

Graver took a deep breath, looking at Raven. "Why do you think I study necromancy?"

Raven's eyes locked with his into a stare. "You want to bring your sister back, but why not ask Father to do it?"

"I did, he said no."

"Why not?" Raven questioned, but wasn't surprised. Wanting to bring back a dead human sister wasn't the behavior of one who had left a human life and mentality behind.

"He can only raise a soul from hell."

She fell silent a moment. If his sister was in heaven, it was pretty selfish of him to want to take her away from that. Maybe he hadn't lost as much of his human self as he liked everyone to believe. "Alright. What's the plan, then?" She asked, playing along with a knot in her stomach. It wasn't right, but she had to gamble that nothing would come of it.

"I have found some rituals that are incomplete or just don't work. But I did find reference to a ritual that did, I just have to find the book that contains it."

"And for that you need…." She reached over, snatching the paper covered in his personal notes from one of the books in the library upstairs. "Hellhound ash." She glanced at the bottle of black ash in his hand. "Kraken oil?" She paused, looking right at him. "What book is this?"

Graver took the paper back from her. "The Book of the Nameless City."

"Is the city nameless? Or did they call it Nameless City because they couldn't think of anything not already taken?" Raven questioned.

Graver stared at her.
"What?"

He scoffed, putting the hellhound ash in his pocket. "You haven't read too many books in the Collins library, if you had, you would know more."

"I guess I haven't made it to the same books you have."

He shrugged, turning to head up the stairs.

"I'm going with you." Raven informed him as she followed.

"No, you stay here, Alex." He turned to her.

"You said yourself, you need me to do this and besides..." She pointed at his notes. "I know where there's a cave." She grinned, a bit pleased with herself.

"If the shop I'm going to has the other ingredients, I'll come back for you."

"And by then, everyone else could be out of bed, and I bet you, the answer to me leaving will be no." She took a few steps back as she spoke, leaning against the door on the back wall, folding her arms with a smirk.

Graver sighed. "Fine, be outside in five minutes." He made his way up the stairs and out of sight. Raven turned quickly, wasting no time checking the door. It wasn't locked.

Slowly, she opened the door. A glimpse, that's all she needed. The missing girls were all in the dimly lit room. Large animal cages held some, and a few were chained to the wall. She took a quick head count before carefully closing the door.

After retrieving her jacket, she met Graver out front. As they headed to the cars, she was already working out a plan in her head. The non-plan needed to change. She needed to ditch him and get to a phone. Doing it around there may be hard, there was no telling who was or wasn't in the cult. Maybe she could do it when they got to Kankakee.

They didn't have to go far before they reached their intended destination, an antique shop in the small historic downtown district. The streets were eerily empty, with the only other cars around belonging to other shop owners. The buildings were aged, many needing minor repairs, but all offering glimpses of days long past.

She glanced at Graver as he opened the door, allowing Raven to enter first. Stepping inside, she was greeted by a large assortment of old world antique furniture and goods and the pungent smell of old wood. The old decorative tin ceiling was open, allowing a look into the second floor. The balcony style feature wrapped the full span of the ceiling and was uncharacteristic of the building's structure. The second floor walls were lined with old wooden shelving. Aged metal rods were along the tops and bottom, with small ladders attached.

"Ok, we have a problem." Graver called after her.

"What's that?"

"I can't get in." Graver explained in confusion.

Raven turned, looking at Graver, who was trying to enter, but just didn't seem able to lift a foot off the ground to do so.

"Sounds more like your problem, not hers."
An elderly woman explained, very matter-of-factly as
she calmly walked down the aisle and past an ornate
antique player piano. The mechanics could be seen
rolling and moving through the glass display down
under the keys that were moving up and down as the
piano played through a tune.

The woman's presence got both of their
attention. She seemed to be a delicate, sweet old lady
with her faded red hair pulled into a bun and a knitted
cardigan held tight around her. "This place is
protected. If you mean to harm me, you can't even
come in. So, what is it? Hmm?" The woman looked
Graver over, completely unimpressed with his very
existence. "The hellhound ash in your pocket? Or do
you have a gun in that trench coat?" The woman
stood there, arms folded, calling him out bluntly.

Raven's brows lifted, looking at Graver
questioningly. "What?"

"I *need* those things, Alex." Graver replied
with no remorse.

"So badly you were willing to hurt a little old
lady?"

"Oh, don't worry about me, I can take care of
myself." The woman assured Raven.

Graver took a deep breath, pulling the list of
what they needed from his pocket along with a roll of
money. "I'm sorry, please, just get the items for me."

Raven took them from him, shaking her head. "Whatever."

The lady gave Graver a stern look. "You can sit on the bench outside to wait, and hope I let your friend buy anything." She turned and headed to the back, not giving him a chance to say anything else.

Raven bit her tongue, following the woman. "I really am sorry, if I had known he was thinking like that, I would have—"

"Have what? Tried to talk him out of it?" She cut Raven off. "What's your name, hon?"

"Alex." Raven replied, continuing to use the false identity to be safe as she peered into the second floor.

"Is that what you're going with?" The woman questioned. "If we're making up names for ourselves, call me Eve."

Raven looked at the woman in disbelief. How did she know?

"Maybe Olivia?" She mused, opening a door that revealed a set of stairs. "Yes, Olivia is good."

By the time Raven got to the stairs, Olivia was already out of sight. "Olivia?" Raven called out, heading up the stairs herself. The second floor housed a large selection of books, charms, artifacts and ingredients. There was a shelf lined with black iron boxes, another had a selection of animal skulls, near the front by the windows was an enchanting display of crystals that reflected colors and light onto the old wooden floor. Jars with herbs and spices lined a shelf, while a cabinet was full of jars and small aquariums that appeared to have different live specimens. Eels, a spider, rat and…was that a fairy? Raven squinted her eyes, leaning over a little to try and see.

A young woman, maybe in her late twenties, was waiting on the second floor. The vibrant beauty had stunning red hair, a fair flawless complexion, and was wearing the same clothes as the elderly woman.

"Yes?" A much younger voice rang out with a smile.

"Wait…are you?" Raven stammered.

"All part of the illusion." Olivia held her smile, amusement dancing in her eyes.

"Why? What's the point?"

Olivia shrugged. "A girl can't look young forever. People will start to ask questions. Then again, in this town, maybe not." Olivia motioned to the list in Raven's hand, wanting to see it.

"In this town?" Raven made an attempt to act dumb, offering the list.

In turn, Olivia shot Raven a look which indicated she knew better. "I have these things, but they aren't cheap." She explained, walking along the shelves.

"How much we talking?" Raven looked at the roll of money in her hand.

"We can get to that in a minute." Olivia carefully collected a few items and set them on a small table before making her way up one of the little ladders. "First, I'm curious. How did a fire and a shadow Nephilim get teamed up?"

Raven tilted her head up at Olivia, watching as she stopped at the top of the ladder. "I'm curious to know how you know what we are."

"Honey." She glanced down at Raven. "No witch worth her salt gets to my age without being able to spot certain things at her doorstep."

"How old is that?"

"Old." Olivia replied bluntly.

"Well, you don't look it." Raven paused, answering Olivia's question. "Unpleasant circumstances brought us together. We'll be parting paths soon."

"Good." Olivia commented, coming back down the ladder, adding one more thing to the table to make a total of four items. "That's everything."

"Ok, how much?" Raven offered her the roll of money.

Olivia took it and placed it on the table. "That's good for a start."

"A start? How much is this stuff?"

"Kraken ink isn't easy to get." Olivia started putting the items into a bag along with the list. "I'll take the money and a verbal I.O.U."

"What do you want?" Raven narrowed her eyes, reaching for the bag.

"I recognize some of these ingredients and have an idea of where you might be trying to go."

Before allowing Raven to take the bag, she placed an empty corked vial on the table. "I want some of the water, if you succeed."

"I'll try my best." Raven took the vial and the bag as Olivia released it. She carefully tucked the vial away inside her jacket before taking another look around.

"I'm sure you will, otherwise I'll need to ask for something else." Olivia smiled and headed to the stairs.

Raven turned as she heard the creak of the stairs as Olivia started down them, and followed her. As the two re-entered the antique portion of the shop, spells and trickery came back into play, presenting Olivia as the older version of herself.

Raven lifted the bag a little. "Thanks for selling these to me, even though my friend's intentions toward you were questionable."

"Desperate men do desperate things, remember that. I hope he gets the answers he's looking for." Olivia responded, sliding down into an old English wing chair behind the counter. "You're welcome back anytime, but needless to say---"

"Don't bring him back?" Raven finished Olivia's sentence.

"It would be preferred, yes."

"Alright." Raven smiled, turning and heading out of the shop. She took another quick look around on her way out. She admired the furniture dating back to the 1800's that featured intricate wooden carvings and overall looked fit for royalty. She saw brass statues on marble bases, chandeliers that looked like waterfalls of diamonds, shelves of fine china, and display areas overflowing with all sorts of antique treasures. Just before leaving, she did a double take at the piano. It was still playing, the keys were moving up and down, but the mechanics that made it run weren't moving anymore.

Graver was sitting on the bench outside, taking the last drag off a cigarette while he waited. As Raven stepped out of the shop, he stood, turning to meet her. "Did you get what we need?"

Raven held the bag up, showing him. "I got it all."

He sighed in relief, reaching his hand out for the bag. "Thank you so much, Alex."
Raven pulled the bag from his reach, smiling wide. "Not so fast! I want something in exchange."

"Anything." Graver offered, keeping his hand out, eagerly waiting for the bag.

"We have to stop somewhere and get coffee." She held the bag out to him with a smirk about her demand.

"We can do that." He snatched the bag, looking inside. The look on his face was that of a child on Christmas morning looking inside the box that had tempted him from under the tree for weeks.

She stepped past him, heading to the car. Her eyes darted over the buildings across the way just before she opened the car door, getting inside. She watched as Graver made his way to the car. "There is a coffee shop just over there." He nodded toward the main intersection.

"Alright, and then we head to the cave." Raven looked toward the intersection, then over at the buildings he indicated. She looked back at the shop they'd just left as the car pulled away. It was a short trip through the intersection and, with another quick turn, they were at the coffee shop.

"You're staying in the car." He informed her as he pulled the keys from the ignition.

"Oh…" She was a bit confused by his logic. She could go with him into the magic store run by a witch that could probably destroy them both with a flick of her wrist, but had to stay put for the coffee shop? "Ok, I'll take a large mocha latte."

"Be right back." Graver headed out of sight into the small coffee shop.

Her hand grasped the door handle as she looked over at the bank. She could easily ditch him here and now. It completely slipped her mind at the shop to ask if there was a phone that she could use. They might let her use the phone at the bank, and if Graver even found her there, he wouldn't make a scene in a place full of cameras, would he? Raven let the handle go, looking at the chairs outside the coffee shop.

The book had her overly curious, something so powerful and important that you needed to cast a spell to get to it, and the location itself had magical properties. She placed her hand over her jacket where the corked vial was. Learning as much as possible was part of the assignment, so maybe it would be best to ditch him once they were done. Maybe even wiggle away with the book in question, if possible.

She slumped against the door, watching for him to come back out. The coffee shop was attached to the local theater, a pairing that reminded her of her regular spot back home, which was located across from a theater. Just as her mind started to creep over a thought, wondering if she would live through this and get back to a normal routine like the one she used to have, Graver came out of the building.

Raven jumped out of the car, smiling at him. "Hey….can I drive? Since I know where the cave is, it would be easier if I did."

Graver stopped, eyeing her in thought with her coffee in his hand. "Sure, why the hell not." He pulled the keys from his trench coat and tossed them to her.

She caught them, running around the back of the car and hopping into the driver seat. Graver couldn't help but smile and chuckle at her excitement over being able to do something as simple as drive.

Getting into the car, he set her coffee down into the cup holder.

Raven glanced at him, starting the car up and pulling out of the parking lot. Getting back on the main road, she headed to the main intersection, flew through the yellow light and took off, heading out of town.

"Whoa, whoa, whoa!" Graver gripped the door as they went through the intersection. "You do know how to drive, right?"

"Yeah, of course I do."

"Well, slow down, our man on the force is on night shift and I don't want a ticket." He explained, watching the road.

"Sorry...guess I'm a bit of a speed demon." She flashed a grin, grabbing the coffee and taking a sip as she drove.

Graver turned on the radio, turning it over to a heavy metal station. They didn't speak as they drove through the countryside. The lack of conversation gave her time to think over and devise how she was going to eventually ditch him.

Raven tensed as she came upon a sign warning the road curved into an s curve just ahead. This was the spot. She slowed down a little, glancing at Graver. He was too wrapped up in the music playing on the radio and going over his notes to notice the change in speed. As she came around the curve, she glanced over a couple of times. There were two crosses on the side of the road. One of them had a wreath of dingy, weathered fake flowers around it. Not far from them was the tree she had slammed into, the large gash ripped into its side from her car's impact a haunting reminder of the accident that killed the person she used to be.

Eyes on the road, she reached over and grabbed her coffee, taking a few good swallows. There was a strange sense of closure in seeing the site of the accident. There had been talk of lawyers, lawsuits and settlements early on. Papers were signed against the trucking company, but the prospect of those things hadn't left her feeling like there was a resolution or an end.

Before she knew it, she was back in the more familiar territory of the Kankakee area. Raven drove back into a residential district. As she started to navigate through the labyrinth of streets that made up the subdivision, Graver started asking questions.

"So, you're from around here?"

Raven glanced at him as they parked in the small parking lot. The only things in sight were trees and a gazebo. "Maybe."

"It would be kind of funny." He smiled as they got out of the car.

"How so?"

"We traveled around so much looking for our fourth sibling and, all the while, you were just miles away from the house." He explained.

Raven glanced over her shoulder as they walked through a large, open area of grass. "I don't see how that's funny. And now that you mention it," she paused as they approached a bike path that led into the forest," Why go around to other states looking? What happened? Why not stay around here?"

"Father said to go, so Brandon and Lucas went." Graver looked over his shoulder to make sure they weren't being followed as they started down the path into the forest. "From what I was told, they were in several different locations until they found me. I lost count of how many towns I saw until we had Austin, Jason and Meg— "Graver fell silent, catching himself.

"I thought there were only four of us?"

"There is." He growled. "A girl named Megan." He explained, pushing branches out of his way and keeping an eye on Raven as they walked, both to keep from getting lost and to protect her if necessary. "She had a charm, or trinket, if you prefer, that was making it appear as though she was half demon."

"But she wasn't?" Raven asked, even though she already knew the answer.

"Freaking light Nephilim. She had a real good story, had us all fooled and probably would have gotten away with it if she had only kept her pants on."

"Wh-what?" Raven laughed a little at his statement, stopping to turn and face him.

Graver stopped walking, welcoming the small break with a huff. "The day we got to the house, she and Jason started fooling around, and the thing she was using broke."

"Fooling around?"

"They were fucking." He stated boldly.

Raven stared at him, genuinely surprised. Jason thought Megan was his sister and still went for it. Not to mention that little rule where light Nephilim aren't allowed to have sex. "So! We're about half way there." She blurted out quickly, wanting to change the subject.

Graver laughed as they started back down the path.

"What's the rush on getting this book, anyway?"

"Father says we are finishing his entrance into this word." He replied simply.

"When?"

"Tomorrow." He answered. "Let's focus on this for now though, ok?"

"Yeah, sure!" She assured him, all the while thinking something more along the lines of how screwed she was. Raven turned around, taking off again, leading Graver to a walking bridge that went over a shallow creek that led from the caves to the river. She stopped just short of the bridge, looking over the rail to the river's bank before going off the bike path to climb town into the ravine-like area of the entrance to the caves and cliffs. As they got closer, making their way past fallen logs and an old rusted out oil barrel, they could hear water flowing over rock.

She looked along the tops of the cliffs and treetops. It was partly cloudy, so the shade from the trees made it darker the farther back they went. Tactically, this was a bad place to be. As they walked through, someone could easily jump down from above to pin them down or corner them. The areas between the cliffs were pretty open, and led to two walls of rocky cliffs with a gap running between them, just wide enough that climbing through was possible. Along that spot was a cave opening barely wide enough that someone could enter, if they didn't mind dark, narrow spaces.

A bit of a waterfall flowed down through the mossy green splotched stone, streaming through to the river. Tiny raccoon paw prints trailed through patches of mud and a couple empty beer cans were next to a circle of stones blackened by a campfire. The sound of knocking on wood brought Graver to look around swiftly.

"It's a woodpecker. Nature, it makes noise." Raven laughed.

"Yeah, yeah, I know." Graver grunted, walking to the cave opening.

"There are more through here." Raven explained, pointing to the narrow path between the cliffs. "If you need a bigger cave than these, that is."

Graver looked at where she was pointing. "This one will work." He made his way to the cave opening. "Get over here, let's get this done before someone comes wandering through."

"Good idea." She hopped over the stream, making her way to him.

Graver handed her the chalk, and he held the instructions, previously copied from the book, up for reference. She started by using kraken ink and black chalk to mark archaic runes around the arch of the cave's opening. Next, she rubbed something known as traveler's root on the stone between each mark. The curviness of the root made it hard to handle as it wore down, but she managed. She poured a bottle of nymph tears in a line along the ground between the arches, connecting them, resulting in the runes illuminating in celestial hues.

"What about the hellhound ash?"

"Keep that for now, we didn't get it for this. It's for something else I want to try with you later." Graver explained as Raven put the small ash filled bottle in one of her pockets.

"We could have asked Atreus for some, instead of spending the money on it."

"No, we couldn't." He responded while checking over the notes one last time, making sure everything was done correctly.

"Why not?"

"Hellhound ash can only be collected when a hellhound dies. The ash can be used to do many things, including resurrecting the hound it came from." He explained thoughtfully.

"That's good to know. If something happened to Atreus, if the option to bring him back is there, I think I'd do it."

"I'm sure he would appreciate knowing that." Graver pocketed his notes suddenly. "I think we're ready." He grinned eagerly in anticipation. "Go on." Not only would he get what he needed to resurrect his sister if they could pull this off, but it would also mean Raven was strong enough to finish opening Mephisto's portal. "Open your first portal."

Raven lifted her palms and pressed them to certain runes drawn on the doorway. She concentrated, focusing on wanting the portal to open. The Nymph's tears on the ground rose up, creating a wall of thin, watery fluid. The fluid started to evaporate as her palms pulled away, and the doorway filled with a swirling vortex of black and deep blue hues that emitted an ungodly echo of sounds. It was constant despite fading back and forth in volume.

"Yes!" Graver exclaimed excitedly. "Alex, you did it! How do you feel? Are you ok?"

"A little light headed." She replied. "A little tingly? But ok."

"Are you good to go?"

"Yeah. It's already passing." She looked over at him and couldn't help but smile at how excited he was.

"After you, m'lady." Graver offered, readying himself to follow.

Raven looked at the portal. Behind the strange noises making their way through, mumbles of a conversation could be heard. She closed her eyes tight and stepped through. The sensation was unpleasant. It felt as if someone latched onto the front half of her body and was trying to pull her skin off, while her back half was trying to stay outside the cave.

With a half scream, she stumbled to the other side. The area was faintly illuminated by a light in the distance coming from a set of open doors. The ground under her feet was solid. The air was cool and musty. The light drip of water could be heard nearby. Even closer was a gentle noise, the slick rubbing of movement over stone.

Graver came through then, shaking off the pain while looking at Raven with a brotherly pride. Feeling a little guilty she turned away, looking around. It was understood that Graver was, in some ways, a victim of circumstance. He had no choice to be born as he was, just like her. There was no way for him to know Mephisto wasn't really his Father. And if the demon really was, by some chance, there was no love there.

"You ok?" Graver asked with concern.

"Yeah." She nodded toward the source of light. "I thought I heard something moving." She paused in thought. "Wait, what if someone comes along and finds the portal?"

"It won't last that much longer. You can't use the entrance as an exit, anyway."

"Good to know." Raven commented, taking a step forward. She froze as something brushed against her leg. "Did you feel that?"

Graver looked carefully over the ground and Raven's legs. "Just keep going, don't look." He encouraged calmly, pushing on her shoulder.

As they moved forward, something brushed against the back of his legs, then slid up diagonally across her shoulder. The closer they got, the more the light made it easier for things to come into focus through the darkness. Two large wooden doors with ironwork inlays towered upward and were open just enough for them to enter. On the other side was a small library.

The area was surprisingly dry for a place accessed through a damp cave. A couple dozen or so wooden shelves lined rough stone walls and made up a few short aisles. Each shelf was full of books. There were books stacked on top of the shelves, on the floor, on the tables and on the large desk in the back.

On the one side of the library there were two tables. One was occupied by a man in a heavy black hooded robe reading a book by the light of a black iron candelabra. He was either too enthralled in his studies, or didn't care as they walked past, as he didn't react to their presence.

Raven stopped, looking at the back of her leg. "Oh, man." She whispered. "What the heck was that?" She started to reach for the thick looking gunk smeared over her jeans, but stopped herself. Maybe touching it wasn't the best idea. Wrinkling her nose, she joined Graver at the back of the library.

Two more doors, both decorated similarly to the ones at the entrance, and an ornately carved wooden desk were along the back cavern wall. Behind the desk was an old reading chair occupied by an elderly black woman. Her hair was a mixture of grey and ebon tones. Crow's feet framed hazed eyes and her fingernails were stained yellow.

"Mmmm?" She mumbled out, looking up from her book at the new arrivals.

Raven looked back and forth between Graver and the woman in the chair. "You're the Keeper of the library?" He questioned, looking the woman over, a bit confused.

"Until I'm released from service, yes." The Keeper explained, setting her book down before grasping the arms of the chair and pushing herself up with a slight groan. "How can I help you?"

"I'm looking for the book of The Nameless City." He answered eagerly.

The Keeper seemed a bit annoyed at Graver's request. She took a hobbled step closer, looking him right in the eyes, studying them before she spoke again. "I recommend looking for the answers you seek within one of the other tomes in the collection, first."

"I've already done research. What I need is in that book, and that book alone. I have proven my worth by getting here, and I wish to see it." He informed the keeper confidently.

Raven tilted her head a little, eyeing Graver as his demands were made.

The Keeper nodded. "Of course. My apologies." She picked up a worn leather journal that was already open to the most current page and moved it over, placing it in front of them. "Did you bring the feather?"

Graver responded by handing the requested item over while looking at Raven. The Keeper attached a quill tip to the angel's feather and reached over, jabbing him in the hand with it.

"Ow!" His eyes flared with a molten hue as his focus shot back to the Keeper.

"Sign the book, please." The calm request was made with not even a blink in reaction to the dark Nephilim's anger. "By doing so, you understand and accept that you are allowed to approach the book.

One hand stays on the podium, one hand can turn pages. When you have gotten your answer, the book will close itself. At that point, you walk away. Understood?" The Keeper fired off the information while holding the feathered writing implement out to Graver using the tips of her webbed fingers.

Calming himself, he took the feather and signed the book without answering the old woman. "Stay here, Alex, and don't get too comfortable. As soon as I'm done, we're leaving."

Raven peered at the signatures in the book. "Fine by me."

Going by the dates, a hundred or so people had signed in the last fifty years. She couldn't read all the signatures as some were written in other languages, but she recognized the names of a well known rock musician and a politician or two.

The Keeper made her way to the door on the right, opening it up to reveal a single room. The floor was covered in a thin layer of dirt and dust, through which it could be seen that the floor was sectioned into large square blocks of stone, each one roughly three feet in width all around. The room carved into cave rock was lit by torches lining the walls. Graver was on cloud nine as he proceeded to the podium and looked at the closed book.

"Many people come through here." The Keeper spoke, getting Raven's attention just as she was about to turn the page to see some of the previous entries in the log book. "Some settle on reading from the library," she explained, coming from behind the desk at a slow, shuffling pace, the worn ends of faded, layered, brown ceremonial robes dragging on the floor. "Few make it past the exit after reading from the book." She stopped in front of Raven. "And through all the years, I can count on one hand how many that ever entered here were able to say they weren't human."

"Is it written on my forehead or something?" Raven's shoulders sagged, glancing at Graver who had just started reading. "I hope it's not a problem."

The Keeper followed Raven's glance. "Not at all." With a half snort she looked back at Raven. "He claims to have done the research, but you got him here. Tell me, child, what do you know of the book?"

"It has answers." Raven replied softly, the words 'and he was willing to kill for them' lingered on the tip of her tongue.

"All the answers to anything you could ever want to know." The Keeper confirmed.

Raven glanced back at Graver and the book, skepticism painted over her features. "I've seen and been told a lot lately, and still find that hard to believe."

"A lot of things are hard to believe. Take reality TV, for example. I can't believe the level of fame and fortune humans obtain from it. Yet, there it is."

"You have TV here?" Raven looked around for a television in surprise.

"And the internet." The Keeper replied.

"Heh…" Raven glanced at Graver again. "How does a book like this work? It doesn't sound possible. Wouldn't it only contain knowledge up until the time it was written?"

"The book was written on leather parchment made from a changeling's skin." The Keeper explained, taking a look at Graver herself as he read. "The ink was formulated from the blood of a shadow demon." She shuffled over to one of the tables, leaning on it for support. "It's bound in sacrificial skin, and the initial passages were written within the city for which it was named." She looked at Raven. "It was written long ago, and the one who created it was so consumed with a thirst for knowledge that, in his death, his very essence became one with the power the book is infused with."

"The book is alive? And it was written with shadow demon blood? Are you sure?"

The elderly woman laughed. "I'm sure. It's a requirement to know about these things in order to become keeper of this place." She shifted her weight.

"But how does it work? Is it alive?" Raven repeated since the Keeper hadn't answered her. "How can it know everything?"

The sound of iron grinding and slamming against stone echoed through the library. Raven and the Keeper turned toward the door that led to where Graver was. He was no longer reading the book, but standing in the middle of the room.

"What the fuck?" Graver questioned in surprise. A set of bars had lowered to cover the doorway.

Raven glared at the Keeper, who didn't look a bit surprised. "What's going on?"

The area shook as the large, square stones that made up the floor lowered, allowing water to fill in their wake. This left nothing but a path of stone blocks stretching from the bars to the area where the podium stood.

"He took the book." The Keeper pointed out, shuffling toward the bars.

"What?" Raven ran over just as Graver hesitantly pulled the book from inside his trench coat. He had it kind of tucked under his arm, hoping no one would notice.

"The spell wasn't here, Alex."

"What do you mean?" Raven pointed at the Keeper. "She says everything is in there."

The water started to bubble and churn as large black tentacles slithered out of the water and over the path. They came up in front of Graver, and behind him, and slithered around the stone podium.

"Is that a---" Raven took a step back as one of the tentacles slithered up right next to the bars. "Are we in the ocean??" She questioned with a half glance at the Keeper.

"Bermuda Triangle, to be exact." The elderly woman replied evenly, showing no surprise at the events unfolding.

Graver pulled the book behind him, raising his free hand as it engulfed in flames. "Alex…" He called out with expectation. His hand motioned forward, flame spewing out, burning through the dark flesh of the creature reaching up from the depths. The ground shook as something bellowed out from beneath them. The sound had a deep bass to it that overpowered all other sound, including Graver calling out for help, and the sound of the tentacle splashing through the water as it burned. Raven grabbed her head, turning her back to the bar. The vibration the unseen creature was causing radiated through her body.

"Graver, put it back!" Raven called out, turning back to face the room and grasping at the bars, trying to lift them.

He ignored her, continuing to try and fight his way out. He dropped the book as a tentacle tripped him, another slapping down against the stone to block his access to the book.

"Graver!" Raven called out again.

Something started to make its way out of the water. Raven could see glimpses just behind one of the tentacles. A hand grabbed at Graver. It looked smooth, white, maybe even a very pale blue. Its webbed fingers curled, pulling itself up out of the water and on top of Graver, spitting thick black gunk at him.

"Alex, help!"

"I wouldn't if I were you, shadowling." The Keeper warned.

Raven gripped at the bars more tightly, trying to pull shadow energy to her hands despite the warning, but nothing came. More of the creatures crawled out of the water. Some of them were completely naked, others had decaying clothes still clinging to their disfigured forms. Their eyes were heavily milked over and they had gill slits behind their ears. Parts of their bodies looked deeply scarred, as if they had been chewed on at some point of their existence.

Graver started to scream as they dug their nails into his face and neck, drawing blood. What little skin was exposed, they were after.

"Stop them." Raven looked at the Keeper.

"I have no control over them." The Keeper said unsympathetically. "His fate is sealed, he will join them in the depths, along with those who came before him and tried to remove the book from its resting place."

Graver was pulled into the dark waters, where his complete submersion drowned out his screams. An onslaught of bubbly water was left in his wake, then quickly calmed. One of the creatures picked up the book and placed it back where it belonged before crawling back into the water. The gate started to move up, Raven's hands barely letting go as it did.

Numbness began to set in as she stood there. When it came down to it, Graver was probably going to end up dead anyway, either as the result of trying to raise his sister, or when it came time for her to put an end to everything going on at the Collins estate. Trying to reason it away didn't help. A sadness crept through her. He just wanted to bring his sister back, and was willing to go to such great lengths to do so. He had trusted her, and she had done nothing. A slow realization set in as she stared at where he had been pulled into the water. She had begun to grow attached to him, and to all three false brothers, in some small way or another.

"Your turn." The Keeper offered as the book opened itself up.

"Oh, no thank you!" Raven spoke up quickly, emotions and thoughts being shoved aside. "I'm fine!"

The Keeper remained at the doorway watching as Raven looked toward the book. The slightest rasp of a whisper floated by. Her eyes darted over the water and around the tentacles, trying to see where they were connected. The water was too dark, hiding away any detail that hadn't reached above the watery depths. "Maybe." Raven whispered, taking a step into the room. Whispers rose around her in a brief, pleasant melody of windswept mutterings.

"Just a little peek, it would be a shame to come all this way and leave without at least looking." She wasn't fine, on so many levels. How was she going to explain this to Mephisto, that Graver was gone? With another step, the tentacle blocking her way uncurled and rose up, allowing her to pass. A better question came to mind. How was she going to push Mephisto back through the portal and close it?

The ground gently rumbled. As she walked, the rest of the tentacles rose, clearing the way. As she passed each one, they draped back over the stone path. The pages turned themselves, flipping to a different page, as if the book knew what she was thinking about as she approached. She stepped up to the podium to take a look.

The pages that were presented spoke briefly of shadow demons, their limitations, abilities and strengths. Some of the text was knowledge she already had, details like how the common shadow demon has no body and often appears as a shadow of a figure. How possession is possible to acquire a tangible existence, but the power the demon wields slowly destroys the host from the inside out over time, rendering it useless.

Sentient dark matter was one way to describe them. Because of their energy based existence, traveling between realms and dimensions was as easy as water passing through cloth. They could adapt to understand any language. Most shadow demons had some form of telepathy or psychic ability, able to look into the minds of mortals.

The book had some new details she had not seen in previous books, and her guardians had failed to mention. Maybe they didn't know? She read the names of shadow demons that had achieved solidarity and presented themselves throughout history as humans, animals and mythical creatures. Black cats and dogs were amongst the favored forms, as were ravens for those able to ascend past their limitations. Shadow demons able to ascend in such ways are also the ones able to manifest, or generate dark energy, just like she can. Another intriguing detail that stood out amongst the scraps of information was that shadow demons predated Lucifer's fall.

"I don't understand how this is going to help me stop Mephisto." Raven whispered, reaching to turn the page. Before her fingers could make contact, it turned itself.

The new pages contained a passage about Mephisto. Originally an angel, he followed Lucifer as he was cast from heaven. The fires of hell reforged the celestial being into one of the arch demons of flame. The fires he commands are derived from the fires of hell. They live within his very being, permeating from his skin. Simply touching someone can incinerate them. Other fire demons were the only ones immune.

"I can't do it." She spoke out loud, closing the book in frustration. "I'm… going to die." Words of defeat trailed off as she looked away. Mephisto would have to be tricked into willingly going back through the portal, or physically forced through, and at that minute she would be consumed by flames. Being half shadow demon would offer no protection from this.

The book flew open again, pages flipping rapidly. "N-no. Bad book, bad." She took a quick step back as she looked behind her at the pool of water that was still exposed along the floor "I didn't touch it again."

Faint echoes of voices danced around the ancient leather bound book. It wasn't the usual whispers that had been recently stirring around her. This was different, and clearly coming from the book. A tentacle slid out of the water, wrapping around the stone podium and her leg. "Shit!" She looked down at it, trying to pull shadow energy to her fingertips but, once again, nothing happened. Another tentacle slithered up and wrapped around her waist and up her backside. The book's rapid flipping made it seem like the pages in it were never ending. More tentacles were slithering closer.

"Enough!" She yelled out, slamming her hands down on the book. The collision of her palms against aged leathery parchment caused a snap of power to ripple through the air as the pages halted.

The book's power could be felt pulsing against her skin. Surprised it had worked, she leaned in, taking a look at the contents of the pages. Instead of words, these pages contained inked strokes artfully depicting a dark scene of demons gathered around a throne. Seated within was a man appearing to be half human, half goat. She kept her hands on the book, but drew them slowly to each side. As more of the picture became visible, a stinging plagued the back of her eyes. Her attempt to lift a hand to them failed. Both hands were being held on the book by an unseen force. The stinging turned to pain that was so overwhelming, it became hard to keep her eyes open.

She closed them tight, keeping them closed until the pain lifted. Hesitantly, she opened her eyes, and gasped in surprise.

Chapter Ten

As far as the eye could see, there were uncountable miles of pits and flames. A mountainous, barren valley, occupied by demons. The ground was made of cracked, burnt stone that had a number of bottomless pits scattered over its surface. There was no sky, but a perpetual sea of darkness. The echoes of screams and crying could be heard on and off as one particular demon made his way through the area.

The demon resembled a man, with horns adorning his head. His skin was stained red, and riddled with burn scars, leaving him bald and disfigured. Wings on the demon's back, tattered and torn, resembled those of a bat. Foul liquids oozed and trickled from a wound on his arm. A sword in his hand was soaked in blood, and battle beaten armor adorned his sturdy frame.

Stopping before his master, he dropped the sword. Falling to one knee, head lowering, he fearfully announced, "My Lord, I bring bad news." An inhuman sound bellowed out through the area in response.

Lucifer sat on a throne carved into the side of a large, jagged formation of rock. His lower body was that of a goat, covered in thick black fur with cloven hooves for feet. His upper body was that of a human, but his head was that of a goat, with large black horns sticking up and curving to the left and right. From behind those horns, another shorter set extended down from behind his ears.

There were short horns extending from his shoulders and elbows. On his back was a set of black feathery wings, which also featured a horn at the joint where they would bend to fold. His arrow tipped serpentine tail started off covered in fur and ended in the same leathery, light grey skin as the rest of him.

"The Nephilim you sent to Bethlehem failed." The demon spoke again, keeping his head down as he did so.

Stillness, accompanied by deafening silence settled over the valley. All looked on in anticipation as Lucifer bellowed out an angry roar. Clawed hands reached up, pulling at the elongated muzzle of his goat-like features, pulling them away from his face and revealing that he was wearing a mask. Fashioned to give the illusion of a true visage, the mask seamlessly covered the human features of the angel once known as 'the most beautiful angel in heaven'. The black horns remained and were not part of the mask. His eyes beneath were a deep crimson.

Setting the mask aside, Lucifer held up a hand, spreading his fingers out, looking over the long thick black claws extending from each fingertip. Those claws were plunged down into his leg just above the knee. They were dragged up into the thigh. Flesh, fur and blood were allowed to gather under the nails before they were snapped off as his fingers straightened, then pushed forward.

The jagged ends remained, sticking up out of bloody, torn flesh. He then turned his hand palm down, hovering over the five cracked bony shards sticking out of his leg. They cracked and snapped. Twisting and fusing with flesh and fur, the writhing lumps folded onto themselves in rapid growth as they fell to the ground where they stretched up, growing until molded into the shape of humans. Each human was fit and beautiful enough to tempt the hearts of mortals, yet each one held features that told of their origins. Deep crimson eyes, smaller versions of Lucifer's horns, thick black hair, deadly nails and fangs.

"Behold!" Lucifer announced. "While God has one son, born of the humans, I have five. Spawned from my very flesh and blood, true extensions of myself. Representations of my power and the might of hell!" The demons watching burst into cheers and howls of excitement. The five new spawns looked around, stretching and getting a feel for their new existence. One of them looked right at the demon who came to deliver the bad news. Through it all, a name was whispered, barely audible through the commotion.

"Damien."

Raven's eyes flew open as the whisper came and went. She had been a spectator witnessing another's perspective of events long past. The ceiling of the cavern library greeted her return to reality.

"Careful, young shadow." The Keeper spoke up, helping Raven to sit up.

"What happened? I was looking at the book, then…" A quick look around revealed one of the wooden tables was now doubling as her resting place. The man that had been reading had left at some point during all the excitement. "I think I had a vision."

"Your first one?" The Keeper asked with curiosity.

"I've seen glimpses, vague and confusing. This was my first full length feature in high definition with surround sound." Raven answered softly, looking at the closed door that led to where the book was kept. "Did it trigger it? The book I mean, did it?"

"I believe so."

"I have to go." Raven slid off the table. "Can……I come back?" Curiosity and a thirst for knowledge was strong in her eyes as she asked the question.

"You are always welcome, young shadow, to seek knowledge here that is denied to the rest of the world."

Raven smiled a little. "Thank you."

"Follow me." The Keeper spoke, shuffling to an empty corner.

Raven followed her carefully, watching as the Keeper's webbed fingers as she lifted them to the wall and hovered over a faded pattern in the stone. The markings radiated the faintest glow, bringing a stirring of energy up around the two as a portal swirled into existence in front of the wall.

"This portal." The Keeper explained, side stepping out of the way. "Will take you to wherever you are thinking of when you step through. Mind your thoughts."

She looked away from the portal, and at the Keeper. "This is what you meant, when you said some who have come to look at the book don't make it past the exit." She looked back to the portal. "The addled mind of one driven to madness will lead them nowhere."

"That is correct, young shadow." The Keeper's voice rasped out in reply.

Raven approached the portal, focusing on a location, Aiden's house. She stepped through the portal, keeping the image of the run-down two story house in her mind. She could almost hear the creak of the front porch's aged wooden boards and smell the thin fragrance of ivy and roses that lingered through the house.

Stepping through, it felt like stepping through a wave of water. The sensation didn't end, throwing her senses off balance. She was through the portal, but instead of stepping through to arrive on the front porch as she desired, Raven stepped through and was now completely submersed in water. A portal that would lead to the desired location of anyone who stepped through it. Sure. Disclaimer: Maybe close to it, anyway.

Breaking through the water's surface, she found that the river near the familiar park was as close to the house as the portal could get her. Raven gasped for air as she felt herself being pulled downstream. It was not an easy swim to safety. The river's current was strong, almost pulling her under twice before she managed to reach the riverbank. Crawling out of the water and collapsing on the grass, she remained still, catching her breath. Laying there a while felt like a good idea.

The calm of the area allowed for some much needed thinking as she stared past the branches of a single tree at the clear blue sky. Aiden and Owen needed to be filled in on what was going on. But then what? Go back to that house and do what, exactly? Different scenarios played out in her mind. She considered a myriad of possibilities so clearly that the line between reality and her mind's eye blurred. All of them involved getting the kidnapped girls out, but each end result came up short of being ideal.

A bit of tension came over her. She needed solutions. Her wandering thoughts finally arrived at a possibility. A whisper, the taste of blood, and the smell of something burning brought her hastily to her feet. Turning around, she spotted Atreus waiting by a tree. She held her breath as joggers made their way past the hellhound. They didn't spare him a glance, reminding her that humans could only see Atreus if he wanted them to.

The afternoon sun felt good and helped to dry her wet clothes and damp skin as she began her walk to Aiden's house. Kids were playing in the park's splash pad and filled the area with laughter. They were jumping around and running through the different multi-colored arches, spraying water all over. A woman chatting on a cell phone while watching the kids triggered the thought to borrow the phone to call for a ride. Instead, Raven kept walking, heading up the road. Too much time had been spent in the Collins' house, and being able to just walk around was enjoyable.

She made her way up to the main street that ran through the heart of Kankakee, crossing over just before the bridge that went over the river she had just crawled out of. She barely acknowledged an ambulance rushing to the multiple buildings that made up a hospital on the other side of the bridge.

Heading into the residential area, they made their way to the street Aiden's house was on. A small child's scream burst out abruptly. Raven looked at the house she had learned to ignore so as to not look at the ghost which was always sitting on the porch. Atreus had looked, but kept going, following Raven as she cut up the alley. As she headed into the backyard, she didn't even make it to the back door. It flew open, both guardians bursting out in a panic.

"Don't move!" Owen yelled out as Aiden pulled a gun, which brought a low growl from Atreus.

"Whoa! What the hell guys?" Raven questioned, lifting her hands a little.

"Exactly, what the hell? We haven't heard so much a peep from you, and you show up with a hellhound??" Aiden questioned, with anger and concern in his voice.

"They took my phone and the car keys." Raven explained, glancing at Atreus. "I was being watched and didn't want to risk blowing my cover by pushing too hard to get a phone. They wanted me to feel content with being there, so I played along. And the puppy is with me. Put the gun down."

"If they took your keys, how did you get here?" Aiden questioned suspiciously.

"Puppy?!" Owen glared at the hellhound. "Puppies are tiny, cute and fluffy bundles of harmless joy. They aren't…this…." He pointed. "….and capable of ripping someone to shreds and devouring their soul!"

"It's a long story… a lot happened."

Aiden took a deep breath putting the gun away. "Get inside."

Raven and Atreus headed to the steps, prompting Aiden to point at the hellhound sharply. "Not you."

"Atreus." Raven turned toward the demonic hound. "It's ok, keep an eye on things out here for me."

The three headed into the house, leaving Atreus on the back steps. Passing through the kitchen, Raven made a pit stop at the fridge, grabbing a bottle of soda before finding her way into the basement. They settled in, occupying the couch and chairs arranged in a corner for studying. Many times the furniture had also served them well as a place to collapse after a rigorous sparring match.

"We should start with the cult." Raven started the conversation, popping the bottle open and taking a nice long drink. She let out half a sigh, the icy cold of the carbonated beverage cooling her off after her walk. "They have a couple hundred followers. I found the girls. It turns out their parents are members of the cult."

"Seriously?" Owen questioned as he leaned forward with interest.

"Smart move, report them missing in case anyone asks why they aren't around or in school all of a sudden." Aiden observed out loud. "How about leadership?"

"Two humans, three Nephilim, and a vampire."

"Walk into a bar?" Owen quipped.

Aiden glared at Owen. "A vampire? That wasn't in the report."

"I know. That isn't the only surprise, either. Mephisto is already here, kind of."

"How?" Aiden asked quickly, appearing to grow more concerned by the minute.

"I don't know. I just know he and the portal are out of phase, and according to Brandon, I'm the only one who can fix it."

"It is in your skill set." Owen pointed out.

"Maybe the portal part, but you're talking about one of the arch demons of hell here. I have to finish the portal to close it and the second I do Mephisto comes with it. I don't have what it takes to force him through the portal and back to hell. I need help."

"I'll call Zaida." Owen pulled a cell phone out, slipping away.

"How are you, otherwise?" Aiden questioned, looking her over.

"Tired." She yawned her answer as her gaze drifted to the collection of books at hand. "I learned some things. I actually have some questions."

"Alright. What's on your mind?" He moved over and sat next to her.

"Were there demons before the first Angels that fell?"

"Wow….straight to the big stuff. What have you been reading?" She caught him off guard with this one, which was a first in her experience.

"That's what I'm trying to figure out." She was treading carefully through territory she assumed was either forbidden or forgotten, not wanting to say too much.

Aiden took a deep breath. "It's complicated."

"Un-complicate it." A darkness crept into her voice as she spoke, eyeing him.

"A lot of things have existed over time that there is no documentation for because all record of it was lost in the flood. Except for what is in the Vatican, which is in a limited access vault." He hesitated. "So it's possible that there were demons or creatures perceived as such before Lucifer's fall."

She nodded a little in response before a moment of thoughtful silence. The answer he provided felt like an attempt to dodge the subject. She had a thirst to know, to understand more on the matter. Why and how does the book of The Nameless City state things about shadow demons that are nowhere to be found in any of the writings he had provided for study? Did he do it on purpose? Does he even know?

"We can talk about it later if you want." Aiden broke the silence. "For now, let's focus on the ritual. When is it taking place?"

"Tomorrow night." Raven followed his lead.

"That soon? Ok, let's see if Owen got ahold of Zaida."

"I'm going to take off for a bit." Raven spoke in an informative tone as she rose from the couch, giving off the impression that it wasn't up for discussion.

"Alright, be back in a bit to go over some details?"

She gave a somber nod in response before leaving to head home.

Home, that is no longer home. She ended up standing in the front yard, trying to work up the courage to go inside. As a family, they had always worked through whatever was thrown at them. It couldn't work out that way this time. Maybe going inside wasn't the best idea. So many lies had already been told. One more wouldn't make a difference, but telling them one more was something unfathomable at this point in time.

Simply disappearing would lead to missing person's reports and possibly flyers on every lamp post in Kankakee County. With a heavy sigh, she headed into the house, only to find no one was around. Relief washed over her. Being able to pack without prying eyes felt like a good idea.

How much do you take when you're abandoning your life?

She crammed everything into two bags. The feeling that she was betraying her family overshadowed thoughts of what should be taken. Family photos and small mementoes were tucked between clothes. The lap top and a stash of money that she'd been collecting to finish restoring the previously destroyed car were also taken. Turning her focus to packing the books she'd borrowed from Aiden's house, there was an issue. They weren't where she left them.

"Shit..." She looked under the bed, in the closet, anywhere they could have been stashed. It suddenly dawned on her.

"Myra, you little shit." She made a mad dash to Myra's room. The youngest of the house, Myra had a habit of going on treasure hunts with her favorite stuffed rabbit. This often resulted in everything from the toaster to Dad's lucky golf ball ending up in her room. Raven searched the bright color themed room. The toy box, under the bed, dressers, she went through everything and none of the books were found. Was it Jaden? She headed out into the hall, looking at the door to her little brother's room. The sound of everyone coming in through the back door brought an end to her search.

It was pizza night. Jaden and Myra were already arguing over who was getting the middle square piece, the best and cheesiest piece. The argument came to an end as Dad led everyone in saying grace.

Eyes falling closed, she pictured them all at the table as they laughed and talked about what they wanted to get from the library and the farmer's market over the weekend. It was a summer tradition. Saturday morning, as a family, they went to the library to each get a book and then go to the farmer's market, since they were right across from each other.

Just leave. Climb out the window and leave, she thought to herself.

She couldn't find the strength to move. The emotional struggle brought tears to her eyes and gave her the overwhelming sensation of being unable to breathe. The desire to see them all one last time grew stronger, and no amount of logical thought was changing that.

"Raaaaven's home!" Myra announced in her tiny voice.

She quickly wiped away her tears as she looked down at the small girl who was jumping up and down at the bottom of the stairs. A smile spread across her pale lips as Raven bound down the stairs and scooped Myra up into a hug.

"Miss me?"

"Bunches and bunches!" The small girl squealed.

She carried the toddler into the kitchen and returned to her seat. "Looks like I got home just in time, huh?" She smiled, taking the coveted middle square.

"Aww man! I wanted that!" Jaden complained as he folded her arms and pouted.
"Oh yeah?" She stuck her tongue out at him before taking a big bite.

Franklin laughed, while getting a piece for himself. "Welcome home. How was the camping trip?"

"You went camping without me??" Myra questioned in disappointment.

"You had a lot of your own fun, though, didn't you Myra?" Their Mother reminded, giving Raven a hug from behind before sitting down.

"We went to this comic thing at the library." Myra explained with excitement.

"Oh man, I missed it?" Raven sat down, listening.

"I helped picked some comics out for you." Jaden smiled.

"He did!" She blurted out. "And we learned how to fight with glowing swords!" The tiny girl's eyes widened as she explained as only a child can.

"Wow…glowing swords sounds amazing, Myra. And thank you, Jaden, I can't wait to read them." Raven smiled, finishing off the piece of pizza. "As for Dad's question…." It felt so good to say the word, Dad, or even think the word Father while looking at Franklin after spending so much time pretending Mephisto was her Father. "Camping was fun. I saw a pack of wolves, went swimming and did a little cooking over campfire."

"Wolves??" Myra looked to Jaden, "Wolves!"

"I heard!" Jaden replied excitedly. "I want to see a wolf!"

"They have some at the zoo, baby, we can go next week." Their Mother piped up.

"Sounds like it was fun, and dangerous. Wolves around here?" Franklin questioned with concern.

Raven finished her piece of pizza, looking at her Dad. "They were on the other side of the river, plenty of distance between us."

"You had me worried for a moment, there." Ellie smiled.

"You sticking around a while?" Franklin questioned.

"We have movies!" Myra informed, leaning forward. "From the magic box outside the grocery store!"

"Yeah, I am." Raven answered as she chuckled at Myra's using that term. Raven had once tried to explain to the child how the machine knows if you return the movie or not.

"How about we take the pizza into the next room and start the first one?" Ellie suggested.

"Really?" Raven looked a little surprised. Food was never allowed outside the kitchen before.

"Yeah!" Jaden grabbed his plate and took off.

"Whoa, wait---" Franklin sighed. "Alright, let's go."

The boxes of pizza were collected and they moved to the couch. Halfway through the second movie, Jaden and Myra had fallen asleep. As Ellie went about collecting them and taking them to bed, Raven headed back to her room. Doubt started to set in. Leaving may not be the best idea. Being there felt right. Another lie or two could result in never having to leave. It would be easy. Just go to work in the morning, like the last few months never happened, and continue with life. Going to a university or college out of state would be good. If anyone showed up that threatened that existence, kill them.

"Raven?" There was a tap on her bedroom door. "Can I come in?"

She shoved the packed bags out of sight quickly, plopping onto the bed, sitting causally. "Sure!"

Franklin came in, holding the two missing books in his hand. "Can we talk about these?"

Raven felt like a deer in headlights. "Yes?"

"Myra found them in here." He sat down in the computer chair, opening one up and flipping through the pages. "Interesting stuff. Can I ask why you have them?"

"I was thinking about studying different religions, so a friend let me borrow them to get an idea of what I'd be getting into." She watched him flip through the pages, a pensive expression on his face.

"You have a friend with books like this?" He lifted them up, disappointment clouded the proud man's face. "Those sacrilegious looking blades in the closet your friend's also?"

"You went looking through my things?"

"You brought the devil's teachings into my house?" He shot back, disappointment turning to anger.

"It's just words, Dad, they don't mean anything."

"Just words? Words can convince even the righteous to commit the most horrible acts." He stood up, shaking the books at her.

"Don't you have more faith in me than that?" She questioned him, surprised at his apparent lack of faith in her. Thinking quickly, she motioned to the books in his hand. "My friend only let me borrow them because if I study religion I have to be comfortable reading different beliefs, not to convert me."

Franklin hesitated. "I do have faith in you….no, I did before you started acting strange and you brought these things into my house."

"I'm sorry, I should have talked to you first. I'll take them back. It won't happen again." She spoke apologetically, standing and holding her hand out to take the books.

"No you won't. I'm going to burn them."

The outstretched hand lowered. Disbelief about how he was acting caused her features to freeze. "Even if you don't like what's in the books, you can't burn someone else's stuff, it's not right. Let me take them back to my friend, ok?"

"No." He said sternly. "I'm getting them out of my house and you aren't allowed to be friends with whoever gave these to you."

"Allowed?" Raven was surprised at his choice of words. "I'm a little too old for you to be telling me who I can and can't be friends with."

"You're living under my roof, you follow my rules. No daughter of mine is going to be hanging around devil worshipers. You stay away from them." He demanded firmly, tossing in a quick…"And you're going to church this weekend."

The expression of disbelief gave way to an emotionless stare as something inside clicked, pulling her mindset in a different direction. "I'm not your daughter, and I don't belong in a church." The words slipped past her pale lips fluidly, a bit of a darkness creeping to her voice.

Franklin was speechless. His anger twisted into anguish as his heart broke. Raven may not have been his biological daughter, but she was his child in every other way. Never had he imagined those words would ever come out of her mouth. He dropped the books on the floor and, without another word spoken, he left the room, closing the door behind himself.

Raven took a deep breath. It felt like the room was spinning and she could hear her parents arguing in the hall. It felt like no matter how many deep a breaths she took, it wasn't enough.

Through the sound of arguing and Myra starting to cry, she could hear a myriad of whispers stirring through the room. A cool, comforting sensation spread over her hands. Hesitantly she raised them, tear stained eyes set on dark energy that had manifested in reaction to the sudden shift in emotions.

Would it be less painful to kill him?

The thought brought fear fueled urgency to everything happening. What if he came back in and the thought turned into reality? Raven snatched everything up quickly. She shoved the books into in to one of the backpacks. After dropping them out the window, she pulled the strap of the laptop bag over her head, securing it across her chest. She climbed onto the window sill, taking one last look around the room before climbing out and down a tree to the ground.

What started as a quick paced walk, heading in the direction of Aiden's house, turned to a run the further she got from her neighborhood. Darting through traffic, she barely saw the cars. The look on Franklin's face haunted her. Why had she said that? In all ways that mattered, he was her Father, so why had she spoken such cruel things out loud?

The world tipped sideways as something sent her tripping and slamming to the ground.

"Fuck!" She cried out, cringing. Pressing her trembling palm against the concrete, she pushed herself up into a sitting position. The laptop bag cushioned her fall, but it wasn't enough to save her lower arm from getting scratched up. Raven pulled the strap to the laptop bag over her head and off before she tossed the whole thing aside. She could hear pieces clatter against each other within the canvas bag.

"Well, that's broken." She mumbled with a defeated sigh as she examined her bloodied arm. With a quick glance over her shoulder, she stood up. As she turned to retrieve the dropped bags, something slammed into her back and ran her into the side of the nearby stone garage. It happened so fast that she didn't see it coming. Four hands clamped onto her arms from behind, hands that radiated heat and grew hotter by the second.

"Get…off me." Her growled demand was met by a low growl. Whatever it was pulled on her, forcing her backward. She jerked an arm away and spun about, pulling her other arm free. As she spun, she got a quick glimpse of the attacker. About six feet tall, it had a wide face with a flattened nose. It had four glowing red eyes stacked with two on each side of the face. The demon's thick and bulky four armed body barely budged as Raven delivered a kick while she kept moving off the momentum of the spin.

She went after one of the bags to get a weapon. Another demon revealed itself, taking her back down to the ground. It straddled her, nearly crushing her under the demon's weight. Her slender fingers stretched, snagging the bag strap and pulling it closer. Like heated iron rods, claws sank into damaged skin as her scratched up arm was wrenched back, while another set of claws sank into the soft flesh of her side.

Her scream echoed through the vacant alleyway. Another set of claws sank through her jeans into her calf. She stretched and pulled a dagger from the bag. Eyes blackening over, she made a rough turn under the demon's weight. All that she needed was an inch or two, and she got it. She slammed the dagger in her hand down into one of the demon's arms. It recoiled, wailing out an awful sound as flesh and muscle was roughly ripped through by the blade being held in a death grip.

The other demon started to crawl over her. She raised her boot, kicking it as hard as possible. There was an audible crack as the boot's thick heel impacted the demons jaw, but it kept coming, opening its fanged mouth wide. As it came lunging down, she thrust the dagger out, stabbing the demon in the eye. Its advance stopped, allowing her to keep the blade as she pulled it from the screeching creature's eye socket.

With the second demon reeling back from her attack, she rolled away, getting up. A third demon suddenly appeared and was met with a punch to the face as it jumped into the fray. The first demon came up from the side, prompting her to duck as it swung its claws wide at her. Rising back up, she swiftly slashed the dark rune covered blade out toward him. It sliced clean through the demon's throat. Blood came pouring out with an awful gurgled growling as the demon crumbled to the ground, grasping all four hands to its throat.

The sound of the laptop being crushed under a heavy foot pulled her attention away from the dying foe. Turning, she ran at the demon making a new advance, meeting it head on, claws clashing against the blade. It leaned in nose to nose with her, snarling and baring its fangs as it pushed against her. Its three free hands grabbed at Raven, lifting her up over its head and tossing her several feet.

She could see the dead demon, and the two still remaining making an approach, and a glimpse of the night sky before hitting the ground. Her head bounced off the cement as she landed, dropping her dagger. Her vision blurred and doubled. With a pained gasp, she closed her eyes tight as the two loomed closer.

The spine chilling call of an incoming hellhound emitted through the area. Raven's eyes rolled open as Atreus leapt from the depths of hell, entering the world of man, appearing in a roll of flame on top of a nearby garage. He ran across the roof, leaping off the edge and pouncing on one of the demons, taking it clear to the ground. The beast's fanged maw viciously sank into whatever flesh it could, ripping mercilessly.

Raven managed to get up and retrieve her dropped dagger. There was no thought, only action in the heat of the moment. Her back had only been turned for mere seconds to do so. Turning back around, she saw Atreus was latched onto the demon's leg. It was twisting around, trying to grab at the hellhound.

She ran forward, grasping the dagger's hilt with both hands, and drove the blade down along the side of the demon's spine. It wailed out, falling to its knees. She pulled the dagger away and brought it down into its neck. Simultaneously, Atreus latched onto the demon's arm, ripping through an artery, sending a spray of fluids over the nearby garage. Raven yanked the dagger out and allowed the demon to fall over.

She spun about to deal with the demon that remained, but it was nowhere to be seen. Blood pooled around the demon as a silence came to the area. Atreus was feverishly ripping flesh from bone, gorging himself. All that noise, and not a soul wandered down the alley. Where were the cops? Her fleeting thoughts came and went as she observed the frenzied eating session. Chunks of flesh were torn away just as violently as the attacks had been when the demon was alive.

"Anger issues?" Raven questioned softly, and Atreus half growled into the corpse in response.

It was just a little further to Aiden's house. Past the hospital, through the tunnel that ran under the streets, a few more back allies and she would be there. As the black cleared from her eyes, she felt as if she could curl up and sleep right there amongst the carnage. The distance she had to go seemed monumental.

Atreus looked up at Raven, blood dripping from his maw. He padded through the crimson pools and stopped at one of the dropped bags. She followed, picking up her things mindlessly. Her body's accelerated healing process had already started, but it wasn't enough to counter a severe concussion.

Atreus led the way, glancing back to make sure she was still following as they made their way past the hospital, heading into the tunnel. Halfway through, they sat down so she could wrap her wounds. Next thing she knew, it was morning.

Raven woke up in her room at Aiden's house. The wounds inflicted during the fight had been tended to, but not by her hand. Everything seemed unreal in reflection, and yet the pain from claws sinking into her was a sobering reminder of just how real it all was. The bags filled with her belongings were on the floor in a pile and Atreus was sleeping on the end of the bed.

"You need to be more careful." Owen pointed out as he entered the room.

"You think?" She shrugged. "Atreus had my back."

"Damn right, he did, he came and got us, took us right to where you were." Owen explained with a new attitude toward the hellhound as he walked to the bed. Hesitantly he reached down and rubbed his hand over Atreus' head in a gentle petting. The hellhound opened its eyes, but gave no other reaction. "I don't think he likes me."

Raven looked down at Atreus, tilting her head ever so slightly. "I think...it's just going to take some time for him to get used to being around people he can't eat."

Owen pulled his hand away from the hellhound, slightly disturbed at the thought. "He shouldn't be eating people."

"Well, last night he ate a demon." Raven pointed out.

He remained silent a moment, watching Atreus, who was watching him. "Ok! Good dog!" He nodded nervously. "So, breakfast? We need to talk about tonight. Come on."

Raven crawled out of bed, half hugging Atreus as she did. The two headed downstairs, where a breakfast of steak, eggs, pancakes, and bacon was waiting. Raven didn't hesitate to load her plate up and sat down, digging right in. Aiden barely glanced up from his cell phone, texting away.

"Do those bags mean what I think they mean?" Aiden asked without looking up from his phone.

"Yes. I'm moving in."

"Excellent!" Aiden smiled, setting the phone down on the table. "I know it wasn't easy, but trust me thi—"

"Can…we not talk about it? I'm here, let's just leave it at that, ok?" Raven interrupted him, trying not to think about the look on her Dad's face from the night before.

"You're right, sorry." Aiden glanced over at Owen.

"What's the plan for tonight?" Owen asked.

"I think someone said midnight is the peak of…something ideal for this kind of thing." Raven motioned her fork as she tried to recall.

"Ok, so we will show up to help at midnight." Aiden caught a glimpse of something from the corner of his eye, slipping past him and Owen before Atreus popped up next to Raven. "Jesus!" He jumped, genuinely startled. "That…." He pointed at the hound. "….is going to take some getting used to."

Raven stared at Aiden's reaction blankly, popping a piece of bacon into her mouth. Should she tell them about the book? He had to have known about how Mephisto's very skin could turn anyone who touched it into barbeque, so why hadn't he brought it up? "What if you're late bringing in the cavalry? Am I supposed to just grab Mephisto by the tail and chuck him back into hell?" She questioned, handing a piece of bacon down to Atreus.

"No, don't touch him." Owen spoke before Aiden could. "You'll burn up. We are going to need to maneuver him back into the portal."

"Or knock him back through with a few good holy blasts." Aiden added.

"Raven could blast him back through." Owen looked at Aiden. "Heck, she could even manipulate her shadow energy to ensnare him and force him through."

Raven blinked. "That's a good idea, actually."

"I don't know." Aiden spoke thoughtfully. "We don't want you to rely on your powers too much. The less you use them, the better."

"Holding back could get her and those girls killed. She has power and should use it, whatever it takes to get the job done." Owen argued firmly.

"She shouldn't need to resort to that. We will be there." Aiden argued back.

"What if we're late?" Owen questioned sharply.

"We won't be."

"How do you know? Shit happens." Owen grew more frustrated.

"The more she uses, the higher the risk we lose her t---" Aiden stopped himself, looking at Raven.

"It hurts me when Mommy and Daddy fight, you know." She spoke with a straight face, watching the two carry on as if she wasn't in the room. She knew what Aiden was going to say, he'd said similar things before so it was nothing new, but there was a stronger gravity to his tone this time around.

Owen laughed. "Sorry."

Aiden sighed. "Ultimately, it's up to you, Raven. Do whatever it takes to get through this, but be careful and don't force anything that doesn't feel right."

"I'm going to head back." Raven stood from the table.

"Be careful." Aiden urged, standing and offering her keys to a car. "Try to bring this one back."

"Sorry." Raven took the keys. "You could get the other one back tonight if you really wanted. It's at the Collins' house."

"Maybe." Aiden looked at the hellhound.

"Atreus." Raven followed Aiden's gaze. "Go back to my house and guard it, just in case any of Mephisto's followers try to track where I have been. Protect them for me until this is over, please?"

The hellhound let out a low woof. He stood, turning and running at the back door. Just before running head first into it, he disappeared in a roll of flames. Raven jingled the keys at Aiden and Owen. "Going to grab my blades and go." She explained briefly, heading out of the kitchen.

"I'm getting the big sword." Owen looked at Aiden as Raven made her way out the door.

"Oh, you think that will help?" Aiden replied.

Raven shook her head a bit as she headed up the stairs, hearing the exchange as she went. Sleep clothes were shed, abandoned to the floor for a pair of jeans and her normal summer go to--a dark toned sleeveless shirt. She grabbed one of the bags, putting it in the chair and opening it to get her daggers. As she lifted the sheathed blades, the framed photo of her family was left exposed. She stared at it a moment.

Her Mom was wearing her favorite dress, the soft pink color matched the roses and mums in the family garden. Her Dad was prim and proper in his suit. Myra was in white, the color made the warm browns of her eyes pop. Jaden was in a green polo shirt that had a wide blue stripe across the chest. She was in a simple plum colored dress, it crisscrossed over her chest and flared at the hips. She lifted the photo from the bag and propped the frame on the desk before gathering her jacket and daggers, and headed out.

Whatever it takes.

Everyone has different lines drawn in the sand they aren't willing to step over. Aiden had many lines. Lines with their own lines, considerations and exceptions. He was wary of the unknown factors and always weighed the pros and cons. Owen, on the other hand, had few. He also didn't mind surprises, and saw them as challenges in the moment, that make for weaving great fireside stories. Raven had to decide, how far is too far for her?

She used Aiden's car to head back to the cult infested house. Things needed to be decided on before hitting the town's border. A bit of anxiety set in as the State Park entrances were fast approaching. The first one she came to, she pulled in and parked.

Her fingers tapped the steering wheel as her thoughts raced all over the place. Aiden's concerns were warranted. As a guardian, it's his job to make sure his charge makes it through alive. In this case, it also entails making sure the charge doesn't go full blown dark side. But what about the people who can't fend for themselves?

The thought of those girls chained in the basement turned her stomach. Who's looking out for them? Certainly not their parents, given that they handed them over to be sacrificed. It's supposed to be Raven and, right now, it felt like she was failing miserably. Raven took a steady deep breath and let it out slowly. "Follow your instincts. Don't think like a human, it can get you killed." Words of harsh previously shared wisdom were repeated out loud.

"Follow your instincts...." She repeated again, getting out of the car. "Unless it breaks one of the conduct rules." A mocking tone took over her voice as the counter-thought was spoken out loud. "This isn't in the rules....is it?" The outward musing came to a stop as she pulled the leather strapped sheaths from the car and strapped them on. She slid the daggers into place, concealed by her jacket. If something dumb had to be done, at least be half smart about it and be ready to defend yourself.

At the first opportunity, she abandoned the main paths. The subtle sounds of the highway and people enjoying the park faded as she wandered deeper into the forest. Coming to a clearing, she took a good look around. It didn't look like anyone had been in the area and it seemed secluded enough.

Crouching down in front of a somewhat flat stone, she pulled a small piece of black chalk from an inner jacket pocket. She drew three symbols on the stone before tucking the chalk away. She stared at her work a moment, thinking on what was about to be done. Her pale fingers reached down, barely touching the marks. A smudge or two would render them unusable. She pulled her fingers back, reaching for the sheaths under her jacket, and drew a dagger. The sun piercing through the canopy of trees glinted off the runed blade as she drew it over her palm, cutting herself. She allowed the blood to trickle down onto the marks as she recited a spell in demonic.

A violent wind whooshed through the area, shaking the trees and stirring up dust before an unsettling stillness overtook the forest. A dark presence stirred up within the small clearing. She stood slowly, turning to come face to face with one of the five sons Lucifer had spawned in her vision.

"Damien." She whispered ever so softly.

The middle child, if you could call them children, and the most attractive, despite the horns and deep crimson eyes. He was clad in black leather pants, boots, wrist cuffs and a sleeveless leather surcoat with 4 buckles up the chest. Thick black hair barely touched the tops of his shoulders.

"You." His voice was just the right mix of dark and soothing tones. "You have some nerve, summoning me."

Raven took a step back, staying alert and watching the being before her. Words on the tip of her tongue moments ago were lost. Damien closed the distance between them swiftly. He stood over her. With a tilt of his head, crimson orbs stared into her eyes with a piercing gaze. "Did you change your mind about which side you chose?" The inquiry broke the tension filled silence as his eyes moved to inspect her full form.

"No." Raven replied, not taking her eyes off him.

His clawed hand snapped out, wrapping around her throat. "Then I should kill you here and drag your soul to where it belongs." His tone darkened to the point that it was no longer appealing to her senses. It plucked at her humanity, causing her to flinch as she lifted the dagger still in her hand in kind, and held up to his neck. Her hand trembled faintly as the son of the devil grinned in amusement at the gesture.

"I know…" She rasped out past his grip. "…where Mephisto is."

Damien let go, his grin only fading a little as he watched in curious anticipation of whatever was about to be said. Raven coughed, lowering the dagger. "I know where he is and I know his plans will ruin that of your Father's."

No arch demon can walk the earth before Lucifer. It could posses anyone it liked, but to physically exist in the human plane of existence before him would prevent the sovereign ruler of hell from doing so himself, and mess up a laundry list of cosmic rules. At least, that was what she had read and banking on to be true.

"You're lying."

"I'm not. I know exactly where he is and how to stop him. I want to make a deal." She explained, getting right to the point.

Damien chuckled, growing even more amused at the situation. "You want to make a deal? The dark Nephilim sworn to the light turns to Hell for help. What's the matter, no angels on duty?" He questioned darkly, watching her like a predator stalking prey.

"My guardian says they won't help."

"Oh?" Feigning surprise, he placed a hand over his chest. "Why do you think?"

"They probably want me dead." She bluntly replied, without any thought.

"It's not just you." He took another good look over her as he explained. "Though I'm sure they are all too eager to get rid of you. The angels of heaven do not help the Nephilim sworn to their side of the war."

Raven tried to hide her confusion at his words. "Well, now who is lying?"

"I'm not." He lifted his chin, his dark gaze unwavering from her. "They see light Nephilim as abominations. Even if they didn't, angels aren't allowed to interfere with the affairs of man unless God tells them to."

"But demons can, you can get involved, especially if there is a deal in place." She pointed out, being mindful of how close he was still standing.

"What do you propose?"

"I need to be able to stop Mephisto and force him back through the portal without dying. In exchange…" She hesitated. "..you'll know where he is and.." Raven trailed off as Damien started to look less amused.

"You didn't think this through very well, did you?" He questioned.

"I'm on a time crunch here." Her frustrations started to show. "And I can't see a way out of this situation alive, which is probably why that dumb book pointed me in your direction."

"Dumb book?" Damien finally took his eyes off her to look around, making sure they were still alone.

"In a cave, under the Bermuda fucking triangle, of all places."

Damien looked back at Raven sharply. "I'm going to give you some free advice." He turned, putting some distance between the two of them. "Don't mention to anyone that you saw that book, at least, unless you can really trust them."

"Right…good advice, thanks." She started to turn as well with the assumption that no deal was going down and he was about to take off.

"I'll be setting the terms of this deal."

Raven blinked, turning about to face him once more.

"You could do what needs to be done, if you were stronger and more experienced." He turned to face her again. "I can give you the boost you need, but there would be consequences."

"There are always consequences. What's the catch? What do you want?"

"Let's call it a favor." Damien moved close once more, looking her in the eyes almost sinisterly. "At some point in the future I will come to you and ask you to do something for me, and you won't be able to refuse."

"Why…can't you just take my soul in seven years like the standard deal?"

His amused grin quickly spread back over his face. "Because, Raven Ashlynn, your soul is already destined for hell, remember?"

Raven took a half step back, her stomach turning at the reminder of that detail. "I dunno…."

"You were fine with the idea of losing your life, and shy away from a simple favor?" He questioned with a chuckle.

"One has potential for a larger impact. You drag me to hell, it only effects me, my family and friends. Your favor, as you call it, could impact far more than that."

Damien held his hand out to her. "I promise I will try not to abuse the favor in that way. After all, this deal does benefit my Father."

Raven reached behind herself, slipping her dagger back into its sheath with a click before accepting his hand. "Deal."

He pulled her closer, turning that hand over to look at her palm. Without warning, he pushed his sharp fingernail into her soft skin, cutting just along the edge under the thumb. "Ow, hey!" She attempted to pull her hand away, only to have Damien tug it back, his steely gaze fixed on her eyes. He cut himself in the same fashion and held her hand tightly, allowing the wounds to press against each other so their blood would mix.

At first it felt kind of like hot water running over the open cut. The sensation seeped into her skin, spreading through the hand and up her arm. Her form tensed, and the longer he held on, the hotter it got, until it felt like fire was rolling through her veins.

"Relax." He suggested calmly, despite knowing full well no one would be able to relax through such an experience. Damien pulled her arm up into a fold to maintain the hold of her hand as he moved behind her. His opposing arm snaked around her waist as he did.

"Stop." She gasped out, shaking against him. The heat spread over her shoulder and swelled into her chest, wrapping around her racing heart. Her head tilted back against Damien's chest as a scream edging on inhuman burst from her lungs.

He pulled his arm away, allowing her to fall in a not so graceful fashion. Her knees slammed to the dirt and her hands barely stopped a full on face plant. She caught a glimpse of his boots from the corner of her eye as her head lowered. The pain started to subside as she steadied her breathing. Her form trembled against the cool breeze brushing against her overheated skin. Sweat rolled down the side of her face. Her pale lips parted to speak but she didn't make a sound. A half glance up revealed Damien was still there watching her, which was the least of her worries.

It started as an itch. A dull, dual twinge of pain on each side of her head began to increase, spreading and twisting into a headache before rapidly exploding into a pulsating migraine. The pain was intense, blinding. Her eyes slammed shut, unable to keep them open any longer. Her fingers curled into the dirt as an audible cracking of bone brought a split second of relief. Another loud crack was followed by a scream. The skin of her scalp felt tight, as if something was pushing from beneath. A piercing pain ripped through the two spots as she felt warm fluid trickling through her sweat dampened hair and down her face. The sound of her own skull cracking, splintering, was deafening.

Raven fell over, her back and head arching backward. Pained broken gasps pushed past her blood stained lips. Flashes of images bathed in sunlight could be seen as her eyes fluttered. The tree tops, the way the green leaves looked aglow in golden light as the sun shined through them. The sky, crisp and blue as ever. Damien, a grin on his face and a sadistic gleam in his crimson eyes as he watched.

She lifted dirt covered fingers to feel her head to see what was happening. They were met with blood slickened horns protruding from the sides of her head. Extending with a thick base from her head, arching back slightly and curling forward to a point that aligned mid cheek, the horns were reminiscent of ram's horns but on a more manageable scale.

Her fingers felt like they were breaking as she pulled them away from her horns. Something solid and black pushed from her finger's cuticles, dislodging her fingernails and pushing them off as something new grew into their place.

Her hand fell limply to the ground as she lost consciousness, and with it the opportunity to ask questions, and several hours of the day.

Upon waking, she was greeted by tall evergreen trees and the sound of trickling water. A corner of the gardens located at the Collins Estate served as a resting place, her back flat to the aged stone around the bottom of the fountain. Damien was nowhere to be found, nor was her jacket or daggers.

It was surreal, laying there. Her whole being felt vibrant and energized. From the sound of the fountain, to the twittering of birds nearby, everything felt new. She lifted her hand up to see if the horns were real or a living nightmare, only to halt once her hand was in sight. Hesitantly her other hand was also lifted for inspection. Stained with her own dried blood, her fingernails were slightly thicker, pointed and blackened.

She'd been warned about consequences, but this seemed extreme. What exactly had been done for a 'boost', and would it go away? Standing slowly, she pushed a hand over the dried blood in her hair and on her face. The world tipped as she started to fall over, catching the edge of the fountain to stop from going all the way to the ground.

Everything was off balance.

She felt stronger, like rising to her feet to run a marathon was completely possible, but at the same time, tilting her head to the left or right made her dizzy, something that would need to be worked through. She remained still, staring at the silhouette of her reflection in the fountain's water.

"Alex?" Jason spoke out with caution as he approached, molten eyes looking her over.

"Yeah." Raven mumbled out, keeping her head down.

"How long have you been out here?" There was concern in his voice as he reached out, gently pulling a veil of hair from her face.

"I…don't know." Genuinely unsure how long she had been lying there, the answer came naturally.

"Are you ok?" He stepped closer, hesitantly reaching for her hair to brush it aside.

"I don't know…I feel dizzy if I try to stand up straight."

"It's ok, I got you." He leaned in, scooping her up gently.

She gasped, cringing as he picked her up. The heat of his being could be felt in a way it couldn't before. Before his body temperature ran higher than it should, but now the core heat of his demonic half resonated from within and contact from her skin to his allowed her to feel it. It was the difference between putting your hand on a hot pan with or without oven mitts. There was nothing filtering the heat now. The sensation brought on a tremble as Jason carried her to the house. There was a hint of urgency to his actions, using his foot to kick the doors to the grand hall open.

"Here..." He moved through the hall, setting her down in a chair. "I'll get Brandon and Lucas, don't move."

"Alright." She whispered softly in response and, as soon as he was out of sight, she looked over at the portal behind the altar. Mephisto was there, still out of phase and staring at her with a pleased grin spread over his maw.

Raven stood, taking a deep breath as she got her footing. She could feel the energy from the portal pulling at her being. Careful, taking slow, steady steps as she walked, getting used to the extra weight on her head, the closer she got, the stronger it felt. The smell of burning flesh drifted through the air and the faint sounds of screams and moans echoed through the hall.

Mephisto reached out, a clawed hand coming to a rough halt just before touching her, hovering. She lifted her own hand, slender fingers outstretched toward him. She could almost feel leathery heated skin through the veil of reality.

Her eyes fell closed as she listened, not just to the sounds escaping the portal, but whispers from Mephisto.

"Look how you turned out." He crooned pleasantly. "You're in pain, though, still confused and lost. I can sense it." He leaned closer, just a little. "It's over, Alex. All of your suffering ends with my arrival. You can rest, and you will be safe under my reign."

Raven allowed her hand to touch his with a cringe. The presence of his being was overwhelming. He lifted his other hand, keeping his eyes locked to hers. "Let me help you finish the transformation." He whispered darkly.

The sound of a gun's hammer being cocked back cut through all the other noise in the hall. "Stop! What are you doing?!?! Not yet!" Raven's eyes opened as Mara screeched out.

Mephisto pulled his hand away, letting out a roar in anger. Raven covered her ears with a wince and turned to look at Mara. The sound of the gun firing could barely be heard through the demon's bellowing.

Raven lowered her head, falling to her knees, grasping at the bullet wound in her arm. The room spun. She could see a glimpse of red high heels clacking across the marble floor right before the gun's cooling barrel pressed against her forehead.

"I've come too far for you to ruin everything now!" Mara angrily yelled at Raven, her finger twitching over the trigger.

Raven's hand uncurled from her arm, and shot up as she stood, grabbing Mara's arm and pushing it straight up. The gun fired, sending the shot into the ceiling. Plaster crumbled and showered down on the two as the woman's arm was quickly pulled down with Raven disarming her. She turned the gun on Mara in the blink of an eye. There was no hesitation, no words of warning or snarky declarations. As soon as the gun was in her hand and pointed at Mara's head, Raven pulled the trigger. Mara's head snapped back from the force, blood and brain matter spraying from the back of her head. Her body fell limp to the floor.

Raven's hand trembled as she looked from the empty expression on Mara's face to the gun.

"Alex!" Lucas called out, running over. He barely spared a glance at Mara's body as he stepped past it to get to Raven. He wrapped his hand around the wound on her arm tightly, looking her over. Following behind him was Brandon and Jason. Brandon froze, staring at Mara. "Mara?" He started toward the body, wanting to hold the love of his life. You could see it in his eyes, the utter despair of his world ending at the sight of her dead on the floor. He fell to his knees, sobbing out her name in disbelief, reaching for her cheek. But his actions altered at the last second. Just before he was about to touch Mara, he stood up straight. The demeanor of a destroyed man was smoothly replaced with a neutral calm as his emotions were taken over by Mephisto's influence. The heat from the arch demon's presence dried up his tears.

"Mara attacked Alex." He informed Jason and Lucas. "Get rid of the body, and get everything ready for tonight." He ordered coldly, approaching Raven. His fingertips lifted her chin to force her to look from the gun to him. "She would have died tonight, anyway. Remember what you are, is this how my child should be acting?"

Raven's eyes looked at his as she reined in frazzled emotions. "No, it's not."

"You're feeling new things, you're changing, do you understand why, Alex?"

"Yes." She replied, her grip on the gun loosening.

Jason carefully took the gun from Raven, watching with brotherly concern. Mephisto reached up, brushing her bangs aside and pulling his thumb over her brow. "By the end of this night, you will no longer be human." He paused slightly before pulling his fingers away from her chin roughly "Do you know how long you've been gone?"

"No." She replied, her eyes focused on him.

"Do you know where Graver is?"

Raven tensed, the mere mention of the name was enough of a reminder of the look on his face while being pulled under water, his pleas for help unanswered. "No."

"Alright, take her to her room."

Jason moved to pick Raven up again, only to have Lucas step in and scoop Raven up himself as the two exchanged looks of distrust. Lucas took her upstairs and straight to her room, setting her gently on the bed. He then strode to the door, locking it. He crept toward her, pale blue eyes trailing up her body, taking in her new appearance. There was an awkward silence as he made his way to her. His pale, cool hands brushed against her skin as he pulled her shirt off, tossing the blood stained garment aside.

"What was that look down there? Everything ok between you and Jason?" Raven questioned as Lucas pushed her hair back to inspect the bullet wound.

"Jason has been worried about you. Things happened while you were away." Lucas explained, digging elongated nails into the wound.

She gasped from the pain and surprise that he was seriously about to dig a bullet from her arm with nothing but his fingernails. "Really, I was gone what, a day?"

"Austin snapped. He tried to open the portal last night in the fear you weren't coming back and we would need to start over. To say the least, it wasn't pretty." He explained just before pulling the bullet out.

Raven quickly wrapped her hand around the wound as the bullet was removed. Lucas set the bullet aside and raised his bloody fingers to his lips, slipping them into his mouth, suckling at them. "Mmm. I must say, Alex, you taste divine." His hand pressed on the bed, leaning forward into her, sniffing at the wound through her hand. "I've never had demon blood before."

"You're surrounded by demons….I find that hard to believe." She remained still, eyeing him.

"It's the truth." He pulled her hand gently from the wound.

"I….really….would like to get cleaned up." She mumbled, feeling more uncomfortable by the second.

"Of course." He smiled, running his tongue tenderly over her fingers. She went still as her eyes looked down at him in disbelief. Was he really making another move? Now? She felt disgustingly grimy, covered in dirt, dried crusted blood, and sweat. It was hard to imagine anyone making an advance on her that didn't involve soap.

"Do you like that?" He questioned affectionately.

"I…dunno." She whispered, pulling on her hand.

He didn't let go, though, pulling it aside as he leaned down, pressing his lips against her shoulder in a soft kiss. "Just relax." He purred softly before pressing his lips against the wound, pushing his tongue into it. The tip of his tongue softly probed, forcing it to bleed. He repeated the action a few times, and with each pass, his tongue drew further up her arm.

"Thank you, Alex." He purred, blood stained lips kissing her shoulder.

"You're welcome." She whispered, fascinated by his behavior.

Lucas kissed at her neck, pushing her hand down onto the bed before feverishly pressing his lips to hers. Her eyes widened and her breath stilled as he squeezed her hand. "Lucas." She pulled back, reaching her free hand up to push on his chest. "I should really get cleaned up."

He bared his fangs at her. "We have time." He spoke dominantly at first, and then backed down a little. "Sorry, if you will have me, that is." He leaned in, kissing her shoulder again. "I've longed for you since I brought you home, Alex, it's been hard."

"I don't think Father would approve." The disapproving Father card was quickly pulled in the hope it was enough to diffuse the situation without getting violent.

"He does, I spoke to him on the matter. If you will have me, I can be yours, Alex." His free hand fell to her inner thigh, gently and slowly exploring upward. Raven's leg tensed under his touch, becoming aroused as he leaned into her neck, brushing his fangs gently over her skin.

"Lucas?" Jason's voice could be heard through the door, accompanied by a knocking.

A mix of relief and disappointment washed over her. While she knew this wasn't something that she should be doing, part of her craved his touch. The advancements were inspiring carnal thoughts and ideas that both intrigued her and sparked fear.

"Yes?" Lucas groaned out, pulling himself away from Raven to unlock and answer the door.

Jason looked at Lucas' blood covered hand, then over to Raven. "Father needs you downstairs."

Lucas turned back to Raven, running his tongue over his fangs. "We can continue this after tonight, I hope." He took a half bow. "I'll come back for you when it's time. Please do get cleaned up and rest." He slipped out of the room, pulling the door closed behind him.

Raven let out a steady breath, resting her hand over the spot where Lucas had put his fangs.

"Yeah, that…just happened."

Chapter Eleven

Raven stood in the window, wrapped in an overly plush bathrobe. There was something comforting about the feel of luxuriously soft fabric against wet skin that can lull you into relaxation and a state of being where it would be easy to curl up and go to sleep. Sleep wasn't an option right now. She observed the cultists as they arrived. Some came by car, others on foot and two even came on horseback. A few of them caught sight of her in the bedroom window and bowed before disappearing out of sight.

From the ground looking up, all they would see is the silhouette of a woman with horns. It didn't faze them, if anything, they seemed excited. The idea felt convoluted, that any human would get excited over the appearance of a demon. A sane person wouldn't want such a thing present, then again, just how sane anyone involved with this could be was now in question, even herself.

She turned away from the window as the arrivals slowed to a straggling crawl. She hovered in front of the mirror, taking yet another look at herself. It was hard to accept. The reflection in the mirror looked like her, yet at the same time, it didn't. Her skin was fair to begin with, but this new tone was almost a pale grey. She dropped the bathrobe a little and exposed grayish freckles that peppered her shoulders. The vibrant emerald tones of her eyes had shifted to hues of dark amethyst. Her canines looked ready rip through flesh and her ears were now slightly pointy.

Getting dressed presented a slight difficulty. The horns were an obstacle to getting a shirt on over her head. Despite that, she got dressed quickly and headed out into the hall. There were a few followers there, but they barely looked at her as they bowed and scuttled away. A week ago such behavior would have felt unsettling, but for tonight she was grateful they made themselves scarce.

Raven took the servant's stairs into the kitchen with caution. If the kitchen was in use she didn't want to alert anyone to her presence. Seeing it was empty, she didn't hesitate and went straight to the basement door. It was unlocked, giving her the opportunity for a quick slide through.

The basement was also empty, not just of cultists, but of the kidnapped girls and the guns.

"Fuck…" Raven looked around the empty holding area. Unsure of what she would actually do once she got down there, the original idea had been to get them all out and as far away from the house as possible before things got started. Now she was clueless once more. She took care not to make too much noise. Closing the door gently, she made her way over to the kitchen counter. It struck her as odd that someone had recently done the dishes. A night they had anticipated for generations had finally arrived, and someone felt dishes ranked as an important task to complete.

Plucking up a knife, she made her way back up the stairs to the second floor, where she could hear an argument coming from one of the rooms. It was a heated exchange of words between Jason and Lucas. From the sound of it, Jason didn't approve of Lucas' behavior and wanted the vampire to never lay his 'unclean' hands on his sister again. The choice of words piqued her curiosity, but lingering by the door wasn't a good idea.

Slipping back into her room, she discovered someone had been in there while she had been out sneaking around. Black and red robes, the representation of Mephisto's cult leaders, had been set out on the bed. The knife in her hand was barely the right size to slip it down inside her boot. With the steak knife safely tucked away, she pulled the robes on and carefully smoothed the material out.

"Alex?" Jason's voice came with a knock at the door.

Raven tensed as she looked over, hesitating.

Another tap. "Alex, it's time, are you ready?"

She made her way to the door, pulling it open slowly. Jason and Austin were on the other side, also clad in their black and red robes. Austin's appearance drew her attention instantly. His hands were covered in black gloves and one side of his face and neck was darkened and heavily scarred in a way that suggested severe burns were the cause. His eyes held a molten hue and small horns had grown in just above the temples.

Austin noticed her stare and turned away, pulling his hood up. "Are you ready?" He questioned in a tone a few shades less than human. He didn't wait to get an answer and headed down the hall.

"Yes, sorry." She looked at Jason, who was also showing some signs of change. His skin had splotches of deep red on it and his canines were enlarged. His clawed fingers reached for Raven's hood, pulling it up over her hair and horns. "The plan has changed a little." He whispered.

Her eyes darted down the empty hall. "What?" she whispered back.

"Your part remains the same." He assured her, pulling his hood up. "Whatever happens, you are safe. No harm will come to you, Alex." He grasped her shoulders, looking at her with admiration a moment before heading down the hall.

A change in their plans meant potential complications for hers. Regardless, she held her head high as the two of them went down the stairs, catching up with Austin. It wasn't the same. Though no one had mentioned him, Graver's absence left a void around them as they moved through the house and to the entrance of the grand hall, which was packed with black robed followers. They went all the way to the very back of the hall, filling it to the walls and windows. The room became quiet upon their arrival. Jason and Austin led Raven down the carpet of the room's divide.

The missing girls were up near the altar, kneeling with their hands tied behind their backs. They had been bathed and were dressed in soft white cloth gowns. A follower stood behind each of the girls, heads lowered and hands clasped on their shoulders to hold them in place.

A black mass had already been conducted, that much was evident as Raven went with her 'brothers' to the altar and turned to face the crowd. Blessings had been given and everyone was waiting eagerly for the grand finale.

"Our day has come." Jason announced, breaking the silence. "For centuries, your families have been dedicated to a shared goal. To bring my Father, Mephisto into this world and begin a new age." He paused, looking over those at the front of the crowd. "For generations you have protected us, his children re-incarnated. At every turn, the Collins family would find us and the forces of Heaven would slay us."

Raven looked down a little while listening, not just to Jason's speech, but the sounds emitting from the portal behind them.

"I regret to inform you all, Graver has fallen in such a way once more." Jason's words brought a few concerned gasps and mumbles from the crowd.

"He died protecting our sister." Jason placed his hand on Raven's shoulder as he flat out lied to those in the room. "He sacrificed his life to make sure we didn't have to start over, to make sure this night happened." He looked at Raven. "Let us begin."

The crowd lowered their heads. Jason gently nudged Raven, turning her to face the altar. The cultists holding the girls in place moved to line up along the sides of the altar area. The hall was thick with excitement from the crowd, fear from the girls, and power flowing in from the portal. Brandon approached Raven, lifting his blood soaked thumb to her brow. He pulled his thumb over her skin in a blessing as he spoke words in demonic. Molten eyes, an indication he was under Mephisto's control, faded back to their normal brown.

Brandon looked confused, as if this time he hadn't been aware of being inhabited by a demon. He stared at Raven before he looked around frantically. The look in his eyes was clear as day, the look of a man trying to find the woman he loves, a woman who, to him, had died in front of him only moments ago.

"Mara?" He called to her in panicked confusion.

Austin stepped forward at a swift pace and pulled Brandon into a strong hold from behind. Brandon struggled, barking out. "Let me go! What are you doing?" Jason pulled a ritual blade from his robe slowly, remaining next to Raven. There was hatred in his eyes as he looked down at the struggling human. He stepped forward and slit Brandon's throat cleanly.

Brandon pulled on his arms, trying to grab his throat. Fear and disbelief flooded his eyes as blood gushed from the wound, flowing down the front of his robes. Austin whipped him around and forced him forward over the altar so the blood would drain out onto it.

Raven remained still, eyes widening at the turn of events. She assumed this was the change of plan and didn't so much as blink. There was an understanding now of Mephisto's words earlier in regard to Mara's death. Neither of them was ever going to live past this night. Brandon's struggle and gurgled gasps for air mixed with his desperate attempts to cry out for help came to an end. Austin let the body go, allowing it to fall to the floor just to the side of the front of the altar.

Jason and Austin turned, looking at their false sister in expectation. The gathered crowd started to hum their strange rhythmic hymn. Raven's eyes darted over the girls still kneeling before the altar and the followers still close enough to snatch them if they moved. She started toward the altar, glancing down at the cut Damien had made on her left hand. It had healed and scarred, leaving a line, a reminder of what she had done.

She stepped behind the altar, looking up at the out of phase portal. It had been a constant source of demonic energy that had been always present in the house since her arrival. Her eyes rolled closed a second, taking in the sounds from beyond and allowing its energy to wash over her; which only seemed to strengthen what Damien had done. The path could be seen clearly now, multiple paths and possibilities, in a way that couldn't be seen before.

It was overwhelming, causing her to take a sharp breath. She almost lost herself to it. Raven pulled back, opening her eyes and lifting her hands. Thick black energy swirled out chaotically, dancing and billowing out around her hands.

She pushed both hands into the portal. An unsettling sensation pulled at her. Her whole body felt strange. She could feel the silk robes against her skin, the hair that framed her cheeks, the soothing heat reaching out from the portal. Yet despite it all, her mind felt fractured between two realities, causing her to question in that moment whether she was alive, or dead.

Her surroundings changed suddenly. The ground beneath her became a charred stone with patches of slick, festering flesh. The sky above became a perpetual night that was only broken by pits of flames strewn across the endless valley. The screams, cries and moans of others suffering could be heard echoing through the distance. And just to the right, out of the corner of her eye, she saw Damien.

Jason's hand clamping on her shoulder ripped her consciousness back to the other side of the portal. He peered at her with a questioning expression. "I'm ok." She whispered softly so only he could hear. Her fingers intertwined in the portal's energy. Demonic tongues were freely spoken as she worked. A new level of excitement came over the room as the portal pulled into view.

Raven glanced in Austin's direction. He was smiling with excitement and approval, but she barely noticed because she was trying to see if the promised backup was out in the garden. It was not.

The girls shook, crying in fear the whole time, and started to become more distressed with the forming of the portal. Raven looked at them briefly before putting her focus on Mephisto. He reached his hands out, much like he had done earlier that day. She glanced at Jason and Austin and noticed they had moved, putting about a foot between themselves and the girls. Raven raised her palms, but didn't touch the demon's outstretched hands just yet. She hesitated.

Before when the portal was out of phase, having her hands this close felt like touching something through several layers of blankets. The portal fully manifested brought the arch demon on the edge of reality, making it all the more real. Why he didn't come through with the portal was unclear.

She pressed her palms against to his. The sudden jolt caused a half scream to push from her lungs. The heat from Mephisto's hands should have burned her skin instantly. While it didn't, it was still painful. She took several deep breaths. Her fingers folded down over Mephisto's hands. He mimicked the action, folding each finger down over her smaller hands as he grinned excitedly.

The arch demon's fingers could be seen by all as they slipped into the world through their contact with Raven. A pull brought his arms, almost to the elbows, into view. Lucas finally showed himself, moving to Jason's side and speaking to him just above a whisper.

"We have company on the front lawn."

Jason turned, looking at some of the cultists in the back. "Take them, take care of it."

Lucas half bowed, doing as he was told. About a dozen or so robed followers broke away from the gathering, leaving the grand hall. Raven was unaware as she pulled Mephisto out of limbo. The entry of a cloven foot brought flames spreading out across the marble floor and a rumbling through the area.

"Yes! Yes! A little further, my child, and you will be rewarded with your brothers!" Mephisto beckoned in demonic.

Raven trembled. Her veins had turned into a molten glow under her skin. A sickening grin was painted on Mephisto's face. One last pull and the demon came fully into the world, laughter bellowing out as his tail slammed to the ground.

More flames consumed the area, erupting under the followers and climbing up the walls. Chaos erupted quickly as many in the crowd started to panic and were running for the exits. They trampled over each other, pushing and shoving to get out. Some were lucky enough to escape, others became trapped as the flames formed barriers across the exits.

The room spun, Raven's grip on the arch demon loosening. The screaming of burning cultists and the cries of the girls still awaiting their fates could barely be heard over something murmuring from the portal to hell. It was indescribable. A sound beyond the echoes of suffering.

"You hear it, don't you?" Mephisto leaned down to Raven. "Don't listen to it, I'm not done with you yet, your place is here with me."

Mephisto started to pull his hands away, the act pulling her attention back to what was going on. She pressed her palms against his as tightly as she could manage, gripping at his larger hands. She pushed on him. Shadow energy swirled up, dancing around her body, strengthening and empowering her. He slid back, laughing in amusement. "What is this?" Raven pushed again, and this time the demon didn't budge.

"Alex, what are you doing?" Jason questioned as he approached her cautiously.

"Oh, fuck my life." She blurted out just before Mephisto started to pick her up. Whose dumb idea was this? Certainly not hers. She pulled on her shadow energy and sent it rushing up Mephisto's arms, which only accomplished making the demon growl in anger.

"Alex, stop!" Austin yelled.

The sound of gunfire rang out from the front of the house in heated spurts. She made a mental note of it as she pulled forth another blast of energy. There was a heat to this one, a heat that wasn't hers. It caused the demon to drop her as the mix of shadow and flame swirled up his arms.

Landing roughly on her feet, Austin bum rushed her, wrapping his arms around her from behind and holding on tightly. "What the fuck are you doing??"

"Don't hurt her." Jason spoke up.

The kidnapped girls were now huddled near the windows, trying to get their bindings off, crying and screaming for help as Mephisto turned his gaze upon his offerings. Raven struggled against Austin's hold, shadow energy kicking up around the two.

"Alex, calm down." Jason pleaded with her.

Austin leaned down, pressing his forehead against the back of Raven's head. He spoke a word or two of a sleep spell in demonic. She looked down and snapped her head back quickly, delivering a reverse head butt to his face, causing him to let her go. Released from the hold, she dropped to one knee, unintentionally dodging Jason's attempt to grab her. She pulled the knife from her boot and spun as she rose to a standing position, kicking a leg out to sweep Jason off his feet. Caught off guard, Jason went down flat on his back.

As Jason went down, Austin advanced again, flames erupting from his hands. Raven thrust the knife in her hand outward as Austin tackled her to the ground. The flames burst over her before dying out. His molten eyes widened in surprise as he came to rest on top of her. He rolled away to the side, grasping the blade sticking out of his ribcage. She tried to get up and strike at Austin, but Jason grabbed her leg, yanking back. She lost her footing, falling to the floor with a grunt.

As Jason pulled on her leg, a blood curdling scream snapped her attention to Mephisto. He had grabbed one of the girls. Her delicate flesh was burning away under the heat of leathery clawed hands grasping the human's arms. Her head was titled back, her face frozen in terror, and tears stained her bloodshot eyes. It was hard to tell if she was screaming or if it was one of the others.

It was oddly beautiful to behold. A stream of untainted light spiraled in a flow from the girl's open mouth into the arch demon's maw. Her soul and very life essence was being sucked away and consumed.

Raven shifted her weight, kicking at Jason, causing him to let go. She crawled to her feet and jumped on Austin, throttling him. She ripped the blade from his ribs. Coughing, blood stained his lips. She drove the knife back down at his chest, but it slammed into a bloody hand as he made a feeble attempt to stop her. Rapidly she brought the blade down at him, stabbing ruthlessly at his neck and chest. A dark raspy hiss pushed past her lips as she delivered the final blow.

Jason just stood there, taken aback by the sudden display of savagery. Austin's head fell to the side, the molten tone in his eyes giving way to his human eye color of blue.

Raven turned her attention to Jason, ready to strike at him next.

"Alex." He spoke amazingly calmly, considering what he just witnessed. "Remember who I am. I'm your brother." He made an attempt to reason with her, being under the assumption that Mephisto's promise came through and nothing human was left in her with the completion of the portal.

The assumption was within the realm of what was actually going on. Her less desirable instincts were becoming harder to resist. There had been a satisfaction in killing Austin. His desperate attempt to stop the blade fueled her desire to end his life. The feel of his heated blood on her skin, coupled with the smell of it, was invigorating.

A second girl went crumbling to the floor. Raven looked away from Jason to the feast taking place. Turning to look at the cultists that remained, she dropped the knife. Some of the remaining few stood in silence amongst the flames crackling around them, waiting for their own fate. There were corpses on the ground, smoldering. A good number of cultists were huddled along the back wall, praying for help.

"Alex, listen to me." Jason pleaded, getting closer and reaching out to touch her shoulder.

She could feel a source of heat, the energy of a half fire demon creeping up from behind. Raven turned, thrusting a hand at him. A torrent of shadow energy rushed out, pushing Jason back and pinning him to the wall. The energy wrapped around his body and up over his mouth, rendering him unable to do anything but watch.

The remaining girls watched on in horror. Some of them were crying, and those that weren't had gone blank because of what was going on. Mephisto snatched up another girl. Whimpers turned to screams. The sleeves of the white cotton gown burned away under the arch demon's touch. Skin blistered, peeled and turned black. A wheeze pushed out and her mouth was forced open by her emerging soul.

"Hey!" Raven yelled at the top of her lungs, running forward. She pulled the cord of her cultists robes away to let it fall open and allow better movement. "Mephisto!!" Shadow energy swarmed around her hands. She grabbed him by the arm, yanking on him with everything she had.

The swirling light that was being pulled out of his victim recoiled from his fanged maw and slipped back into the girl's body. As she was dropped, she fell on top of the two dead girls. While she frantically scrambled away, Mephisto spun to face Raven, who immediately started backing up. "I killed your sons." She cockily taunted, glancing at the portal to measure the distance, though it wasn't exactly easy for Mephisto to see that with her eyes filled in with black.

He roared out, stomping forward faster than she was able step backward. It was only a matter of seconds before he was close enough to lash out. Razor sharp claws aglow with heat ripped through silken robes and flesh from her right shoulder, down and across diagonally to about mid-chest. She screamed, tripping backward over Austin's body. Her fumble and fall prevented any severe damage from being done.

While his claws cut deep enough to draw a good amount of blood, they hadn't gone quite deep enough to stop her from finishing what she started. It felt like her chest was on fire, but she pushed through the pain. He kept coming at her relentlessly. She managed to rise to her feet in a less than graceful fashion, the tips of heated nails brushing past her back as he tried to latch on to her, but she kept moving.

She ran to the portal, grabbing the corner of the stone altar for support as she half slid through the blood around Brandon's body, putting herself between the portal and altar. Mephisto's tail slammed to the floor, cracking it even further. It jetted out like a spear aiming to run her through with the flaming barbed tip. Raven dropped down behind the altar, covering her head. Mephisto's tail skimmed over the altar's surface, flying into the portal. He roared out in frustration, turning to rip the appendage away, but the demon's bulky frame jerked as something started to pull him in.

Raven peered up to see the underside of Mephisto's tail being used to reel him into the portal. "Oh, thank God." She whispered, crawling out from behind the altar. Mephisto latched onto the edge of the altar, holding on, trying to pull himself back and fight against whatever or whoever was pulling him back into hell.

She tore her eyes away from Mephisto and turned to the windows. The lower set of glass panels were sealed, but the middle set were opened. In the heat of the moment she couldn't recall if there was a way to open the bottom panels. She got up, making haste to the girls before the observing cultists decided to stop being statues.

"Come here….let's get you untied."

"You're h-helping us?" One of the girls questioned, looking just as confused by Raven's actions as she was scared of her appearance. Despite that, the brown haired, wide eyed girl turned so the ropes were exposed.

"Yes." Raven pulled the knots apart, keeping an eye on the others. "Untie everyone else and get out….run the first chance you get, run away from town."

"Alright, thank you….thank you." Another managed to say through hyperventilation and tears.

Her attention returned to Mephisto. His claws were digging through crumbling marble, the whole altar sliding with the force being put behind pulling the demon back to where he belonged. Striding forward, Raven lifted both her hands up. A heated glow was still present in the veins of her hands and half way up her arms. She thrust both hands down to her sides as she moved, shadow energy exploding out around her.

Raven leaned over the top of the altar, placing her hands over his. The shadows wrapped around his heated flesh, seeping in, bringing a visual decay in their wake as the energy traveled up his arms. A glow of amber welled in the arch demon's chest, his maw falling open. Letting go, she ducked down and used the altar for protection once more as flames spewed out.

The top of the altar gave way, causing Mephisto to lose hold of the crumbling structure. She managed to stand and turn in time to see his twisted expression of anger just before he disappeared from sight. The portal fell closed. Some of the flames burning away at the hall were immediately snuffed out, including the barrier of flames at the exit.

The ten girls that survived were visibly exhausted, emotionally and physically. The white cotton gowns draped to their bodies were stained with soot. They did as they were told, and made a desperate run, as fast as they could push their bodies, to get out into the garden and out of sight into the night.

The remaining cultists didn't even bother to give chase. What few that managed to survive by huddling by the back wall desperately ran away in the same fashion as their victims. Those that had been observing split up into three groups. One group headed into the front of the burning house. The second left out into the garden, and the third approached Raven.

Their approach came to a halt as she raised her hand for them to stop, shadows trailing behind blackened fingertips. Jason was still pinned to the wall and looked furious. Raven moved her raised hand in his direction. This could play out two ways that she could see. Kill everyone that was left, or let Jason go in the hope that his words still held meaning, that no matter what happened, no harm would come to her this evening. She pulled her hand to the side, pulling the shadows away from Jason and allowing him to fall to the ground.

"Why?? Alex, why did you do this?" He yelled out, getting to his feet and moving toward her frantically.

One of the followers moved closer, distracting her and giving Jason the advantage. Able to get right on top of her, he pulled her into a tight hug. It lingered on, his body shaking through the clutched embrace. "Why?" He distraughtly whispered. The words as to why didn't come. The answer was complicated and time was drawing short.

"Jason we nee—"

"Master Jason, we need to go. Kill her, or leave her." Someone interrupted with the suggestion.

The heat of flames manifesting around Jason's hand as he lifted the blade was unmistakable. Raven tried to pull away, but wasn't fast enough. Jason pushed the now heated ritual blade into her stomach. The hot steel painfully seared everything it cut through. A pained half gasp, half scream roughly escaped her lips. Jason held tighter, pushing the blade in deeper.

"I can still hear my Father's command. My sister will be going with us. If this doesn't kill her, we will figure out how to control her and start over."

Jason spoke with authority that was met with zero argument.

Her trembling fingers curled into Jason. Thin wispy strands of shadow energy gently stirred around her hands. Pain that rivaled that of the blade burning in her shot through every fiber of her being as she drew on the power. The shadow thickened, seeping into Jason, causing him to release her. Backing away did nothing to stop what she had started. Streams of the energy flowed from Raven's hands into him.

One of the followers grabbed Raven, but the woman pulled her hand away the second she made contact. Dark energy had latched on to the human's skin and began a seeping crawl up her arm. Raven shot a look at a second cultist approaching. He froze mid-step, seeing what happened to the woman who already tried what he'd had in mind.

Raven just stood there, watching. Her hand fell to her stomach and around the blade sticking out. A scene from a movie came to mind, she remembered seeing a scene where pulling the blade out could do more damage, so she left it alone for the moment. Jason fell to his knees, clawing at his chest. Blood started trickling from his nose. Coughing brought speckles of blood to his parted lips. His desperate attempts to breathe brought deep, broken, wheezed gasps as he was suffocating. Shadows flowed out of his mouth, reaching out through the air in that ink to water fashion. Falling over, decaying skin split, releasing more of the energy out into the air. The woman who had been foolish enough to touch her was suffering the same fate at Raven's feet. Gut wrenching sounds were being emitted from both of them as they choked and suffocated. Suddenly, it stopped. The molten glow in Jason's eyes went out.

The shadows faded from their bodies and from Raven's hands. She said nothing, staring at Jason's body on the ground.

"Where is Mephisto?" Someone called out as they entered the hall.

While turning to see the new arrival, she noticed the positions of the other cultists. They had knelt down on one knee, their heads lowered and arms folded. The man demanding answers was pointing a gun, his free hand holding a gunshot wound from the fire fight playing out on the front of the property.

"He's gone." One of the cultists spoke up. "Alex is to blame."

The man wielding the gun looked around at the burning bodies of friends and colleagues, then at the bodies of Jason, Austin, Brandon and two of the girls taken as offerings. "Let's go. Everyone get out of here." Those who were left alive wasted no time standing and taking their leave. The gun was fired several times blindly as the man holding it turned, running away.

Raven turned herself as the gun was fired off, moving behind the altar for cover. Bullets slammed into her arm and the back of the leg. One zipped past, grazing her arm. Another pinged off one of her horns. She collapsed against the altar, gritting her teeth.

Silence overtook the area, the gun fire at the front of the estate had come to an end.

"Out the back, hurry." The man with the gun told everyone who remained, this time with more urgency.

Glass panels shattered. Window after window breaking mixed with the sound of bullets impacting the walls, people screaming, and bodies falling to the floor. The hall fell still. The sound of wood buckling could be heard in the ceiling above from the fire still burning through the rest of the house. The faint sound of emergency sirens in the distance came in and out of focus.

The blackness faded from Raven's eyes as she sat there. Luckily, most of the grand hall was constructed from stone, marble, iron, and glass. The wall with any wood had already burned away and fed the fire to the rest of the house. Flames weren't an issue, heat and blood loss were.

Raven looked down, wrapping a hand around the blade protruding from her stomach. A half laugh mixed with a harsh coughing pushed past her lips. She had made a deal to make sure the contact with

Mephisto wouldn't burn her to ash because of her human side. The deal didn't cover blades and bullets.

"You surprised me." Damien's voice crooned out at her.

She barely looked up at the demon prince standing over her, one foot on either side of her legs. Slowly, he crouched down, looking her in the eyes. "Look at you….dark and beautiful like the very shadows you command." He spoke with admiration, pulling a finger along her jaw line. "You took to using them so easily, so quickly. What will your Grigori say?"

"Probably nothing…." She coughed. "…pretty sure I'm going to die."

He chuckled. "Hardly." The singular word came out darkly, sinisterly, even. His hand shot out, grabbing the blade and pulling it out in a quick, fluid motion. He showed no concern over the blood that came rushing out. Raven pulled her hands over her stomach, pressing down on the wound. He tossed the blade aside with a flick of the wrist. "Let me get this back, now." He rested his hands over hers and squeezed until the molten glow in her veins faded away. The sudden shift in body temperature caused her to shiver. "There you go, it's all you now."

Raven looked confused. "Wait….I don't feel any different."

"Still feel like you're dying? Blood loss does that." He sneered, still holding her hands.

"No...I mean--"

"I told you there would be consequences." He interrupted her with a knowing smirk. "Which…. I'll help you with one of them, think of it as a gold star sticker for a job well done."

Raven's brows rose at his choice of words. Before she could question or say anything else, a pain pierced her palms. It felt like someone stuck a small, fine blade into each one and was pulling it through the skin, carving into it. There was nothing left to give in reaction. It hurt. The pain registered and was there. At the same time, there was numbness dulling the different pains, cold shock, and sheer exhaustion.

"There you go." He let go, taking a satisfied look. She barely caught a glimpse of her own hands as consciousness waned. They were pale from blood loss. Normal human nails tipped blood covered fingers. Damien stood, keeping his eyes focused down at her. The arrival of little red dots of light popping up on the wall behind him drew his attention to the front of the hall.

"See you soon, Raven." Damien stepped back, phasing out of existence with a roll of hellfire.

"This one's down." She could hear a voice from the front of the hall accompanied by the subtle sounds of movement. She could make out the sounds of the body armor shifting over itself, the gentle rustling of a body being turned over, clinking from a gun, and faint gasps of shock.

"So is this one. No movement in here, proceed with caution." Another spoke.

"Raven?" Zaida's voice called out

A red light from the beam of a high powered rifle's scope being pointed right at her flashed over her emerald green eyes. A guy in tactical gear stooped down cautiously in front of her.

"I got a live one!" He called out.

Another man showed up, keeping the aim of his gun on her. "What's your name?"

Her eyes rolled up, glaring at the gun pointed at her.

"It's Raven." Aiden answered on her behalf, coming into view.

The man lowered the gun and raised his hand, waving at someone. "Medic over here…. now!"

"We got to move, this place can come down any second." Aiden pointed out.

"Oh, my God!" Owen blurted out, stepping around Aiden.

A paramedic came running up, sliding down to her side and immediately inspecting her wounds. He pulled thick gauze from a medical case and handed it off to Owen as he knelt down next to Raven. The leg with the gunshot was pulled up to better allow a tight wrapping of the wound. Owen pulled her hands away from her stomach. The medic used a pocket knife to rip open her shirt so a gauze pad could be taped down to the spot. "Stay with us, hold that there, ok?" He urged, putting her hands over the pad.

The house sounded like it was groaning right before the wooden beams could be heard splitting overhead. The house shook as part of the upper level caved in. The paramedic and Owen picked Raven up, carrying her through the grand hall.

They stepped past corpses and smoldering bodies. Smoke hovered in the air, along with the smell of freshly burned flesh and wood. Raven glanced down at Jason's corpse as they passed it. His skin had turned a decayed grey, the veins in his neck and temple were blackened, and his mouth was soaked in blood.

"Don't look." Aiden suggested in an overly protective tone, stepping in front of the corpse. They were moving too fast to argue or get more than a glimpse of the bodies strewn about. The group burst out of the door and into the garden, meeting up with a stretcher. The sound of a helicopter roared overhead, making it near impossible to hear anything. Zaida grabbed Raven's hand, motioning and speaking to someone. It was a blur, and even though Zaida's lips were moving, Raven could hear nothing, not even the helicopter, anymore.

Chapter Twelve

"Dark and beautiful, like the very shadows you command."

She heard Damien's voice, the dark and alluring tone that brought a calm through the darkness. The statement carried over as she opened her eyes. It resonated as if Damien had been leaning next to her ear, speaking the words at that very moment. The light pouring through the window into her bedroom stung her eyes. She lifted a hand to shield them, but pulled it away, seeing the IV taped to the back of her hand.

Something else also got her attention. At first glance it looked like someone had scribbled all over her palms with a marker. Barely recalling Damien's actions, she turned her hands over to inspect her palms.

Each palm was covered in a circular seal. They looked like black tattoos and they were far from discrete. In the middle was an introverted pentagram. The six sections within the pentagram each had some kind of symbol inside that nearly filled it. Through the inner circle where the star was housed, two vertical lines ran through the branding. At each end was a small open circle. In the middle of each line on both sides, another line extended out, each ending in another mark. Each point of the pentagram had three dots around it. The outer double circle was filled with runic writing.

Sitting up, pain shot through her stomach and across her chest. "Ahh…shit." She gasped out, grabbing at the bandages. "Wait." It dawned on her. She's at Aiden's house, in her bedroom and there was medical equipment. It was a combination that didn't make any sense.

"Hey, you." Aiden came into the room, smiling.

"What happened?"

"Well, we were a bit late, but we got your backup. By the look of it, we got there just in time." He leaned against the bed, motioning a hand at the equipment. "They let us borrow this stuff."

"They?"

"Yes. The backup." He replied with a vague explanation. "How do you feel?"

"Who…are they?" Her eyes narrowed a bit at him.

"CIA Division Six."

"You called the government??" She questioned him in disbelief, hoping he was only making an attempt at a joke. "This is too much, you're bullshitting me."

"Yes." He paused. "I mean no. No, I'm not bullshitting you, yes I called the government. I did say I would get you backup."

She leaned back on one hand, wary of this bit of news. "They know about all this stuff?"

"Not every detail, but more than the council is comfortable with…enough to help, now and then." He paused a moment. "Think about it. This isn't one of your comics, or one of those television shows where people, demons and the like get killed in a massive battle and no one notices. We got a house fire and a bunch of kidnapped victims saying a demon tried to eat their souls. Someone has to explain that away."

"Ok…" Raven rubbed her eyes. "How do they know? I mean…."

"One of the presidents was attacked by a demon." Aiden started.

"Really?" Raven questioned.

"Yes. A light Nephilim saved his life before his election. Later, once he was president, Division Six was started. The administration that followed put it under the CIA to better hide the spending from the public eye."

"And Area 51 is real." Owen piped up, entering the room. "But it's not full of aliens." He made a bee-line for the bed and crawled up onto it. "About time you woke up."

"How long was I out?"

"A few days." Aiden answered, sounding and looking guilty about the fact. He moved from leaning against the bed to the bedside table. He picked up an envelope and held it out to her. Raven hesitantly accepted it, peering inside. There was a business card that only had a phone number on it, and a credit card issued in her name.

"I was asked to pass that along to you. The phone number is in case you need a cleanup, or even backup. The credit card is, well, anything you need."

"I would use the credit card, but not the phone number." Owen spoke up, drawing a glare from Aiden.

"She shouldn't use either." Aiden had that tone he gets when it came to a subject that could have too many pros or cons to be considered.

"Yeah, I can't accept this." She closed the envelope, holding it back out to Aiden. "It doesn't feel right, blindly accepting an open line of credit."

"It's part of why the division exists." Owen snatched the envelope before Aiden could take it. "You're not going to be able to hold down a job doing what you do. But…." He sighed. "I half agree with Aiden. You shouldn't use these." He looked at Aiden with an expression that screamed 'you can't argue with me on this.' "Unless it's a last resort."

Aiden stared at Owen, taking a deep breath. "I can agree to that for now."

"It's so nice to see Mom and Dad getting along for the sake of us kids." The familiar Aussie accent cut through the tension.

Raven looked up at Zaida, cracking a small smile. "Hey."

"Hey, you…I turn my back for a minute and you try to die on me. What gives?"

Raven shrugged. "You need a faster horse. Pretty slow for cavalry."

Zaida laughed, moving to the other side of the bed opposite from Aiden. Raven glanced between them, feeling grateful to simply be there among friends. There was an underlying heartache to the moment. It reminded her of the hospital stay after the car accident that started it all. Her Mom, Dad and siblings hovered around the bed in the same way to talk.

"I can imagine you have some amazing stories about all of this that sometime soon you have to share. Maybe write it down?" Owen said with a bit of excitement at the idea. "But in the meantime." Being the closest with his seated position on the bed, it was all too easy to grasp Raven's hands and turn them palm up. "Care to explain this?"

Raven looked down at the seals on her palms. "Well…there was this book…."

About the author:

A Kankakee IL native, Mandy grew up on scifi, fantasy, horror and videos games. A lover of things horror/occult/supernatural themed, she has been writing since high school. Nephilim House of Mephisto, is her first published novel.

Find Nephilim online:
Nephilimnovels.com
Facebook.com/nephilimnovels
Twitter.com/ nephilimnovels
Nephilimnovels.tumblr.com